Scavenger

By

Michaelbrent Collings

Written Insomnia Press
WrittenInsomnia.com
"Stories That Keep You Up All Night"

Sign up for Michaelbrent's Minions
<u>And get FREE books.</u>

Sign up for the no-spam newsletter
(affectionately known as Michaelbrent's Minions)
and **you'll get several books FREE**.
Details are at the end of this book.

DEDICATION

To...

Good people who strive to make the world better,
for nothing but hope's sake,

And to Laura, FTAAE.

Prelude

1

Life was perfect, and that was as it should be.

Some people believed otherwise. Thaddeus "Tad to my friends" Sterling knew that, just as he knew that most if not all of the people who said that worked terrifically hard to make sure it was so. Consequence was a natural result of action, as sure as the sun revolved around the center of the Milky Way, the earth revolved around the sun, and the whole of the universe revolved around Sterling's family.

He watched them now, the smile often hinted at among friends and business associates rearing into full view as he watched his child and wife play.

His wife was beautiful. There was little chance she would have been anything other, given who Tad was, and where he came from. But as beautiful as she was – she had been a runway model in Europe, turning away from that lucrative and glamorous position to take up the far more lucrative, glamorous position as Mrs. Thaddeus Sterling – the child Tad had given her far outshone her.

Perhaps the universe doesn't *revolve around us. Maybe it's just all turning to get a look at the beautiful child that has made us all orbit around and around, all of us just hoping to get a look, a smile.*

Some people would believe otherwise. Some people believed life was hard, and that it should be. They believed that family was a tenuous thing, and had to be clawed at like a loved one strapped to an anchor, falling below the surface. But some people – *most* people – were fools. Most people…

Tad's eyes, wide open as he watched his family with fully focused delight, now somehow managed to widen still more. His thoughts fell from their musings.

The sun revolved around the center of the Milky Way. The earth revolved around the sun. The whole of creation orbited his family. And that meant the whole of creation saw as the center of that unit – the center of the perfection he had created – stumbled.

The child was graceful. The child was like a dancer who spun not along terrestrial planes, but through the wind and the aether. The child did not stumble.

Yet that was what Tad's child did now. Stumbled.

And then fell.

Tad was up and running as it happened, launching off the rattan chair he had had brought so he could sit and watch his family. He was only a dozen yards away, but each running step toward his family somehow contrived to draw him away from them. Creation had orbited the three of them so long, but now it was spinning off its axis. The thread that had kept the universe close – and watching over them all – had somehow frayed.

Tad had done nothing to deserve that. To deserve *this*. Yet it was happening. Cause and effect, action and reaction – they had all disappeared, and the laws of physics along with them, because how could fifty feet be taking so long to cross?

He heard himself muttering, but could not hear what he said. It could have been a prayer, a curse. It could have been yesterday's stock prices. He didn't know for sure *what* he was saying, because as his child fell, his mind fell apart.

He finally reached the thing that had fallen. The angel. Something was in his way. He didn't know what it was. He couldn't focus on anything save the *one* thing.

He pushed the blur that had blocked his path. Heard a high shout of surprise and terror and pain as the thing in his way went flying. He heard sobbing in the background.

He gathered his child. The child of his loins, his mind, and his heart. The child that had danced through life, and made all of life a place of music.

The child danced no more.

The music went away, and all that remained was silence, and screaming, and the dance was replaced by nothing at all.

Nothing. And then something…

Rage.

Tad looked up and screamed. He screamed so hard he felt his throat tear. Felt blood froth in the back of his mouth. He felt the pleasant baritone of his voice switch to a surly whisper. He felt the vocal cords tear themselves apart.

His scream faded to a hiss. Then to nothing at all. No music, no dancing. No cause, no effect. No child, no family.

Nothing but the rage.

FBI REPORT FILE FA2017R2

Appendix A

First interview with subject, night of incident, by Detectives Hernandez and Dehghani.

HERNANDEZ: Come on. Please. We just want to –

DEHGHANI: He hasn't said a word in hours. He ain't gonna talk. We should just toss him in a cell until –

HERNANDEZ: Shut up, D.

(addressing witness) My partner really wants to put you in a cage and throw away the key –

DEHGHANI: Hernandez, go f –

HERNANDEZ: – but I don't want to do that. I want to find out what happened. We have a bunch of dead people; a bunch of dead, mangled people; and a few things that we think are people, but haven't been able to scrape up quite enough to verify. Just tell us what happened. Is there anyone else out there? Anyone in danger?

DEHGHANI: He ain't gonna talk.

HERNANDEZ: Look, we know you didn't do it. Not all of it. We think there was someone behind this, but can't pin down who it was. If you know, tell us his name, please.

DEHGHANI: He could barely stand when we found him. He mighta fried a circuit or –

WITNESS: (laughter)

DEHGHANI: (addressing Hernandez) You ever see something like this?

HERNANDEZ: (unintelligible)
        (addressing witness) What about Thaddeus Sterling? He was seen near where we found you -

DEHGHANI: Not his usual stomping grounds –

HERNANDEZ: And we know he's missing.

DEHGHANI: He one of the bodies?

WITNESS: (laughter)

Following completion of transcript, N.B., NOTE FROM DET. DEHGHANI, investigating officer:

Please note in file that transcript reads "laughter." Witness was not merely chuckling or laughing as at some joke. It was loud, hysterical laughter.

PERSONAL NOTE: I have been an LAPD officer going on 22 years. I have never heard someone laugh like that. Because I can't think of adequate words to describe it, I will refer anyone reading this transcript/file to the video record, and will add that the laughing was scary as hell.

3

FBI REPORT FILE FA2017R2

Appendix B

Reproduction of YouTube comments on pertinent videos – see Appendix AA for list of videos, both active and since archived, Appendix AB for list of videos no longer available, and report sections 18 through 20 in re actions taken to recover videos that disappeared during hours following incident.

See also Appendix AC list of known commenters as matched to YouTube designations, and Appendix AD for list of YouTube designations belonging to persons still unknown.

For list of known homicides attributable to YouTube commenters, please see report for File FA 2018R2.

See also Appendix AD and files referred therein to list of Portobello Road videos, comments, and homicides. N.B.: Hard copies of the files must be relied upon, as *all electronic files are subject to corruption by parties unknown.* See Internal Report FA 2019R43.

Comments to YouTube video designated A1

4 COMMENTS   SORT BY

Gamercity69humpty
First!

👍 👎 REPLY

mYm0MMAHatezU
First!

👍 👎 REPLY

InMorning83
Was that real?

👍 👎 REPLY

MissingU4Evah
WHAT THE HELL DID WE JUST SEE?!

👍 👎 REPLY

ONE

1

The first voice was a woman. The next belonged to a man.

"Wake up, mister. Please, wake –"

"Wake *up!*"

"That's not help –"

"No *shit* it ain't!"

Clint did not hear what came next, if anything. He had been close to consciousness, but now that consciousness receded. It became a dream, and the dream pulled him to it and became his world.

2

The darkness is gone. Just for a moment.

For a moment he is standing at the place he does not want to be, and at the place he *must* be.

He looks down. The grass here is slightly weedy. Brown patches show among the green places – a water pipe burst three years ago, and since then the grass has been watered by hand, a chore which the gardener seems unwilling to do regularly. Or perhaps he is willing, but no one has paid him to do so.

Other places here are green, evenly trimmed, impeccably maintained. Those are the places where the rich lay. Even a few feet away, the graves switch from cheap plaques set into the ground to full headstones and even an ornate crypt or two.

The man stares down at his feet. Of all the markers set flush with the ground, this one is the cheapest. It was all he could have hoped to afford. More, in fact. He ate nothing but ramen noodles and rice for several weeks after he purchased it.

It is nothing.

It marks nothing.

It hides nothing.

But it is all he has of what was once his everything.

The engraving on the marker is simple:

CLAIRE – 1999-2007

There should be a longer space represented by that simple hyphen. There should be many years; in fact, there should be no hyphen at all. She should be alive.

A great many things *should* be. Few, in the man's estimation, ever *are*.

"I'm sorry I couldn't find you," he murmurs.

Then he looks up, and sees the blue sky swallowed in sudden darkness and has a single moment in which he realizes he is not here at all. He has not been here for hours, he suspects. He *was* here, then...

What?

He does not know the answer to his own question. And he has no time to ponder it, for he is not real. He is a dream, and the blue sky darkens and then the darkness reaches down and swallows everything: the grass, the stones, the marker, and – last of all – the man who is nothing but a dream.

3

The darkness he had awoken to was still there, but this time something felt different. Clint Walker could feel it. The cemetery was gone. He *had* been there, but was there no more. He would not return, either, until another year had passed. He would go back then, and look down, and be able to do nothing but mourn for what remained still lost.

The darkness still held him, but he felt it thin and weaken. He surged toward it, reaching out ghost hands to peel it apart like a spiderweb – or a cocoon. A chrysalis from which he would emerge to find… what?

More voices, first of all. One was that of the sweet-sounding young woman, another the gruff voice of the man who had spoken to her before Clint's dream/memory took him away for a moment. Another was thick with accents Clint recognized from his youth: the voice of someone with little education, but a great deal of anger.

He couldn't hear what they were saying. Only the tones. Anger, confusion… fear.

It was on the borrowed strength of this fear that Clint finally pushed out of the darkness.

4

He tried to sit up, felt like puking, sank back, then tried to sit up again. This time it was a little better. He still felt like vomiting all over the floor, but was able to choke it back and go from flat on his back to bent at an awkward forty-five degree angle, then sat up fully.

He looked up.

Looked ahead.

Looked to his right.

Even glanced down for a moment.

The sight that greeted him was essentially the same in all these directions, and that was what drew the first words from his dry mouth: "Where...?"

White. That was all he saw. White ceiling, white walls, white floor. All of them were obviously metal. The ceiling was corrugated, the waves reminding him of the shipping containers he'd seen on trains or at ports.

No doors. No windows.

One wall had a strange item beside it: a water cooler. The kind in any office or waiting room in the country. Just as white as the walls, with a single spigot in its center.

The top held a five-gallon water jug. The word "SPARKLETTS" was written across it – a sight so mundane it was beyond jarring when compared to the rest of the room.

Beside the cooler, five paper cups sat rims-down on the floor. Another odd sight, and one that drew the eye nearly as much as the final ornamentation.

Nearly.

The final thing was bolted directly to the wall. It was a wire mesh that reminded Clint a bit of some of the cages he had seen covering clocks and air conditioning controls in some of the places he had stayed as a kid. The metal cages provided access to anyone with the key, but kept mischievous – and sometimes straight-up malicious – fingers away.

This one, though, had no keyhole that Clint could see. Just a set of bolts holding it fast to the wall.

The metal looked sturdier than those other cages, too. There were gaps that allowed Clint to see what the mesh cage held, but the metal itself was thick and somehow forbidding – though not as forbidding as the thing that hung inside it.

Clint had seen such things before: it was just an iPad. But for some reason *this* iPad seemed less like an innocuous bit of personal electronics than an open eye. The dark, huge pupil of a shark, staring through a hole in the wall. Something waiting a moment more before it came in and ate what it found inside.

Clint realized abruptly that he had been laying – and now sat – on a hospital-style bed. A nice one, too. Nothing like any he'd ever been on himself. The ones he had found himself in on the one or two occasions he'd been so ill he had to go to the doctor were usually the cheap, ratty kind. Free clinics didn't have a lot of dough to invest in comfy resting.

All this Clint took in in a moment. That was something he had learned as a child: take in the details, figure out the goods and the bads whenever you land in a new place.

Movement drew his attention. He had been aware he was not alone in this place, but now he focused on the others in here.

One of the people in the room was pacing relentlessly back and forth. The entire room was only about thirty feet long from wall to wall, but the man was using every bit of it. He was black, darker even than Clint, only where Clint was about five-ten and a hundred-seventy pounds after a meal and before taking a crap, this guy was at least six-five and two-fifty. Tattoos writhed up his neck and onto his face, ending in a stylized "52" on each cheek. The tattoos were old, too; darkened with age to the point that they made his face look bruised. Like the tattoos represented something that had beaten him in over time.

They probably had. Clint knew what that number meant: the man was now or had at one time been a member of the 52 Hoover Gangster Crips, a gang that operated out of South Los Angeles, not far from where Clint had spent a large chunk of his youth.

Not many people got out of the gang, short of prison or feet-first into a coroner's van. But this guy maybe had. Certainly active members of the Five-Deuce didn't tend toward wearing suits. Light, worn weave that had turned shiny at the elbows and knees. A dark tie that hung low across the man's neck, like a noose waiting to be drawn.

The guy saw Clint looking. He shook his head. "This isn't... how can this be happening?" he asked. No reply was wanted or needed, though, since the guy turned away in the same moment and resumed his pacing.

Clint wouldn't have answered regardless, he suspected. His attention was taken by the other thing the man was wearing on his neck. The tie was down far enough, the collar of the other man's shirt open wide enough, to allow Clint an easy view of the dark collar that ran around the man's neck. It looked like a dog collar, or something you might find in a sex shop that catered to extreme fetishes. Not leather, but some kind of plastic-looking mesh.

A green light blinked, steady and inexorable, on one side of the man's collar.

Clint's hand rose automatically to his own neck, spasming slightly as he found a similar ring around his throat. It was tight. He could breathe easily enough, but couldn't get a finger between the collar and his skin without compressing his windpipe.

Is there a green light on mine, too?

What happens if it changes to a different color?

Green lights were usually a good sign, he knew. But they had a disturbing tendency to change to red. And somehow he doubted that, if such a change occurred on his collar, it would signal a party or a lotto win.

There was no seam or buckle of any kind on his collar. Just a perfect circle, bound to him for some unknown purpose.

Clint realized, too, that he was wearing a smartwatch of some kind. No buttons, but clearly electronic, with a band made of the same seamless material as the collar on his neck. He swiped a finger over the face of the watch, hoping to activate it. It remained dark.

"This ain't happen –" began the gangster again.

This time, though, he was cut off by another of the room's occupants: "Yes it is. And maybe this guy can help us figure out what 'it' is."

Clint looked at the woman who had spoken. A bit younger than him, he suspected. She was gorgeous, if a bit on the used-looking spectrum of beauty. Blue eyes, blonde hair. A fit-looking figure that was hinted at but not overtly displayed by the inexpensive jeans and white t-shirt combination she wore. Long, bangly hoop earrings hung nearly to her shoulders, adding just the right dose of trailer-trash vibe to a feathered haircut that obviously was still striving to make it to the late 1990s.

She wore a collar and a smartwatch, too.

She smiled ruefully at Clint, and when she spoke again he realized her voice was thick with the accent of someone from back east. He wasn't an expert in such things, but he figured it was probably New Jersey or New York. Maybe Boston. None of the upper crust tones he had heard on movies and TV shows, though – this was strictly working-class. The kind of voice that screamed of an upbringing in a home where Daddy worked a blue-collar job and Mommy held two more jobs to make ends meet.

"I'm Noelle," she said. "Noelle Morgan." She extended a hand. Clint shook it automatically. She had a firm grip. "Don't suppose you know what's going on?" She must have seen the answer in Clint's expression, because the small hope that had illuminated her features darkened. She chewed her lip.

Clint tried to pull at his collar again. Wondering why even as he did it – what was the old saying?

The definition of insanity is doing the same thing over and over again, but expecting a different result.

He forced his fingers away from his throat as Noelle nodded and said, "Some kind of weird plastic mesh. It feels, like, *military* or something. Something that don't feel like it'll cut or break or nothing."

"No seam, either," said Clint. "How can it –"

The gangster, still pacing, shook his head and interrupted with a, "This ain't happening. It ain't –"

Again he was cut off. This time not by Noelle but by a fourth occupant of the strange white room. The man looked to be in his fifties, his eyes and skin tone marking him as someone of Chinese descent. Though Clint had rarely seen someone of that ethnicity as big as this guy. The dude looked like a dock-worker, wearing a wife-beater tank-top, shorts, and a "life-screwed-me-so-screw-*it*" expression. "You say that again," he muttered at the gangster, "and I'll twist your head off." He shook a ham-sized fist in the direction of the man who had been pacing.

The guy with the tattoos stiffened. He shook his head like he was shaking away a bad dream, then focused on the big man who had challenged him. "Go ahead and try it," he said, and stepped toward the other guy.

The fifth – and last – occupant of the room stepped forward. She looked like she was in her late thirties or early forties. Plump, but pretty in a matronly kind of way, with eyes that Clint suspected could be wide and caring, or hooded and severe, depending on her mood and the needs of the moment. She wore a fairly shapeless gray dress familiar to him – the look of any of a million office workers or government employees in any of a million offices.

She looked Latina, and sure enough when she spoke there was the trace of rolled "r"s and long, melodic vowels that marked many native Spanish speakers' tones.

"This isn't helping any of us," she said, stepping between the two men who were busy having a stare-down.

Clint almost laughed. The woman was half the size of either of the other guys, but she showed no fear at all as she got between them. He almost laughed again when both men looked at her, then looked at each other, then back at the woman. It was clear they were trying to figure out what that woman was doing between them, and whether it would be worth their time to knock her aside before going at each other in earnest.

The black dude turned away first. The Chinese-looking guy stared at his back, scowling as the gangster resumed his pacing.

The Latina woman turned to Clint. "I'm Elena Ruiz," she said, the brightness of her voice strange in this situation.

"He's charmed, we're all sure," said the big man in the wife beater. Another odd moment as Elena Ruiz glared at him and he seemed to wilt away, cowed by the force of her stare.

Elena turned back to Clint. Gesturing to the black man wearing a furrow in the metal floor, she said, "That's Solomon Black." The big guy in the wife-beater guffawed at that. Barely batting an eye, Elena said, "And our resident optimist won't tell us his full name."

"Chong's good enough for me," said the big man. "It should be good enough for you." Fishing in the pocket of his shorts, he came out with a lighter and a half-crumpled package of cigarettes. He shook out a cigarette and lit it.

"Can you not?" said Noelle.

Chong glared at her. The tip of his cigarette glowed as he inhaled deeply, then exhaled forcefully in Noelle's direction.

For a moment, Noelle looked like she was considering mayhem, then she just sighed and looked back at Clint. "Can you tell us anything?" she asked.

At the same time, Elena said, "What's the last thing you remember?"

"I… " Clint's brows bunched together. "Not really. I do remem –"

His voice cut off suddenly as he swiveled to his left, and saw for the first time what waited there. For some reason, he had assumed he was at the outer wall of the room. He usually had a good feel for spaces – another product of his upbringing in places where you never knew when you might have to fight or run, so you stayed aware of the geography of your surroundings – but supposed that whatever had knocked him out must have robbed his mind of a bit of its normal function. Because he definitely wasn't at the edge of the room. He was at its midpoint.

There was no one to his left. Everyone else in the room had stationed themselves on one side, and Clint couldn't blame them for their choice of position. What lay in the other half of the room was disquieting, to say the least.

Not disquieting. Nothing so gentle. It's weird. Creepy.

Terrifying.

5

The other side of the room was decorated almost identically to the one Clint had first seen. No water cooler, no paper cups, no iPad behind a mesh cage on the wall.

But the beds were there. The same expensive-looking, white, hospital-style frames with the same expensive-looking, white, hospital-style mattresses. The head of each mattress was propped up to a forty-five degree angle, as though whoever had prepared this place wanted to display the occupants of those beds.

And there *were* occupants in them. Just none living.

Five beds. And in each, a mannequin.

Each mannequin was positioned the same – propped up at forty-five degree angles by the hospital beds – but each was a different size and wore different clothing. Three "men" and two "women." And just in case it hadn't already been obvious what they represented, whoever had placed them so carefully on the beds also had dressed them in the clothes similar to those worn by the breathing occupants of the room.

A big, dark mannequin wearing a cheap suit. Another big one, "skin" a yellow-gold, wearing a wife-beater and shorts. Another one, a bit smaller than the others, also dark and wearing jeans and a button-up. The others – the "girls" – wore jeans and a white t-shirt, and a boring gray suit, respectively.

All wore collars. All wore smartwatches.

Creepy. But none of that was as bad as the last little detail: each mannequin had had a huge red smile painted over its lips. Clownish, the kind of grin you'd expect to see on Ronald McDonald. Only no fast food chain in the world would dare to feature a mascot who also had huge white circles painted over their "eyes," with a small black dot in the center of each to represent a sightlessly staring pupil.

The mannequins smiled, and their wide eyes stared at nothing at all.

Clint shivered and turned away. "What the hell is going on?" he asked.

"None of us knows," said Noelle. She shrugged, her shoulders bouncing up and down in a jittery, nervous motion.

"What's the last thing you remember?" asked Elena.

"Shit, lady," said Chong, "who died and made *you* queen? What's the last thing *you* remember?"

Elena took no visible offense at Chong's attitude. She shrugged her shoulders. "I was working in my office."

"Bet you didn't expect your workday to end this way," said Noelle.

Elena's face took on a strange cast. "No. But it didn't start out well, so for what it's worth, at least the day was consistently crappy." When Noelle cocked her eyebrows in an obvious question, Elena shook her head and said, "I work in a place that's constantly on the edge of bankruptcy. Today was one of those days where we realize the money we need for things like rent isn't there."

"Sounds fun," said Clint.

"Not really." Elena laughed. "Here's the funny part: I was looking at the ledger, and thinking what bad luck it was that the bank balance was at six-hundred-sixty-six dollars. 'Bad luck,' I thought. Then...." Her eyebrows drew together.

"What?" prompted Noelle.

"Some noise. Like... a bee? A swarm of bees?" Elena shook her head. "I was emailing, then I...." She frowned. "I don't remember what happened. Just that buzz, and then I woke up in here."

"Where do you work?" asked Noelle.

"What the hell does *that* matter?" demanded Chong.

Solomon Black had stopped pacing for the moment, and now stared at Chong. "Dude, just shut your –"

Before either man could resume their short-tempered feud, Elena answered Noelle. "St. Jerome's," she said.

Even though he was the one who had just objected to the line of questioning, Chong asked, "That the hospital near Sepulveda?"

"No," said Elena.

A moment of silence prevailed. Chong cleared his throat. "Anyone want to know where *I* was when it happened?"

"Not really," murmured Noelle. But it was so quiet Clint barely heard it, and he suspected it was too quiet for Chong to register.

"I was watching the game at my place," said Chong. "Doing some work –"

"I thought you said you were watching the game," said Solomon.

"Multi-tasking, bro," said Chong, the civility of his words given lie by the clipped tone of his voice. "You ever hear of a home office?"

Another tense moment. Then Solomon sniffed dismissively. Chong nodded like he'd just scored a three-pointer in a pick-up game. "Dickhead team wasn't doing shit for playing anyway. Eyes on the prize, guys, I always say, and their eyes weren't even close, so I bailed for a minute. Went into the office while the eighteenth huddle-up was happening and…." He shrugged.

"What do you do for a living?" asked Noelle.

"I package and distribute cans of mind-your-own-beeswax," said Chong.

Another staredown, this time between Chong and Noelle. The young woman looked away first. "Just thought it might matter," she said. "Maybe we're here because of something we do for a living."

"Maybe," agreed Clint. He looked at Chong. "So…?"

"So I still package and distribute cans of mind-your-own –"

"Good heavens," said Elena. "What would it hurt to tell us?"

Chong glared at her. Then shrugged and said, "I'm a broker. I put people who need stuff in touch with people who have stuff. For a commission, of course."

"What kind of stuff?" asked Noelle.

Chong's only answer was a grin that Clint had seen before. Never from someone doing something legal, though. It was the smile of people who considered themselves outside – and usually above – the rules. People who thought of the world as something they could, and should, take bits and pieces of as they wished.

"Did you hear bees?" asked Elena.

Chong almost laughed. Then he squinted as though trying to see into the distance. Past the white walls of this place and into a faraway memory, Clint suspected.

"Maybe."

Elena nodded, then turned to Solomon. "And you?" she asked.

"I was coming home from work," he said.

Chong snorted – a sound that Clint was quickly coming to realize must be one of his trademarks. "A job, huh? What kinda job? Boosting some old lady's car? Rolling a gas station?"

Solomon looked away, but not before Clint caught the guilt in the guy's eyes. "I don't do that stuff."

"Sure," said Chong. Another snort. "You're probably an accountant. Wait, no – insurance salesman, right?"

Clint's jaw dropped at Solomon's answer. Turning a fierce glare on Chong, the big black man said, "I'm a motivational speaker."

The strangeness of that statement was enough to quell every sound in the room. Chong was first to recover. No snort, though; this time it was an ugly, derisive laugh.

Noelle tugged at the collar of her shirt. "Damn, it's hot," she said.

Clint realized he was sweating. They were in a metal box with no visible vents or other outlets for the body heat in here, so of course it was hot. But he suspected that the box itself wasn't outside. A roof and walls like the ones surrounding the group would have turned the place into an oven if they were exposed to direct sunlight.

Or maybe it's just night. No way to know what time it is. No way to know anything.

"What about you?" asked Elena. "What's the last thing you remember, Noelle?"

Noelle had been looking at the water cooler as she tugged at the neck at her shirt. Now she turned back to Elena. "Work."

"Where?" asked Elena.

"I work at a bar on Cienega."

"Anything unusual about it?"

Noelle's lips pursed. After a moment, she shook her head. "No. Just the usual crowd of drunks busy grabbing drinks when they're not trying to grab my ass." Her eyes took on the same faraway squint that Chong's had held a moment ago. "I went out to the alley behind the bar for a break, and then...."

"Bees?" asked Elena.

After a moment, Noelle nodded. "But I don't remember anything else. Just work and –"

"I bet you like your work, too," said Chong. Clint was really starting to not like the guy. "What do you charge for 'work'?" he asked.

Clint stood up. "Back off, man. You're not –"

"Who's gonna make me, kid? You?" demanded Chong, striding forward until he was inches away from Clint.

"*So* hot," said Noelle. She was obviously trying to shift the focus away from yet another imminent fight. It worked. Everyone turned to look at her. She was staring at the cooler next to the wall. At the paper cups on the floor. "Anyone want a drink?" she said with a nervous titter.

Clint did. But he wasn't willing to give in to the desire. It *was* hot, but not intolerably so. And drinking water in a place like this... not a great idea, he suspected.

"Not me," said Chong.

Solomon grunted. "You worried it's poisoned or something?" he asked Chong, the tone of his voice making it clear that he thought Chong was a candy-ass, gutless wimp.

"No," Chong said easily. "Not at all. It's like Mom always said: 'Don't take candy from strangers, but if you wake up in a windowless, doorless room with a suspicious water cooler sitting there while dummies do Joker grins at you, be sure to drink up.'"

Noelle took half a step forward, and Clint realized now how damp the tiny hairs on the back of her neck were; how her skin glistened. "Whoever did this could have poisoned us while we were asleep if they wanted –"

"We don't know *what* the guy could –" began Chong.

"Who says it's a guy?" demanded Noelle, her accent thickening with ire. "Maybe a woman –"

Chong had been cut off by the question. Now he returned the favor, yelling over Noelle's words, "Sorry, *princess*. Did I offend the social justice crowd?" He bowed low, a mocking parody of the kind of gesture you might see in a movie about English royalty.

Clint shook his head. He didn't know what was happening, but he was sick enough of the bickering already that he was willing to do just about anything to shut it up. And he was getting thirsty, too, and figured that whoever went to all the trouble to set this up hadn't done it just to poison them as soon as they woke. So he pushed forward, picked up one of the paper cups, filled it with water from the cooler, and upended it into his mouth.

He paused when he was done. He realized that everyone was staring at him. Waiting, no doubt, for him to keel over or begin frothing at the mouth. He kind of expected something like that to happen, too.

But nothing did. After a moment, he poured another cup. Drank it. Smacked his lips and said, "Tastes a lot like water. And it *is* damn hot in here."

Solomon's hands opened and shut, like he was grabbing phantom cups of water for himself as Clint drank for a third time. The big ex-gangster stepped forward, obviously deciding that if Clint survived the drink then *he* could.

Before he had taken two steps, Chong shouldered past him. "Hey!" shouted Solomon.

"Let it go, *hermanito*," said Elena.

Solomon frowned at her. "*No soy tu hermanito*," he spat.

Elena, visibly surprised, said, "*Hablas español?*"

"My old lady was Mexican," said Solomon.

"'Was'?" parroted Noelle.

Solomon glared at her, his eyes full of anger and, Clint thought, more than a small measure of hurt. The big man finally shook his head, grimaced, and picked up a cup. He filled it with water then, surprisingly, didn't drink. Instead, he held out the cup to Elena.

"*Gracias*," murmured Elena, taking the cup and drinking deep.

Solomon nodded, then filled another cup and handed it to Noelle before filling the last cup and drinking it himself.

"Hey," Chong said to Clint. He sipped at his cup and said, almost conversationally, "Where were you today? When you got grabbed?"

"Cemetery," Clint said quietly.

"Doing what?"

Clint ignored him. Chong shrugged and poured another cup. Drank. Belched. He crumpled his cup and tossed it in a corner. Noelle rolled her eyes. "Doth I offend, milady?" asked Chong, then belched again.

Noelle turned away. She met Clint's eyes. "What?" she demanded.

Clint realized he had been staring at her. It surprised him – he wasn't the type to just stare at a girl, even when *not* confined in some lunatic's playpen – and it took a moment for him to answer, mostly because it took a moment for him to understand the answer himself. Then it hit him, hit him like a hammer upside the head. "You remind me of someone is all."

For a moment he saw the marker. The words – so few words! – that were such an unfitting synopsis of a life.

Noelle shoved her hands in her pockets, obviously embarrassed. "Who?" she asked a moment later.

Clint didn't want to answer that. And as it turned out, he didn't have to. A voice, bright and cheery and oh-so-strange, said, "Well, aren't you all just the *cutest* thing ever?"

Scavenger Hunt

6

The voice was high-pitched, gleeful in a macabre way that sent a shiver wriggling up Clint's spine. Five pairs of eyes turning to look at the iPad on the wall – the one that had been dark until now, but which was dark no more.

The voice had been strange. Disconcerting. But not nearly as much as the face it came from, because it was not a face at all. Yet at the same time it *was* a face of a kind; and a famous face, at that.

The man who stared out of the screen behind the wire mesh that secured the iPad to the wall was wearing a dark suit and tie. Or at least a dark *jacket* and tie. He was only visible from the shoulders up, so below that he could be wearing shorts or chaps or nothing at all for all Clint knew.

Clint couldn't make out *where* the man was, either. The backdrop behind him was nothing but a white wall, featureless as the walls that now surrounded Clint and the others in this place. But the combination of white background and dark suit made the simple yellow of the man's "face" stand out brightly, almost painfully so.

The man wore a yellow circle over his face. A perfect circle, marred only by a black line, curved in an upward arc near the bottom, and two black dots close to the top. The simple yellow "smiley face" that could be seen on keychains, bumper stickers, and – most of all – was the first emoji on phones the world over.

Though Clint admitted that none of those smiley faces were spattered with blood the way this one was. The red-on-yellow was nearly as jarring as the yellow itself against the white background. And twice as terrifying.

Clint felt the moment stretch out. Utter silence as five strangers were stared down by a man in a suit, wearing a yellow cutout over his face. The smiley face twisted on its center axis as the head below cocked to the side: whoever was under there was waiting.

Chong rushed forward with a sudden scream, his fists pummeling the cage that protected the iPad. "Let us out of here!" he screamed. "I'll kill you! I'll find you, and when I do I –"

The cage didn't give under his fists, the silvery metal easily resisting his attack. Still, some of the vibrations must have made their way through to the iPad, because it glitched for a moment. The smiley face twisted, and the shoulders of the man on the screen bunched together as though he were flinching away from Chong's attack. "Stop," he whispered. Then, louder, "Please, just *stop*."

Chong's only response was to roar even louder, and renew his attack. "Stop, stop, *STOP!*" shouted the man on the iPad.

And Chong did stop. Suddenly and completely. Not because of the words, but because of the sharp tone that suddenly rang out through the room.

Everyone spun to face the five empty hospital beds... and toward the five occupied beds beyond. The beep sounded once more as they turned, and Clint had a moment to see that the light on the collar worn by the "Chong" dummy had shifted from green to red.

And then it exploded.

Smoke filled the white room. Clint coughed and waved away the sudden plume of darkness that surrounded him. A few moments later, the darkness withdrew. There was a hum, and Clint realized that there must be some kind of hidden venting system somewhere, because the smoke was clearing away. Letting him and the others see "Chong."

The mannequin's head was mostly gone. Half the collar hung from the thing's melted neck, the underside of the mesh criss-crossed with silvery lines, and it didn't take a brain surgeon to intuit that they had led to, and caused the discharge of, the explosives packed in the collar.

As Clint watched, the remaining bits of the mannequin's head sagged, melting from the heat of the explosion. His gaze flicked to the side, catching an open-mouthed Chong who stared in horror at his avatar, melting and blackened on a bed that smoldered beneath it.

Everyone turned back to the iPad. The man there stared out through the small black dots. "When I give an order," he said quietly, "I expect to be obeyed. Understand?" His voice quavered, as though he was holding himself back from hysterical screaming only by the greatest of effort.

Clint nodded. So did everyone else, their chins going up and down in perfect sync. The smiley face moved, too, nodding as well. "Wonderful," said the man, his voice still strained and strange. "Then let's begin."

7

"First: introductions," said the man. "I already know your names. And as for me…." He giggled, a jagged shard of a laugh. "You can call me Mr. Do-Good."

Clint felt like the world was spinning too fast. He wondered what would happen if – *when* – it finally flung itself loose of its moorings.

Again, he was taken back to the cemetery. To the time staring at the reminder of the last moment the world had spun away beneath him. He went once a year, every year. That was not enough to honor what was there, but he could not stand to see it more often than that.

He had thought those times were the worst; that what the marker represented was the lowest possible point of his life. And he realized now how wrong he had been.

"Please, mister," said Noelle, her voice small and faraway. "Why are we here?"

Mr. Do-Good's mask did not move, and of course Clint had no idea what his face looked like beneath it. Even so, he had the distinct impression that the man was beaming at Noelle like she was a prize student. "What a good question!" he half-shouted. "We're going to play a game, of course!"

"What kind of –" began Noelle.

"Please, dear," said Mr. Do-Good, "don't interrupt. It's rude." Then he cleared his throat. "But to answer your question… I guess you could call it a scavenger hunt. You've all played those, right?" He paused a moment. When no one answered, he continued, "You get points for going door to door and getting people to give you things, or doing something ridiculous in a public place?" The words ended in a question. The kind of sentence a host at a party might utter when in doubt that the party game he had chosen might not go over as well as hoped.

No one spoke. Clint didn't know if he *could* have spoken, even if he had wanted to. The world was still spinning too fast, and if he said anything at all he thought he might just fly away and be fully and finally lost.

And would that be so bad?

He was spared the need to answer his own question as Mr. Do-Good continued. "Excellent!" he shouted, as though everyone had answered his last query with overwhelming knowledge of and excitement about the prospect of playing his game. "But I must warn you: this scavenger hunt is a little different than most. You'll have tasks that will be sent via your smartwatches."

Clint saw lights flare in his peripheral vision as everyone's watches brightened. Clint looked at his. No time, no music or email apps. Just a familiar symbol: a smiley face. The face winked as Clint looked at it, then he looked back at the iPad on the wall as Mr. Do-Good spoke again.

"You like them? They're super-*duper* cool." Another laugh, so intense it sounded almost panicked. "So you'll be given a place, and a time to get there. When you arrive – assuming you arrive in time! – you'll get a task, and another time limit in which to accomplish it."

Elena whispered something under her breath. Clint couldn't hear what it was, but he suspected it was a prayer.

Chong whispered as well, though his words were loud enough for Clint to make out: "The hell's wrong with this guy?"

"Shhh!" hissed Noelle.

Mr. Do-Good laughed again. "Now, assuming you get to the place, and finish your task, you'll receive your next challenge, then your next, and so on." Then, as though to forestall questions that no one had asked, he added, "There *are* a limited number of tasks, I promise. And if you get through them all, you get to go free. Isn't that ever so nice?"

No one answered.

No one moved.

The world kept spinning, spinning. Clint's knees felt rubbery, his guts hot and loose inside him.

"Now, the rules," said Mr. Do-Good. Another mad, pained giggle. "We've already covered that you have to complete the challenges. Some will go to everyone, some will be for a specific person. You have to stick together as you play. Finish the game, and like I said, you're free."

"What if we don't play the game?" Noelle whispered.

Mr. Do-Good leaned a bit closer to the screen. "I really hope that doesn't happen, Noelle. If it does...." The circle twisted slightly, as though the person behind it was looking beyond the group.

Clint turned for just a moment. Long enough to see that the "Chong" mannequin had slumped forward, the burnt nub of its neck resting against its own knees.

Mr. Do-Good spoke again, and sounded suddenly... lost. Like he had forgotten who he was for a moment. Clint wondered if the world was spinning under the man on the other side of the screen, just like it was for him. "Okay," said Do-Good, "so where were we? Oh, right. You have to do what the watches say. And there are a few other rules, too. First: no police. Anyone says a word to a cop and *kaboom!* Also, you have to go wherever I tell you on foot. No cars, bikes, roller skates, scooters, or unicycles." He laughed, sounding suddenly angry – as though he was saying words he himself hated, but was helpless to alter. "Oh, one more thing: you can't talk to anyone unless they talk to you first. But even if they do, you can't mention me, or the scavenger hunt, or anything relating to it. Just say whatever you need to, to get rid of them, and keep on your merry way." He breathed audibly, inhaling a shaky, strained gasp of air. "And remember, too, that any conversations you have will necessarily keep you from completing your tasks in that time, so you might want to restrain yourself to a quick hello-and-goodbye, rather than extended conversations about French impressionism, mmmm*kay?*" He paused. "Okey-dokey then!"

Another beep rang through the room, and Clint jerked in place, his hand going automatically to his throat. Chong and Elena did the same, while Solomon and Noelle simply went rigid.

But it wasn't the collars. When Clint realized it, he did what everyone else did. He raised his hand, looking at the smartwatch on his wrist. The smiley face was still there, but it had shrunk and moved to the top right corner of the watch face. It spun around, like an image on a video game's load screen.

As it did, Do-Good spoke again, from the watch this time: "Do-Good says, *LET'S HAVE SOME FUN!* Your first challenge is to go to 1514 North Chambers Street. Time: 15 minutes."

As he spoke, the exact words he used also scrolled across the watches.

The words blinked, then numbers appeared below them.

15:00...

14:59...

14:58...

8

As the numbers counted down, Clint heard the *whirrrr* of some kind of motor, and a second after that –

(14:57… 14:56…)

– two of the walls began sliding back, separating at the corner where they had come together a moment before. Everyone took a hesitant step in that direction, propelled by the knowledge of what would happen if they failed to meet Do-Good's deadline.

Poor choice of word.

"I don't want to go," whispered Elena. She flicked a glance in the direction of the iPad, as though this entreaty might make Mr. Do-Good throw up his hands, laugh, and say, "Oh, okay, then let's just call the whole thing off."

Noelle was shaking her head, obviously agreeing with the sentiment, hands jammed deep in her pockets – what Clint guessed was a nervous gesture, a defensive posture that she hoped would keep her unnoticed in times of stress or danger. "This is a bad idea," she said.

Do-Good didn't say anything. The smiley face just stared. But a second later, four explosions rocked the small white room as the four remaining mannequins' heads blew apart.

The shock glitched the iPad again. "I recommend you get a move on," said Do-Good from the screen.

Clint didn't look at the others.

He just ran out of the room. From the small white cell into the greater, more dangerous prison of Mr. Do-Good's game.

Scavenger Hunt

9

When he exited the white room, he found that his earlier deduction had been correct: the white room was not outside.

The thing was a boxy structure, painted black on the outside as though to counterpoint the whiteness of its interior. The whole thing hunkered in the center of a large space that Clint guessed was the floor of a deserted warehouse somewhere. The entire place had a dilapidated, abandoned air. The roof, high above, had hanging lamps and spaces where fluorescent bars must have nestled, all of them broken or missing entirely. Beyond the lights, a long row of windows – also largely broken or missing – showed nothing but empty air and darkness. Night outside.

The light that flowed from the white room was the only illumination, and it spilled over dirt and refuse and the occasional pile of old office furniture and a few filing cabinets that tilted drunkenly against one another: evidence of the business that had once been done here, but had apparently died off long ago.

Solomon Black was looking around, spinning almost wildly in place as though to catch any attacker that might be sneaking up on him. "What is this place?" demanded the ex-gangster.

"No idea," said Noelle.

Elena, looking at her watch, said, "Then how far is it to…?"

"Everyone, outside," said Clint. "Let's find out where we are first, then we can go from there."

He expected someone to fight his suggestion, if for no other reason than because Chong and Solomon, at least, tended to fight *every* suggestion. But no one said a word, and everyone jogged after him as Clint quickly made his way to the closest door that looked like it might lead outside the warehouse.

His guess was a good one. The door opened with a squeal of rusty hinges, and when Clint stepped through he found himself in a run-down street. Refuse similar to that inside the warehouse lay all over, as though it had lined up to get inside the building where it could lay down and die with others of its kind.

To the sides sat more large buildings, all industrial in appearance, all run-down in maintenance. A seedy-looking street of a type that could be found in the commercial areas of any large city. Clint didn't recognize it by sight, and realized that he had no idea where the white room was. He had assumed it was close to the place where he had been taken, but this might not be Los Angeles. It could be New York or Chicago or *China* for all he knew.

He spun around, looking for… there! He ran toward the metal bar that jutted out of the sidewalk nearby. Looking at the green placards that jutted from it, he asked, "Anyone know how to get to where we need to be from here?" He gestured at the signpost showing the cross streets.

"I do. I know this area," said Solomon, his gravelly voice somehow deeper now that they were out in the open. He pointed to the right. "We're about a mile away."

"And we have only fifteen minutes?" breathed Elena, fear squeezing her voice up a few notes.

Chong took off. Running in the direction Solomon had indicated, not waiting as he shouted, "*Fourteen* minutes, actually."

He ran fast, but not far. When he was about fifty feet away, that same beep Clint and the others had heard before slashed the night sky. Chong halted so fast Clint could practically hear the big man's feet bite into the pavement below as the beep came again.

"What happened? What color? What –" demanded Chong.

"It's red!" shouted Elena. She hustled after Chong, the others hesitating only a moment before following.

Clint wondered why any of them *would* follow, *would* get close to Chong when his collar was now flashing red. Then he realized the answer his body had already known, even as Noelle said, "We have to stick together, remember?"

As they approached Chong, the big man's collar flashed once more, then went green. He must have seen that fact on the others' faces, because he heaved a sigh of relief that quickly became a sharp exhale of purest irritation. "Shit. Hitched my wagon to a buncha –" He shook his head. "Come on."

He turned and began jogging in the same direction he'd been going. He moved fast enough that everyone had to hustle to keep up, but not so fast that he left them behind.

The collar on his neck stayed green. Clint cast his eyes over the others' collars. All green. When he got to Noelle, she nodded and smiled weakly. "Looks like we'll be having some together time, huh?"

Clint couldn't help but chuckle.

They continued forward, keeping pace with the slowest of the group. Clint would have figured that to be Elena, since she was the shortest and roundest of them. But she turned out to be surprisingly quick, her legs pumping like pistons as she continually outpaced everyone else, moving ahead a dozen paces before seeming to remember the rules of the "game," allowing herself to fade back and letting everyone catch up.

No, the slowest person was Solomon. He was tall and rangy, but his long legs moved slowly – torturously so, given what was waiting for them if they didn't make their journey. Clint gritted his teeth, knowing that saying anything wouldn't make the big guy move any faster.

Chong didn't have the same inhibitions. "Hey, *motivational speaker*," he said, turning the title into some kind of slur. "Can't you motivate yourself?"

Solomon managed a short glare before turning his attention to putting one foot in front of the other. "Doesn't... work... like that...." he said in between breaths.

"You're a pretty shitty motivator, eh?" said Chong. "Doubt you bring home the bacon." He paused, and his mouth curled in a sour grin. "Going back to boosting cars, I assume?"

"Shut *up*," shouted Noelle. She looked around, obviously surprised at her own outburst, then her shoulders stiffened as she added, "He's *good*," to Chong.

Clint blinked in surprise, a motion echoed by Solomon himself. "You... you heard me talk?"

Noelle nodded. To Chong she said, "He used to be a gang member. The...." She looked at Solomon. "What gang was it?"

"I'm Five-Deuce," Solomon said, spitting out the words as a combination curse and challenge and shield. Then he blinked as though surprised. "*Used* to be Five-Deuce." He gestured around. "This is actually their territory. It's how I know it."

"Banged a lotta hookers here, huh?" said Chong.

"Shut up!" Noelle shouted again. "Didn't you hear him? *Used* to be a gang member. Now he talks about getting out. He's got a good message. Better than anything *you've* said." She turned to Solomon and added, "Your wife must be proud."

"She is," said Solomon.

Chong laughed. Clint sighed. "What's so funny now?" he asked.

"He said that his wife *was* Mexican," said Chong. He waggled his eyebrows at Solomon. "She leave you? That what happened?"

Solomon's eyes flashed with sudden rage, and he took an angry step toward Chong. Before he could get there, though, Clint surprised himself by launching toward the bigger man. He shoved Chong, feeling the man's tank top rip under his hands. "Shut up, man! Don't push him! There's no reason to –"

Chong, staggered back by the surprising force of Clint's push, now surged forward. "What's your damage, kid? Not like I was making fun of *your* family – if you even have one left after your little visit to the cemetery."

Clint felt his features twist liquidly, washing back and forth between the twin shores of anger and hurt. For a moment he was back in an office – *the* office. Back in front of the nicked-up desk with the placard on it that said "DAVE

HIGGINS, DIR." over a logo with the name "Eighth Street Children."

Dave Higgins was behind the desk. Gray. Always gray, like he had been born in a stormcloud and had carried a bit of that storm with him everywhere he went. He leaned forward over that crappy, tortured desk and Clint heard his own voice – high and tight, the way it always was in this memory – say, "She's dead, isn't she? My little sister is dead."

The bit of his past inserted itself into Clint's present, throwing him back and twisting in his guts with a sharpness that hurt. Then that pain became a tightness, and the tightness shifted quickly to anger. Clint shoved Chong again, shoving the memory away at the same time.

Clint lunged forward, following Chong as he stepped back in surprise. Other than an ability to take a punch, Clint didn't have any particular skills as a fighter. He doubted he could face down a guy as big as Chong. But he had to do something. Had to make the nightmare memory go away. Pain could do it. He'd fight, he'd maybe lose. But the memory would go, and hopefully would stay gone.

He took another step, and looked down as he felt something touch his arm. For a moment, he was looking at Claire.

No. Not her. She's dead.

It was Noelle. The young woman squeezed his bicep. "Don't," she said. "He's not worth it."

Clint stared at her, seeing his sister's face superimposed over Noelle's, existing both in this place, this *now*, and in the *then* of memory.

Claire faded. She always did.

Clint nodded sharply, then turned away from Chong and resumed walking. The timer was still counting down.

Seven minutes and change.

Interlude

1

Her name was Hope, and it was more than a name. For Hope Sterling, her name was a beacon that pointed at a brighter tomorrow.

For a long time it had been nothing *but* a name. She recognized, even at a young age, that she enjoyed blessings of a type and on a level that most people could only dream about. That was part and parcel of being the only child of one of the richest men in the world. But recognizing one's elevated station was not the same as truly appreciating it, or of having the hope that tomorrow will be as bright – or brighter – than today.

Then she fell. She fell into Mommy's arms, and then she had a moment where she thought she heard Daddy's voice. Then all went quiet and all went dark but somehow Hope knew she was still falling. Falling and falling forever, until there was nothing but the darkness, pressing her down farther and farther, faster and faster.

She hit the bottom of the nothing-place with a jarring jolt that she felt from her toes to the top of her head. It hurt. Every cell in her body screamed, and even though she could see nothing of herself, she felt herself turn into a clenched fist. One solid line of muscle, pulling itself tighter and tighter and so tight it felt like she was going to die, and then tighter still.

Then the fist opened. The darkness fled.

Hope opened her eyes.

She was in a room she recognized, though she had no memory of ever visiting such a place before. But she knew what the bright lights and white, naked walls and the *beep-beep-beep* nearby all meant: she was in a hospital.

She didn't understand what was happening. She was seven, and she was a bright seven-year-old – everyone said so, and some said she was something far beyond merely *bright* – but even the smartest child has her limits. That was something she knew, too, just as she knew that it was no crime or shame to ask for help.

She tried. She wanted so badly to open her mouth, to scream and cry, but when she tried her mouth stayed closed, her words remained locked in her throat, no tears came to her eyes.

Hope panicked, but only for a moment.

This will end. I'll be able to move again in a second.

She had no idea if that was true or not, but she chose to believe.

That was the first, smallest hope.

She stopped struggling, and listened. At first there was only that steady beep of a heart monitor. Then other sounds came to her: the hum of machinery, the different but no less distinct babble of voices – people going about their business in this place.

She heard Daddy a moment later. He sounded like he was far away. She had to concentrate to hear him, and no matter how hard she tried, she missed every few words. The blackness into which she had fallen kept threatening to come back, and whenever it did it dampened out sound and sight for precious seconds.

"… -most died," Daddy said. "How did this happen? I can't believe –"

Daddy faded for a moment. Hope didn't understand the words he had said. What had died? Was *she* dying?

Daddy's voice returned then, and he sounded lost. "I don't believe it. How can this be possible? I can't... I can't believe that...."

Hope heard something that sounded like a sob, and for the first time she felt afraid. Even in the darkness, she hadn't really felt fear. The darkness was nasty and thick and felt like it was shoving into every part of her, but she hadn't really *feared*. She had known that Mommy and Daddy would find her, and would pull her out of that darkness sooner than later.

But the sound of Daddy crying... that was something she had never heard, never thought she *would* hear. And if something had made Daddy, with his money and his thousands of employees and the dozens of people who ran his house and above all with Mommy at his side... if something made Daddy cry, how terrible and frightening a thing it must be.

She felt a hand on hers. She still couldn't move, but her soul jumped at the touch. She heard Daddy again, and finally realized that he wasn't far away at all; he was right here beside her. But he still sounded like he was on the other side of a thick wall when he said, "This can't happen. I won't let this happen."

She looked for a moment. She saw Daddy. He plastered a smile on his face, so wide and so red and so fake she knew it could not be real. Daddy never smiled like that, and that meant something was wrong. It meant Daddy was afraid.

"Mommy?" she said. Because shouldn't Mommy be there, too?

"She's not here, honey. But I am. I'll always be –"

The darkness reached out. Hope didn't know if it would keep her this time. Whatever had happened had terrified Daddy, so she no longer knew if he could fix whatever it was.

She could only hope.

FBI REPORT FILE FA2017R2

Appendix B

Reproduction of YouTube comments on pertinent videos – see Appendix AA for list of videos, both active and since archived, Appendix AB for list of videos no longer available, and report sections 18 through 20 in re actions taken to recover videos that disappeared during hours following incident.

See also Appendix AC list of known commenters as matched to YouTube designations, and Appendix AD for list of YouTube designations belonging to persons still unknown.

For list of known homicides attributable to YouTube commenters, please see report for File FA 2018R2.

See also Appendix AD and files referred therein to list of Portobello Road videos, comments, and homicides. N.B.: Hard copies of the files must be relied upon, as *all electronic files are subject to corruption by parties unknown*. See Internal Report FA 2019R43.

Comments to YouTube video designated A9

---

2 COMMENTS   SORT BY

Lost1tY3st3rday
I think… I think that shit was real.
👍 👎 REPLY

HansomeMuthah92
I think it was.

Can we do that? You think we can?
👍 👎 REPLY

TWO

1

"Gotta live the dream, boy."

Those were the last words Solomon Black heard his old man say. The dude had knocked up Solomon's mom and then bolted when he found out she was pregnant. He came back when Solomon was five, ambling into the apartment like he owned the place; like he hadn't even been gone. He pulled a beer from the crappy fridge, tossed his feet on the chair, and said, "Hey, girl," to Solomon's mom before turning on a football game.

After five minutes he turned it off, said, "Cocksuckers couldn't win a game if the other team didn't even show up," then took Solomon's mom behind the curtain strung up in the middle of the single room that served as living room, dining room, and kitchen on one side of the fabric... and the "bedroom" on the other.

A couple seconds of murmured conversation. Solomon heard the strange dude say, "Baby, please," a couple times. Then he heard sounds he never heard before. Sounded like his momma was maybe getting hurt, so he went to the other side of the curtain and then a heavy, man's boot flew out and hit his head with a dry, painful thud. Both Mom and the stranger screamed for him to get out.

He did, but not before he saw what was happening beyond the curtain. It scared him. Mom *had* to be hurt, right?

But she came out ten minutes later and was all smiles. She got the stranger another beer, then sat on the arm of the chair he'd apparently adopted as his own and whispered to him and giggled and then giggled more every time the dude pinched her bottom or squeezed her boob.

Solomon did not like the guy.

"He's your daddy," his mom said after the dude left, maybe a half hour later – a half hour during which the stranger had not looked at Solomon even once.

"Daddy?" Solomon remembered saying.

"Yes. Your daddy. He'll be around more now."

She said it like that was that, like it was all the explanation anyone could want, need, or hope for. That was how she acted, too, because Solomon certainly never heard nothing more about the stranger who was his daddy.

"Dad" showed up every week or two. Never sent no money Solomon's way, or his mom's – least, not from what Solomon saw when he ate his dinner or went to school with no lunch after a breakfast of water and wishing.

In fact, near as Solomon could tell, money actually went out the door every time Dad showed up. He drank whatever beer was in the house – and Mom started stocking up, too, so as to have "everything nice and nice" for him when he showed up. And when he left, Dad usually whispered something in her ear and waited 'til she handed over whatever money was in her purse. If she didn't hand it over, he just took it. She complained once.

Black eyes are a good way to stop someone's complaining. That was the first of two things Solomon learned from his dad. The second was that taking things was easy, and no one said shit to you if you did it with the right attitude. The attitude could get you money from a woman who could barely afford food, and turn that money into new Jordans or a limited edition Lakers hoodie.

Solomon didn't have that attitude. Not yet. But he was getting it. He wasn't as big as the other kids, but he figured that was because he was barely getting started. At five years old he knew he was tiny, but he also knew he was tough. One time Darius – a second-grader whose daddy was a different kind of no-show, 'cause he was doing a dime in Folsom for armed robbery – cut Solomon with a knife he brought to school. The knife wasn't too big, thankfully, but it still cut Solomon pretty deep. Even so, when he got home he didn't say a thing until his mom asked (screamed, actually) what had happened and why blood was running down his arm and staining the carpet.

"Dad" came home while Mom was sewing him up. Hospitals were too expensive, so when Dad walked in Solomon was sitting quietly as Mom ran black thread in neat crosses along the length of the cut.

Dad watched for a minute. He stared at Solomon, and Solomon could tell that his dad wanted to say something. Didn't, though. Just shoved a knuckle into Solomon's head and gave him a noogie that hurt near as much as the knife cut did, and said, "Tough little shit," before taking Mom into the bedroom and making their noises again.

It was the only compliment Solomon's dad ever paid him. He hated his dad, he knew that. But he couldn't help feeling all glowed up inside, like he had a candle or a fire or something in his chest. Felt good.

Dad left. But before he did, he took Solomon aside. "We gotta have a man talk," he told Mommy when she came out of the bedroom. "Go to the store."

"But –" she began.

"Now, woman," he growled. She went. After she left, Dad pulled Solomon close and said, "Who did that?"

Solomon was only five. But he knew the rules. "Snitches get stitches" was one of the first things anyone learned – shit, he knew it before he knew how to curse, and *that* was pretty damn early. So he shook his head.

Dad nodded. "No snitch, huh? That's good." Then he gave Solomon a single shake. Just one, but it snapped his head back so hard he worried it was broken. "But I'm your dad, boy, and I ask you a question, you *answer*, you hear me?"

Solomon bit back tears, and tried not to whimper the single word: "Darius."

"One-Ton's kid?" asked Dad. He used the gang name Darius' dad went by – that was how most of the growed-up dudes Solomon knew of called themselves. They wasn't Aaron or Joe or Mike or Pete or none of that – they was Killer Bee or Joey Cholo or Thirty Mil or whatever name they got when they joined one of the gangs that ran things in the hood.

Solomon hesitated another moment – not long, less than a second, but it earned him another quick shake. "Yeah," he said. "That's him."

"Huh," was all Dad said. But the next day when Solomon went to school Darius was gone and all the teachers acted weird and the second graders had a special assembly and then got to go home for the day and when they came back the next day Darius *still* wasn't there and didn't come back ever again.

Dad did something. Solomon didn't ask what. His mom never did, neither, even though he heard her talking to Mrs. Greenway down the hall and heard Darius' name a buncha times so he knew she knew what it was.

Rumors spread through the school. That was what kids did, because even in elementary school they learned that rumors were an important part of staying social, staying connected, and sometimes even staying *alive*. Some said Darius got hit by a truck, coming back from school. Others said that he *jumped* in front of the truck, 'cause he knew what an asshole he was and that he was such an asshole none of the gangs in the area would want him so he was as good as dead anyway.

But the story that Solomon heard most was that Darius got hit in a drive-by. According to the story, Darius, his older brother Z-Dawg, and one of Z-Dawg's homies were hanging out on the corner. Probably arranging for a drug run – the gangs used kids to run their product a lot, 'cause cops was less likely to stop a kid than a tatted-up homie, and the younger the better – but the run never happened because an old brown car drove past, a shotgun stuck out of it, and boom-*BOOM*.

Solomon couldn't be sure whether this last story was true or not. But he knew that sometimes Dad rolled around in a crappy brown ride that he called Foxy Brown. And he knew that Dad had a shotgun.

And those things… they made Solomon feel all hot and good in his chest, too. So he hated Dad, but he felt somethin' warm for him, just the same.

That was when Solomon Black learned three *new* lessons. The first was that life was complicated, and you could love and hate a thing all at once. The second was that, though a black eye could stop an argument, a double-blast from a shotgun could stop a *person*.

And the third? The third was that stopping a person could be a fine damn thing.

2

"I dunno. Looks like a pussy to me."

"Nah, he ain't no pussy."

"Says you."

"Damn *right* says me."

Solomon listened to the two dudes arguing over him, and wanted to say somethin', but SFD told him before they got here that Solomon shouldn't say shit. SFD was his sponsor – the member of the 52 Broadway Crips that first took notice of Solomon and had been using him to run product for the last three years. SFD stood for Six Feet Down, which SFD told him he got as his name 'cause that was where he put the dude he shot as his audition for the 52s. Solomon heard another homie say it stood for the size of SFD's dick – and that the "S" definitely stood for "Small" – but he never told SFD that.

SFD was too scary to say that shit to his face. He was a stone-cold killer, a full homie with the Five Deuce, and no way an eleven-year-old kid was going to give him lip. Good thing, too, 'cause SFD had taken a liking to Solomon Black. Got him out of school all the time, which was the shit 'cause Solomon hated school. Everyone talked like there was a future if you stayed in school, but that was crazy talk because the only future in this part of town was getting in a gang and having your homies' backs so they'd have yours.

So when SFD came up to him and asked if he was Face's kid, Solomon – who rarely referred to his dad at all, and never once since Zeke "Face" Washington got lit up by a dozen cops after trying to roll a liquor store – answered immediately. "Yeah. So?"

Even then, Solomon knew who SFD was. Everyone did, just like everyone knew that Dee and Chuck, two fifth-graders, ran for him a lot. Dee and Chuck were the kings of the school, when they bothered to come at all; and their prestige was one-hundred-percent because SFD picked them up in his black BMW twice a week, and kept them in comics and made sure they always had current passwords to the best porn sites.

Solomon had been ditching that day. Hanging out at the 7-11 and trying to figure out how he could distract the towelhead who worked the counter long enough that Solomon could fill up a Hefty bag he'd brought with him with cherry Icee. He'd just about decided on pulling the fire alarm at the back of the place, hiding in the bathroom, then coming out after the clerk bugged out and getting to work on his Icee heist, when SFD rolled up.

The windows of his BMW were all tinted – even the front one, though not so dark as the sides. The side windows looked completely black to Solomon, which added to the cool effect when the driver's side window dropped with an electric *whrrr* to reveal SFD himself.

He wore the usual outfit: black tank top, tight on his muscled upper body; camo pants, pockets bulging with all sorts of secrets and all sorts of promises; shades with gold rims; and a chest full of bling. His nine-mil was tucked in his waistband; and just like the stories said, it had "S.F.D." in gold letters on the handle.

"You Face's kid?" asked SFD.

"Yeah. So?"

SFD leaned over and pushed the passenger side door open. "Get in," he said. It was not a request.

Not that Solomon woulda refused him anyway. He was eight years old, so he wasn't a full-growed man yet, but he wasn't *stupid*, neither. He slid into the seat, luxuriating in the smell of weed and cigars and some other, earthier and somehow more *dangerous* scents he caught running under it all.

"Close the door," said SFD. Solomon did. SFD waited. Waited. Waited. Finally he growled, "Buckle the hell up." Solomon did, and SFD shot him a toothy grin and said, "Safety first, little man."

Solomon felt that warm feeling again. Only this time, there was none of the hate he felt whenever he thought of his dad. It was just warmth.

SFD's watchin' out for me. Holy shit, *large as legend and I'm in his BMW and oh, man, the guys at school are never gonna believe this.*

The ride was short. Just a few blocks. But when SFD dropped him off, Solomon had already grown up – he was ten grams heavier, to be exact. And when he lightened his load that night, delivering the bag to a dealer after sneaking out of the house, he felt even more like a man.

The guy he dropped the drugs with clapped him on the shoulder, grinned, and said, "Any trouble?"

"Five-oh saw me, I thought they was gonna stop me."

The guy, whose name Solomon never learned, shook his head. "Nah. You too young. They only give shit to the *big* boys." Then he laughed as Solomon's expression darkened and clapped him on the shoulder again. "Lighten up," he said. He held up the small plastic bag and shook it. "You passed the test."

"Test?" said Solomon warily. "SFD didn't say nothing about no tests."

The guy laughed. Another clap on the shoulder. "My *man*," he said.

Next day SFD turned up with another "errand" for Solomon. And the next. Then a week off. Then another errand.

The errands got more complex, and the drugs got heavier in Solomon's pocket each time. But the extra weight never dragged him down none. The more he carried, the faster he ran – and not 'cause he was scared. No, he was just *excited*. SFD was the shit, and that meant Solomon was the shit, too.

And maybe someday he'd be more. Maybe he'd even be Five-Deuce like SFD. That was the dream. But it wasn't like you just walked into a Five-D crib and said, "So you holdin' tryouts today?" Nah, you had to be *invited*. Had to have a *sponsor*.

Maybe SFD would sponsor Solomon. Then he'd be on the way. Then he'd be the shit not 'cause he was a reflection of SFD, but as his own man.

Solomon worked hard. Got Ds in school, which was fine with him since he never figured on staying there long. But he was an "A" student in Street 101. SFD was his teacher, his mentor, his friend, and – in every respect that mattered – his father.

Three years of running. Three years of doing whatever job SFD asked, and doing it better and faster than any of the other kids. That was why it wasn't a surprise when SFD rolled up the night of Solomon's eleventh birthday. Solomon's mom had saved up and was going to take him to McD's, and had already promised to get him anything on the menu that he wanted. But when she saw the BMW outside, she just sat down and said, "You gotta go," in a quiet voice.

Solomon loved his mom. She'd always been there. And she understood the street. Didn't give him a hard time about his grades, 'cause she understood. She'd been Face's old lady, after all. She knew what it was to love a gangsta, and Solomon knew she hoped he'd do even better than Face ever did.

He planned to do just that. He'd get into the Fifty-Twos, he'd be street royalty, and he'd take care of his mom and show her what a *real* man was. Not some loser who showed up to leech beer and petty cash. Nah, Solomon would show her what it was to have the favor of a king.

He got into SFD's ride, buckling up like he always done ever since that first day, and they drove a mile or so. SFD got outta the car, gesturing for Solomon to follow him. They both marched into a store. Sold fish – not very good fish, either, from the smell of it – but they walked through the store without stopping, into the alley behind it, and up the fire escape on the building across from the fish shop.

Solomon knew that this was normal precautions. No sense telling enemies their exact whereabouts. And since the world was full of enemies, that meant you always dodged around. Never went in a straight line if it could be helped. Never went anywhere important when someone else could be watching.

Solomon followed SFD up the fire escape, clanking up six flights, then crawling through an open window barely big enough for him to fit. He had finally caught some of his growth. He wasn't a muscular type like SFD – not yet, anyway – but he was already five-foot-ten, and sure to get another six or seven inches taller before he finished.

The window he crawled through had been covered with aluminum foil, so it was dark inside. The dark was thick and, for some reason, Solomon thought it gave the apartment a *bad* vibe. Like the place had its own personality, and that personality was the kind of thing that would pull legs off a cat to see what would happen if it could no longer land on its feet.

The paint – what little could be seen between posters sporting images of rappers, cars, and the women who loved said rappers and cars – was peeling, and dark patches of fungus spread across the ceiling.

Yeah. A bad place.

"I dunno. Looks like a pussy to me."

SFD had told him on the way here – "Don't say nothin'. Not a single damn word," so Solomon managed to bite back the words that came automatically. He just stared at the guy who'd said it. He was dressed similar to SFD, only he was *huge*. Only a few inches taller than Solomon, but the guy had to be three hundred pounds of solid muscle. He sat on a sofa in the corner of the room, seated dead center and his arms splayed out so no one else could possibly sit there 'less they wanted to try and cuddle.

"Nah, he ain't no pussy," said SFD.

"Says you."

"Damn *right* says me."

The last sentence was where Solomon wondered if the dude on the couch was something big. He was wearing Five-Deuce colors, so he was part of the gang, but that didn't mean much. But the way SFD talked to the dude... same kind of words Solomon had heard him say a million times, but there was something about SFD's voice that made him worry a bit.

SFD was the shit. He didn't walk, he *strutted*. And the strut was in his voice, too – the words bounced up and down, bobbed and weaved like they was constantly dancin'. But now they was strangely flat, and SFD kept looking away from the dude on the sofa.

The dude leaned forward, elbows on knees and hands folding together like he was about to pray. He squinted at Solomon. "Nah. Pussy."

Solomon said, "Say it again and you'll find out how true it ain't."

Beside him, SFD took in a breath so fast and hard it sounded like it probably hurt.

3

The man on the couch looked surprised, but only for a moment. Then he laughed hard and loud, and that was when Solomon saw the dude's two front teeth had been capped in gold. He knew now who this was: Two-Teeth.

He wished he could take back the words he'd said. Two-Teeth was laughing, but Solomon was wise enough to know some dudes laughed when they was happy, and others laughed at the idea of shoving a blade into someone's guts. From what he'd heard, Two-Teeth was definitely in that last group.

But Two-Teeth surprised him. He held out a fist, and after a moment's pause Solomon bumped it. "My man," said Two-Teeth. Then the laughter disappeared and he sat forward and said, "You want to be Five-Deuce? That's what SFD tells me." His eyes flicked toward SFD and again Solomon marveled to see his friend's eyes cast down, avoiding Two-Teeth's own.

"Yeah," said Solomon. "Dad was Five-D, so I figure that's where I go, too."

"Face was a good dude," agreed Two-Teeth. He smiled again. "I ran with him for a while. When I was about your age. Taught me a lot, and I figure I owe him for that." His smile widened. "So you ready?"

"For what?"

The smile didn't disappear, but it hardened. Two-Teeth's face now looked like a stone sculpture, the creation of some artist who was dying of cancer and wanted to tell the world what he thought of it. A smiling face that was all rage and madness and the deep, dark things of the world. "For whatever I say to do," said Two-Teeth.

Solomon felt like he was on the edge of a cliff. On one side, the foundation that he'd known. The life he had. On the other, there was a darkness that could hide anything within. This was the moment to jump… or to crawl back down the mountain and hide at the bottom, knowing he was nothing and never would be anything.

He jumped. "Whatever you say's okay with me," said Solomon, trying to sound casual.

"My man," Two-Teeth said again. He gave Solomon a package. "Go to the corner near Bobby's where the crackheads hang out. Tonight. Don't tell no one, and don't be seen. You do good with what I tell you, and you got a future."

Solomon nodded, and then SFD was practically yanking him outta the place. Back out to the fire escape, back out to the street.

SFD took him to his car, but didn't offer him a ride. He just got in and looked at Solomon for a long moment. "You do this…." His voice drifted away, and for a second Solomon wondered if maybe SFD was still on that mountain, still hadn't jumped all the way himself. Maybe he was even figuring on pulling Solomon back to firm ground.

But the darkness… that was where the promise was. Where the street kings lived.

Solomon walked away from SFD. Even an hour ago, such would have been unthinkable. But now, Solomon knew he wasn't SFD's no more. He belonged to Two-Teeth, and maybe – if he was lucky – to the 52s.

He looked in the package that Two-Teeth gave him. Saw what was there and expected it to scare him. But it didn't, and that night he was right where he was expected to be.

Bobby's was a corner store whose awning boasted of "GROCERIES! EGGS! MEAT!" in faded orange letters, but which Solomon knew mostly held liquor, cigarettes, and a magazine rack in the back for anyone who didn't know what the internet was. It was also a regular hangout for some of the dealers from the 59 East Coast Crips, which were sworn enemies of the 52s.

Solomon walked to the corner across from Bobby's and sat on a bench. He waited. There were two 59 ECC dudes in the alley just behind Bobby's and just seeing them there burned Solomon inside. They was way out of their territory. They shoulda stayed near Hooper Ave, the center of their strength... and if it was up to the 52s, Solomon knew, they'd all be dead and gone.

He watched the dudes. One was a short, fat dude who wore a black, old-school LA Raiders jersey, jeans slung low, and bright blue Nikes. The other was tall, lanky. His stick arms hung from the blue tank top he wore, and hisshou stick legs could be seen poking out of his low-riding shorts. Both wore blue bandanas around their necks, ready to be pulled high to cover their faces if the five-oh showed up.

At first Solomon figured the short, fat dude was the leader. But after a while he realized that the thin guy was the boss of the small crew. He watched 'em both, though. They took no notice of him, which was, he figured, at least part of why he'd been tapped for... whatever was coming.

A buzz sounded. Solomon pulled out the burner phone that had been the first item in the bag Two-Teeth gave him. He flipped it open – thing was so basic it was a *flip* phone, for Jesus' sake – and answered.

Two-Teeth spoke to him. Fast and quick, and Solomon didn't say a word back. Just listened until Two-Teeth was done, said, "Werd," and hung up.

He waited, and though it was already full night, the sky seemed to get darker somehow. A few streetlights flickered and then went dark. Solomon took that as a good sign.

A while later, both the dudes in the alley bumped fists. Just like Two-Teeth had said they would. Fatso walked away. Just like Two-Teeth had said. Skinny Boy stayed behind, and rolled a joint. Just like Two-Teeth had said.

Solomon waited five, then crossed the street, pulling out the second item Two-Teeth had given him. He held the gun at his side until he was close. He walked like he was heading for Bobby's as he crossed the street, but veered off at the last second and went to the alley.

Skinny Boy looked at him in irritation. "The hell you think –"

That was as far as he got before Solomon unloaded the gun. He missed the first two shots, but figured the last seven went into Skinny Boy just like they was supposed to. He straight-up *knew* the last two did, because Skinny Boy was already down, and Solomon put the gun against his head as he gasped and pulled the trigger those last two times and then Skinny Boy didn't move.

It happened so fast that Solomon was away – running down the alley and around the far corner – before anyone else appeared. And that was like Two-Teeth had said, too.

4

He met Two-Teeth the next night. Strolling down near Skid Row, and Two-Teeth pulled up. That was the first time Solomon realized that SFD's BMW wasn't that great after all. Two-Teeth's ride was tricked out beyond belief, with mag wheels lit from behind by blue LEDs, icy blue xenon headlights, a custom grille, and an oversized spoiler. The chariot of a king.

Two-Teeth pushed open the passenger door and nodded at Solomon. Solomon got in.

"It went good," said Two-Teeth. Solomon nodded. "The phone and gun?"

"Got rid of them like you said."

"How?"

"Laid out the phone on the street until I saw a few cars run over it, then broke down the gun and tossed each part in a different Dumpster."

Two-Teeth stared. "You know how to break down a gun?"

"YouTube, man."

Two-Teeth smiled his flashing smile. He nodded. "Wise, man. Big wise. Just like the first Solomon in the Bible, man."

Solomon gaped. Two-Teeth smiled, a gross parody of innocence, then held one hand over his heart, another high up as to heaven, and said, "What, yo momma never make you go to church?"

"Nah. Not ever."

"Too bad. Not for me no more, but some of those dudes was righteous. Solomon was the smartest dude in the world, richer than God, and had hundreds of bitches." He smiled and pulled a rolled joint from a small cubby under the Sony digital multimedia receiver set into the center of his dash. He lit it up, toked, then offered the blunt to Solomon.

Solomon took it. Breathed in deep. He coughed, and Two-Teeth laughed. "First time?"

"No way, brah."

Two-Teeth laughed again. "Well, you get better at it, little man."

He put the car into drive, then pulled away from the curb. Solomon kept at the joint, getting a little better with each pull. A pleasant buzz filled the empty spaces of his brain, which was *almost* enough to mask the anxiety of what he thought was coming next.

Two-Teeth pulled into a residential neighborhood that sat near the edge of 52 territory. The place was close to an area zoned for industrial buildings, the kiss of death for many neighborhoods, but even without, that Solomon knew this was a neighborhood without hope. Houses didn't so much line the street as lean awkwardly beside it. Roofs that had been built straight now lurched to the side or drooped in the middle. Lawns were scrub brush and dirt and a weird collection of lawn ornaments that Solomon guessed were meant to brighten the place up but instead just made it all seem like a scene from a horror movie.

Two-Teeth stopped at one of the nicer houses on the block. No grass here, either, but the walls and roof looked sturdy, as did the bars over the still-intact windows. It had a porch, too, with a few planters hanging from the eaves.

Two-Teeth pulled up in front of the house, got out, and motioned for Solomon to follow him. Solomon followed the man to the porch, expecting to be led inside. Instead, Two-Teeth swerved right, going to one of the planters. Nothing but dead plants sat in the planters, Solomon realized, and that thought for some reason made the buzz he'd been enjoying withdraw. Made the fear come alive, and come out to nip at him with sharp teeth.

Two-Teeth rammed his fingers into the dirt in one off the planters, pulling something from inside. He shook it off, then showed it to Solomon. It was a key, and when Two-Teeth pushed it into the lock on the front door, Solomon felt the fear grow to something close to terror.

He had done what Two-Teeth had asked. *Everything* he had asked. And now the man was showing him the way into what was obviously a safe-house, a crib meant to be away from prying eyes. That meant that Solomon was going to come out of this a full member of the Five-Deuce, or a corpse.

Two-Teeth tossed open the door. It was dark inside. He went in. Solomon followed.

He'd been expecting it to happen, but it came much sooner and much harder than he could have imagined. He had barely set foot into the front room of the crib when something angular slammed into the side of his head. Pain exploded along Solomon's temple. He slid to the side, woozy and suddenly nauseated, but didn't fall completely. He righted himself.

Another fist hit him on the other side of the head. Solomon *did* go down this time. He felt heat on the side of his head and knew the strike had split his skin wide open.

Gonna have a scar.

He was on hands and knees now, and gritted his teeth against the pain and dizziness as he tried to right himself; to stand. One hand left the floor, and he tensed to push himself upright. Not standing yet, but the first step.

The next strike came. A kick to the gut. Solomon vomited, immediately and violently. The kick rolled him to the side at the same time, so puke got all over him and he had an insane moment where he realized that some of it musta got on his new shirt and his mom would be pissed at that. Then the next kick came. And the next. The next.

He didn't know how long it went on. Only seconds. Forever. Both at the same time. But each time he felt a kick or punch, he just let it happen. He rolled with it, and tried to get up.

Finally, a pause came. Spitting blood, sure that a few ribs were broken or cracked, Solomon levered himself up again. He couldn't help but flinch when a hand dropped into his red-veiled sight. But it wasn't a fist. It was an outstretched hand. Solomon took it, unsure. Two-Teeth's strong hand levered him up, pulled him to a standing position.

"Tough," said one of the others in the room. Solomon knew there were others, but could never remember how many, or their faces. He just saw Two-Teeth. Saw the gold grin.

"Big tough," said another voice.

"Nah," said Two-Teeth. "Big *Wise*."

Beaten and bloody, dazed and more than a little confused by pain and violence, Solomon grinned. Because he wasn't Solomon anymore. He was Big Wise. He'd been given a final initiation test, then been jumped-in. He was a 52.

5

It was easy. For a while.

Big Wise wasn't a full homie, let alone an O.G. – and he knew that he was years away from that title. But he knew he would get it. He'd be an Original Gangster, and maybe he'd even run the area that Two-Teeth controlled.

But for now he was just a little brother. Just the newest member of a gang that was sprawling ever wider, whose hands and fists were reaching ever farther. A foot soldier.

Still, Big Wise *had* been brought into it all by Two-Teeth. Not just SFD or one of the lower-ranking dudes, but Two-Goddam-*Teeth*. That lent him some immediate cred, and his rep shot even higher as he did job after job.

None of them bothered him. That surprised him a little. He figured that killin' that 59 asshole would have kept him up a night or two, at least, but he slept soundly. He figured that knifing the dudes in the crackhouse down on 7th Street would have made him at least a *little* sick, 'specially since one of them twisted during the stabbing and instead of just getting shanked in the gut he straight-out opened himself up and his guts tumbled out in purple coils. But the only thing Big Wise felt was anger that his Converse All Star high-tops went from immaculate white to a greasy red.

None of it bothered him.

Until one night, when something did.

6

The Five-Deuce were expanding, and that was exciting. That meant room for growth – not just for the gang, but for Big Wise. He just had to play the game, play smart, and keep himself moving up.

Big Wise really *was* a pretty smart kid. And he was growing into a smart young man. At seventeen, he had a good rep, hadn't pissed off any of the serious players, and most of all knew he could be counted on to get the job done, no matter what.

At first it was just dope. Extortion. Throwing a beat-down on any rival gangs who tried to come into the Five-Deuce's expanding turf. But as the gang grew, Big Wise heard a word from Two-Teeth he had never heard before. Big Wise's sponsor was on the phone, and though he had made it a practice not to listen in on things that didn't concern him, he did catch one word: "Diversification."

Big Wise looked it up on his cell, and recognized immediately that the word represented the growth of the Five-Deuce. It wasn't just beatdowns and drive-bys and drugs anymore. The gang had its fingers in extortion, prostitution, and other ventures that Big Wise could only guess at.

Two-Teeth, apparently, was heading up a "diversification" effort of his own, because Big Wise was moved off the duties he'd been seeing to. Now he delivered strange packages. Some was stuffed with money, he could tell. Some was sent in packages, others in brown-wrapped packages that were cool to the touch.

A lot of the deliveries was to cops. That was nothing new: the five-oh had to be in for their cut. Everyone had a cut, that was the baseline rule of Gang Economics 101. The cops varied: some were uniforms, some were detective-types. A few times he delivered to dudes who wore tailored suits but still had the eyes of any and all pigs: beady, needy, and greedy.

Most of the time the money Big Wise delivered fell into the hands of a dickhead named Patrick "Pat" Pattinson, which was about the whitest name Big Wise ever heard, and which fitted the cop perfect, 'cause the dude was *white*. White teeth, white skin, white hair. One of the brothers who knew Pattinson said he was an albino. Big Wise didn't think so, 'cause he thought albinos had red eyes, and Pattinson's were the bluest he ever saw.

Albino or no, Pattinson was a weird-lookin' dude. And he was a dude that no one liked to screw with. Wasn't just the way he looked, though that was enough of a mind-bender to make most folk think twice before messing with him. No, it was also the fact that Pattinson gave off a legit crazy vibe. Standing with him was like standing next to a furnace with a leak in the gas pipe. Too much heat, too much ragged flame.

Anyone warming themselves there ran the risk of getting caught in the inevitable blast that had to come.

But this was the man Big Wise had come here to meet tonight. He handed the cop a roll of bills, then the cop handed him an address. That wasn't normal, and the cop said, "Tell your master I'm not his errand boy or his message service."

Big Wise took the paper. There was an address on it, and below that the words "**PICK UP**" in dark, blocky letters. It wasn't unusual for instructions to come this way, especially not from Two-Teeth. He still wasn't O.G., but he was getting there, and part of his business model was distance. He stayed away from direct action, and as often as not when something needed doing the homies assigned found out via anonymous Facebook message or texts from some burner phone.

Big Wise turned away. Pattinson called out, "Hey!" Big Wise turned back. "Tell Two-Tits that it's gonna be fifteen next week."

Big Wise felt his blood turn to a strange mixture of cold and hot. It felt like ice inside him, yet at the same time he felt that if he'd been cut in that moment, nothing but red steam would have come out. Part of that was the diss to Two-Teeth, part of it was the sudden raise in the cost of a blind eye turned to Five-Deuce's business dealings, and part of it was just the fact that this shithead was acting like a street king, even though he was less than trash. Not even a joker, a jester in the court of legit players like Two-Teeth and – it had to be said – like Big Wise himself.

He took a step in Pattinson's direction. The cop didn't blanch, and didn't back down, not even when Big Wise muttered, "The hell you playin' at?"

Pattinson smiled, and Big Wise thought for a moment how much like Two-Teeth's own grin that smile was. "Things are different now. You know that. You can feel it. Five-Deuce are expanding. That means more work, and more work for us honest cops to not notice it."

Big Wise thought about killing the fool, even though the thought was rejected as fast as it came. It wasn't his job to knock off fools like this – not without being ordered to. Pattinson was a pain in the ass, but he was *Two-Teeth's* pain in the ass, and Big Wise wasn't going to stick himself between them. Not until he was asked.

Then it would be a pleasure.

Big Wise nodded and turned away, leaving Pattinson whistling something Disney-sounding as Big Wise left him behind.

He went to the street on the card, only to find that the address was for a number that did not exist. The pick up was set for number 1542, but the buildings here jumped from 1540 to 1554, with nothing but an alley between. That wasn't too surprising, and Big Wise had experienced this before as well. Two-Teeth was careful. Had to be when you was *diversifying.*

Big Wise went into the alley. He looked around. For a long moment he saw nothing, then at last he spotted a blue bandana. Five-Deuce colors, wadded up in the end of a drainage pipe that jutted five inches from the side of building number 1540. Big Wise yanked the bandana out of the pipe, which had a rough, sharp edge to it and nearly slashed his hand open as he jerked the cloth clear.

When the bandana was out, he put his hand into the drainpipe. The thing was oversized – probably part of why it was chosen to hide the drop – so Big Wise reached in without much trouble. Up to his elbow before he found what was hidden away in there. Then he pulled it out: a manila envelope with the telltale rectangles of stacked, bound bills.

On the envelope, in the same block letters as on the first piece of paper Pattinson had given him, was written another address: the real destination, and no doubt the place that Big Wise would drop off the money he'd just pulled from the pipe.

Big Wise knew the general area, but wasn't too up on the details. It was on the edge of 52 territory, part of a big chunk of the hood they'd grabbed from the 59s during the last round of turf battles. Not the kind of place he'd ever had reason to be before. But now it was property of the Five-Deuce, so it was home.

Home or not, he was surprised at what the address turned out to be: a big, industrial/government-looking building. Larger than any other place on the block, and it even had a ring of grass around it that marked it as a place with some extra flow.

Still… Big Wise double-checked the address.

Right place.

The hell am I picking up?

He went through the big wrought-iron gate that surrounded the place, expecting to hear a shout, to hear someone scream at him to leave and that they had already called the cops, who would be there in less than a minute, strapped and ready to blow away a brother.

No one appeared.

No one spoke.

Big Wise grabbed the handle of the front door. He expected to find it locked. Again, he was surprised. The door opened, pulling roughly away from the jamb with the squeal of poorly-maintained hinges.

Big Wise walked in. No one said nothing. Not even the white dude waiting at the end of the hall just inside the building. They stared at each other for a few long seconds. Big Wise could feel the other guy taking his measure, and almost laughed. A flabby, soft dude in a ratty suit could *never* understand the measure of a real man like Big Wise.

"Who are you?" the man finally asked. His voice was nasally, higher than Big Wise expected. The kind of voice that made a brother want to punch the hell out of its owner.

Big Wise bit back that feeling. Still, it was through gritted teeth that he said, "Two-Teeth sent me."

The white dude frowned. He looked like he was around forty, which made him straight-up *ancient* to Big Wise's seventeen years. Balding prematurely, his mousy brown hair frosted with uneven patches of gray here and there. It made the dude look not just old, but *used*. Washed up.

"Two-Teeth was supposed to come himself, I thought," said the dude.

Big Wise didn't say anything back. He just stared at old whitey, and waited for the inevitable. It happened quick, only a second or two going by before the other guy nodded and sighed the kind of sigh that said he was doing the universe in general – and Big Wise in particular – a huge favor by continuing to live among them.

"Fine. Where's the money?"

Big Wise handed over the package. The white dude pulled out the bills, and it was all Big Wise could do to mask his surprise. Wasn't tens or twenties inside. It was *hundreds* – at least a hundred Gs worth.

Whitey flipped through one of the wrapped bundle of bills, flipping their edges with one pale thumb like he was the world's fastest money-counter. Then he grinned sourly and said, "Come on."

He took Big Wise deeper into the place. Through a series of corridors, then up the stairs, then through a final door. Big Wise followed the white guy inside, then stopped moving when he saw the rows and rows of bodies that lay silently in worn beds strewn throughout the room.

He didn't know what he was picking up. That happened sometimes. But a painful knot started forming in his gut, which had never happened before.

Five-Deuce is growing. Changing. Diversifying.

The word had been one of promise. Of growth and money and women and dope and anything else Big Wise could wish for.

Now the word felt like poison. Like a world that was about to disappear from his grasp just when he was on the verge of owning it all.

Whitey kept on, threading his way between beds, passing by them all as if they had no import to him. He realized after a moment that Big Wise wasn't following. Turning, he gave another one of those patronizingly patient sighs. "Don't worry. They all got something with their food tonight. You could piss on their faces and they wouldn't move. The girl's over here. Name's –"

"No names, dude." Big Wise said the words fast and loud, biting them off like they hurt. They did. Suddenly he felt like Solomon Black again, a little boy wondering what was happening beyond the curtain. Wondering if the sounds he heard were pleasure or pain. "I don't need that shit in my head."

He thought about leaving. But the old white dude's face creased in a look of patronizing pity. Like he was looking at a retarded dog or something. That look firmed up Solomon's –

(Big Wise I'm BIG WISE)

– backbone. He walked forward. Saw what the old guy was pointing at. *Who* he was pointing at.

Diversification.

First a little bit of robbery. A bit of mugging. Then dope. Then guns. Then… what?

The answer was obvious, and was now literally staring him in the face. The 52s had graduated from things to people. He had heard of this – not in the Five-Deuce, but in other gangs. Grabbing folk off the street, selling them into bondage of one sort or another. Girls mostly, who would be sent to men who would get them hooked on drugs – not weed, neither, no, the hard stuff, crack and heroin and worse – until the girls would beg to do anything, whatever it took to get their next fix.

The lucky ones would end up in porno. Maybe a few would even break free of the prisons created in their minds long enough to kill themselves.

That was the lucky ones.

The unlucky ones would be sold for more personal encounters. Some would end up on the street, discarded when their looks or their willingness dried up and their money-making potential disappeared along with them. Others… unmarked graves, bodies dumped off boats a few miles off the coast.

He looked at the girl. At the face of *diversification*. And he was back on the cliff's edge again. Staring into darkness, understanding for the first time that that darkness was staring back at *him*.

At the thought, the girl moved. She sighed, and her eyes opened, and Big Wise had a moment of sheerest horror when it felt like she was looking at him, *into* him, into his soul. But her eyes were glazed, her pupils almost nonexistent in the blue field of her irises.

She closed her eyes. She moaned a bit.

Diversification.

Big Wise picked her up. She was light in his arms. How young was she? How young could people *want* them to be?

He closed his own eyes for a moment. Then opened them and looked at whitey and said, "You got something to carry her in?" The man looked surprised. That look drove a bit of anger into Big Wise's brain. He was glad. Better that than the guilt that threatened to overwhelm him.

On a cliff. But not jumping. No, I'm being pushed. *Falling in.*

"Did I stutter, asshole?" he asked. "Or you want me to just carry this little girl out in my arms so the whole world sees?"

Whitey blanched. He left for a moment, and when he came back Big Wise almost wished he hadn't said anything. The old dude was trundling a bag – a piece of *luggage*, for shit's sake! The kind of thing you'd see at an airport or on a bus, if the person taking the trip had blown all their money on the ticket and had little left over for a suitcase. Ratty, soft sides that looked old and pretty beat-up. But it had two wheels on the bottom, and a handle that extended out of the top.

"Someone left this behind a while ago. I kept forgetting to get it back to her or throw it away." The white dude smirked like he knew a funny joke – but one he'd never tell to someone like Big Wise – and added, "Glad I did."

He laid the bag on its side. Unzipped it to show the dark space inside. He gestured. "She should fit in here just fine."

Big Wise hesitated.

He thought about the money he had. The nice shoes and nice clothes and bling. The car he was saving up for. His mom was gone – died last year – so she wouldn't care, but....

For some reason, that last actually made him hesitate. What would mom think? She'd been fine with him in the 52s – proud, too, that he'd risen so far and so fast.

But would she stand for this?

He saw Two-Teeth, handing him a joint. Saw the big man laughing, and saw the lack of laughter in his eyes. "Big Wise," said the man in his head.

Then he heard one more voice. His dad. Zeke "Face" Washington saying, "Gotta live the dream, boy."

Big Wise put the girl in the bag. She was young –

(*so young so young nah man don't think of that don't think of* nothing *just do what you gotta do live the dream live the DREAM*)

– and small. Big Wise folded her in on herself, crossed her arms and legs and then tucked it all together into something that looked like the pictures of fetuses he saw in eighth grade health class on one of the rare days he actually showed up.

He zipped her in.

He trundled her out of the building.

He realized when he was out that he had no idea where to go. He just started walking, trying to ignore how the suitcase bumped over each rut in the worn sidewalk. Trying to think of anything but what it held.

The darkness stared into him. Then it wasn't just looking at him, it was leaking *into* him. And then it *was* him. Jumped over the cliff's edge, pushed off it – it didn't make no difference. Only thing that mattered was that for the first time in his life he couldn't see anything of what waited ahead, or even what he himself was.

7

Two-Teeth must have had people watching for him, because a black van pulled up beside Big Wise before he made it a block away from the place where the girl had been sleeping.

He jerked as the van pulled up beside him, so lost in the darkness that he hadn't heard the van approach. Hadn't even heard the door slide open. But he did hear the scratchy voice that said, "Put it in here."

There was no question what the dude was talking about.

It. Not her. It.

Big Wise looked at the dude who'd spoken, surprised to see a brown face looking at him. Not a brother, certainly not a 52. This was a Mexican dude. Tats on face and arms, but they didn't look like any gang tags that Big Wise had ever seen. He didn't know *what* they looked like, and he didn't care.

Diversification. Two-Teeth's got new partners.

Big Wise thought about refusing. But saw, too, that the Mexican was packing: a pair of shoulder holsters worn over his white t-shirt, the dark butts of two handguns sticking out. Just like he saw the driver – not a Mexican, but a white dude – staring back at him with eyes so dead that Big Wise figured the dude could give crazy lessons even to someone like Two-Teeth.

He held out the handle. Waited. The Mexican didn't move. "Inside the van, *pendejo*."

For a second Big Wise balked, thinking the guy wanted *him* to get in the van. No way he was going to do that. Turned out there were things Big Wise wouldn't do, after all, and he knew he would die rather than get into the vehicle with the tattooed man and the dead-eyed man wearing a live man's skin. "Come on, Zonker," said the man.

"Shut up, Mako," said the Mexican before turning to Big Wise and grabbing at him – only no, that was wrong. He was grabbing the handle of the bag. The man wrested the cheap metal out of Big Wise's hands, then yanked the suitcase up into the van. It banged against the lip of the cargo area as he wrestled it in, and Big Wise nearly groaned.

Then the side door of the van slid shut. The van disappeared. Nothing was left. The girl was gone, and Big Wise stood alone in darkness.

Two-Teeth paid him. Two-Teeth was good to him; he always reminded Big Wise of that fact when handing over clothes or dope or cold, hard cash. "Two-Teeth takes care of his bruthahs," he said every time. "I got your back, Big Wise."

He said it now, handing over a fistful of cash. It was a lot – more than Big Wise had ever gotten as "thanks" for any of the jobs he did for Two-Teeth. He shoved it in his pocket without counting it. Two-Teeth smiled and clapped Big Wise on the shoulder. "Good job tonight. We on the move, boy. On the *move*." He nodded at Big Wise's pocket, which bulged with the wad of cash. "Go find yourself a party. Get laid. Take a personal day." He winked. "On the *move*."

The personal day lasted about twelve hours. Then Big Wise got a call. Two-Teeth was on the other line – himself, not one of the underlings he got to deliver most messages. "Bro, gotta deal with something."

"What is it?" asked Solomon.

Solomon? Wasn't I something else? Wasn't I Big Wise?

"Gotta feed a pig."

"Which one?"

"The albino."

Big Wise – Solomon? – sighed and kneaded his forehead. He hadn't done any drugs last night, but he'd downed enough booze to float a ship in. He hoped that would drive away thoughts of that little blue-eyed girl in the suitcase, and what would happen to her in the coming days and weeks and years.

It didn't, but at least now he had a big mother of a hangover to divert his thoughts from the girl's future.

"When?" he asked.

"Now good for you?" asked Two-Teeth. But it wasn't really a question, and he didn't wait for an answer before adding, "Be at 6th Street in fifteen."

Big Wise went. He waited on the corner – it was a spot he often waited, when Two-Teeth had something for him to do. Another layer of care, because Two-Teeth almost never phoned in his instructions – they always came in person, usually delivered through someone else.

Solomon had always admired this. It was part of what made Two-Teeth such a great leader, and such legit street royalty. But suddenly he realized another thing: it also meant that anything Solomon or any of the other lower-ranking dudes did, they'd be doing on their own. Solomon and the others would know who gave them the orders, of course, but would they be able to prove it? No. And would anyone other than the homie who got pinched dare to name Two-Teeth? Not a chance. In fact, now Solomon thought of it he remembered numerous times when Two-Teeth sidled up to him at the crib, then said nonchalantly, "Anyone asks, I was with you last night, all night."

And Solomon had always nodded. Always agreed. And never thought once about the *why*. He assumed it was because Two-Teeth had been involved in something deep and dark. But now he wondered: had it been because someone *else* was up to something – at Two-Teeth's request – and now the man with the easy smile was preparing to deny any knowledge or blame?

A day ago, Solomon wouldn't have believed that Two-Teeth would do such a thing. Would leave a homie out to dry. But then, would someone who had sold a little girl into prostitution think twice of just leaving a man – even a "brother" – out in the cold?

Nah. Solomon didn't think so.

So every passing moment that he waited got worse. Every second on the street he felt more exposed.

A car pulled up. SFD rolled down his window and said, "Big Wise."

"What?" he managed.

SFD handed a bundle to him. It was wrapped in tin foil and could have been a sandwich or some leftovers or anything at all. But it wasn't. It was money. Probably a lot. Two-Teeth knew when Pattinson got paid, and today wasn't that day. Which meant that the bent cop had either performed extra services for the Five-Deuce, or he had gotten wind of something, and was shaking down the boss for extra hush money.

"Pattinson's on a stakeout," SFD said. "Go find him and give him this."

"Where?"

SFD told him, then rolled up his window and left a trail of rubber a quarter-mile long as he peeled away from the curb.

Solomon stared blankly at the money. A lot of money.

Enough to buy a girl? No. But enough to buy silence if Pattinson got wind of last night's goings-on? Probably.

He didn't think about what he was doing next. He just did it. He opened the package, staring with dark, haunted eyes at the two thick stacks of bills. Twenty-large. More than Solomon got for any job, that was sure. White man's world, even when the world was a dark one.

He moved to an alley and, after checking carefully to see if anyone was watching, he teased most of the bills from the centers of each wrapped bundle. He left a few behind, and those became the tops and bottoms of the new bundles, made of ones and fives and a few tens from the stash of cash Solomon always carried.

He looked at the results. The bills were a little loose, the bands not as tight as they usually were. And certainly if Pattinson dug into the bills and took more than a cursory glance at them, Solomon was screwed.

But if he was lucky…

He didn't deserve luck, he knew that. But he hoped for it. Even prayed a little, and that was a first. God didn't answer, but neither did a lightning bolt come from the heavens to strike Solomon down, which he figured was a good sign and a good start.

So he walked down the street, heading toward Pattinson and toward what he hoped would be the first step to freedom.

8

The closer he got to where Pattinson was waiting, the more nervous he became. Pattinson was a suspicious type. Dirty, and dirty dudes – especially dirty *white* dudes – always counted the money that was handed to them. Solomon thought about just taking *all* the money and high-tailing it, but worried that Two-Teeth would have someone watching. If that was the case, then he took a single step outta line he'd be in trouble. Taking a little side trip to an alley wouldn't be an issue – any watchers would figure he was taking a piss, or puking up whatever alcohol remained in his system. But moving away from a straight-line path between him and Pattinson would be noticed. A call would be made. And that would be it for Solomon.

He knew. Because he'd done it to others. Hadn't thought twice. Hadn't thought twice about a *lot* of things. But now he was thinking twice. Three times, even four. Thinking over and over, replaying the things he'd done, and coming up with a picture that had no future at all, other than eventually being dropped in a cop's lap when it became convenient, or simply dropped in a hole if he became powerful enough that Two-Teeth felt threatened.

That was something he'd done, too.

But that was then. Now, he had to figure out a way to keep a suspicious, dirty, very white guy from counting the cash that Solomon would give him. Once Pattinson had pocketed it, then Solomon knew that any watchers would peel off. Their job would be done, and Solomon would be of less interest than their drugs, or their next job, or whatever woman they were seeing.

So if Pattinson did take the money – if Solomon could figure a way to get the suspicious bastard to put it away without counting it – Solomon would have a little time. Maybe even a few hours. Enough?

Maybe.

So many maybes.

And the closer he got, the more he knew in his gut that Pattinson *would* count, *would* know, and that *would* be the end of Solomon Black.

He saw Pattinson's car.

The cop was sitting low in his seat, smoking a cigarette and splitting his attention between a nearby house and the street. Maybe because he was looking for crime, but more likely because he was performing guard duty for Two-Teeth. The house he was "staking out" was a crackhouse that Two-Teeth ran, and so Pattinson probably was supposed to watch the area to make sure that anyone inside had plenty of warning should a cop show up who *wasn't* in the pocket of the 52s.

Watching him, Solomon realized what he could do. And it wouldn't even be hard, or unbelievable to anyone watching.

Clutching at his stomach, he ran suddenly to the side of a building. He'd wanted to puke all morning, but was good at forcing that kind of thing down. Now, though, he let it come. And come it did, in a huge flood of Jiffy Super Chunk, all over the side of a building. He heaved again, making sure to let himself be as loud as possible, knowing that Pattinson would see it. Would hear it. And would know that everyone else in the area had seen and heard as well.

Solomon straightened and staggered toward the car, a dumpy, puke-green thing that no self-respecting brother –

(*Don't think like that, you ain't gonna be a brother to no one if this goes right, and if it goes wrong you ain't gonna be nothing at all.*)

– would be caught dead in. As he approached, he turned away as though to puke a few more times, gagged, but continued on.

At last he reached at the car. He leaned on the trunk, willing himself to puke, knowing that Pattinson's eyes had to be on him. But he'd emptied his guts on the wall before, and now managed only a few heaves. Not good enough, he knew. He had to –

He heard the sound of the car door opening. The cheap shocks bounced as Pattinson got out of the car. "What the hell are you –"

As he spoke, Solomon turned to face him. He saw the disgust, the anger, and even the fear in the cop's eyes. He knew then that this *was* about the girl. Something had happened, something had gone wrong, and the money that Two-Teeth had sent was to make sure that Pattinson stayed quiet about it, or maybe even to insure that the cop buried any further investigation into what had been done.

That thought brought up the next round. Solomon's mouth opened so wide it hurt, and if what had happened before was a flood, this was an ocean emptying. The emotions on Pattinson's face all turned to disgust as he danced back, but it was too late. Vomit bounced off the cracked blacktop of the road, and more of it spattered Pattinson's shoes and pantslegs.

Pattinson screamed wordlessly, then glared at Solomon as he said, "Sorry," and added the last touch: wiping his dripping mouth with the back of his hand, and not-accidentally getting some of what was there all over the tinfoil bundle that he still held.

He looked at the package, as though just now remembering it was there. "Shit, man," he mumbled. "Sorry." He wiped it (poorly) on his shirt, then held it out to Pattinson.

"Two-Teeth –"

"Yeah, yeah, I know." The cop looked genuinely conflicted, and for a moment Solomon worried he'd refuse to take the foil-wrapped money at all. That would be a problem.

But the man's greed overwhelmed his disgust. He took the package between a thumb and forefinger, looking at it the way he might stare at a cockroach that had crawled outta his asshole. He twitched, and Solomon could practically see the guy trying to decide if he should open it and count the money or not.

Solomon hitched. Gagged again.

"Jesus Christ, man. Get out of here."

Pattinson waved him away, tossing the package through the still-open door of his car, into the footspace on the passenger's side. Then he said the most wonderful words Solomon had ever heard: "I find any puke on the actual money when I get home and I'm going to take it out of your hide."

Solomon nodded. Gagged once more for good measure, then staggered away. He felt Pattinson's eyes on him until he turned the corner.

Once out of the cop's sight, he kept up his lurching walk for several blocks, turning aside to dry heave every fifty or sixty feet. He got a few glares from people on the street, but not many. He was known in this area. No one would say shit to Big Wise.

But to Solomon Black?

He didn't know, and he didn't aim to find out.

After a few blocks, he stopped staggering and fake puking. A few blocks after that, he started to run. He figured he had an hour, maybe two, before Pattinson's greed and suspicious nature won out over his disgust. He'd look at the money, see a few hundred instead of twenty thousand. He'd know Solomon took it.

And then Two-Teeth and the rest of the Five-Deuce would be after him.

9

He felt the minutes burn away as he ran. He hadn't really known what he was going to do, only that he couldn't do what Two-Teeth wanted. Not anymore. Not in a world where *diversification* meant making little girls into hookers.

Now, though, Solomon needed to *think*. He needed a plan.

(*"Livin' the dream," said the man in his mind, the man behind the curtain with his mommy, the man who hurt her and made her love him at the same time.*)

First thing: he ran as fast and as far as he could. The Five-Deuce turf was growing, but it still had its limits. He ran to the closest one. That was passing into a rival gang's territory, and that was risky, too, but better that than Two-Teeth.

As soon as he stepped over the invisible line that marked the end of Five-Deuce turf, Solomon stripped off the bandana he always wore. Crip colors, and to ditch them was a straight-up diss, that no Crip would dream of doing.

Solomon dropped the cloth in the gutter and ran on.

He knew he needed distance, first and foremost. He thought about boosting a ride, then realized that would cause even more trouble, because if he was caught then he'd be in prison and there was no way a traitor like him survived the first month.

Traitor.

I'm a traitor.

He was surprised how much that thought hurt. And surprised how quickly he was able to shove it to the back of his mind and turn back to the question of what to do next.

He couldn't boost a ride, so how was he going to get out? How could Solomon Black escape this –

He almost smacked his own forehead in that moment. He'd been thinking of how to get away, but thinking the way Big Wise would have thought: all about thieving or maybe even forcing someone to drive him out of the city at gunpoint. But he wasn't Big Wise. Not no more.

And Solomon Black? Why, Solomon was a law-abiding citizen. He'd get around the same way any other law-abiding citizen would.

He ran a few blocks. Then ran some more as he saw the bus pulling away from the stop. Didn't have a bus pass, but he had plenty of money, and it was the work of a moment to shove a bill into the till and then pass to the back of the bus. Even better, there was only one other person on the bus: a housewife-lookin' sister who got visibly nervous when he sat near her.

He smiled at her. A Two-Teeth kinda smile.

She got off at the next stop. Solomon waited until she was gone, then moved to the front of the bus. The driver was a fat chick with beady eyes, a unibrow, and a peach-fuzz mustache that would have been the envy of any teenage boy. "Can you take me to the terminal, no more stops?" Solomon said to her.

She didn't even glance at him. "I look like a freakin' taxi?"

She didn't glance at him when he held up two hundred-dollar bills, either. Didn't even look at the bills. "I ain't no freakin' taxi," she repeated.

Solomon added another bill. She took the money. Still without looking. "No passengers up front," she said.

Solomon sat down in the back. He stood up again when the woman pulled the bus to the curb. "What are you –"

She silenced him with a glare that woulda made Solomon's mother proud. "You think I can just roll into the terminal without stopping? I'd get *fired*, man." She grabbed a wrench from under her seat and hopped off the bus.

A moment later, Solomon saw her in front of the bus. He heard the sound of metal hitting metal, then a moment later the driver got back on. She switched off the digital sign that spelled out the bus's next destination, and pulled a CB from under the dash. "Mike, the freakin' bus is making that noise again."

"Mike" sighed audibly on the CB's speakers. "Shit, Maria, can't you –"

"Don't you cuss at me, you freakin' idiot. What am I supposed to do if the LA Transit issues piece-of-crap buses to hardworking people? Huh? *HUH?*"

Mike had no answer, other than, "Bring 'er in."

Maria slammed the CB mic home in its cradle, then grinned at Solomon through her rearview mirror. "Can't just *roll* into the terminal. I ain't a freakin' taxi."

Solomon grinned back. She wasn't royalty, but Maria was definitely street, and he could respect that, even if he was running from that world himself.

They pulled up to the terminal a half-hour later. Maria stopped the bus a block before she got there, pressing the button that opened the back door of the bus. Solomon didn't move for a moment, until she glared at him in the mirror and said, "I ain't no –"

"Freakin' taxi," he finished. "I know."

"Can't just roll up with a passenger in a busted bus."

Solomon nodded and bounced. Maria pulled away from him, but he kept walking to the terminal. He had to get away from the hood – far away. Going home was a bad idea, and since his mom died there wasn't anything waiting there anyway.

So he was going as far from home as he could get.

The terminal had a few short-line buses that were pulling away, most of them going back to the places Solomon wanted to avoid. There were two buses going farther, though. He bought a ticket on the first one leaving. It took him to San Pedro. From there, he hopped on another bus. A longer trip this time, after which he grabbed another bus and another. He ended up in Sacramento. Crashed a few hours on the benches there while he waited for the bus that would take him to his final destination, because he figured that a place like Boise, Idaho, wouldn't have much in the way of gangs, and that meant he wouldn't have to look over his shoulder quite so often as if he went to a bigger place like Chicago or New York.

The Five-Deuce was strictly local, but the Crips were nationwide. Wouldn't be beyond belief if Two-Teeth arranged for some brothers to visit Solomon Black if he went to a big city.

Idaho sounded about right.

10

For a while, he thought it might work.

Nineteen thou and change wasn't enough to live on forever, but it went a helluva lot farther in Idaho than it did in California. He figured he had a few months, easy, before things got dicey on the money front. That had to be enough of a cushion to start life as a regular guy.

The trouble was, as he quickly found out, that while Big Wise had a resume on the street, when he was being Solomon Black he had something called a "rap sheet." No felony convictions, but he'd been arrested a dozen times, and everything from international companies to the local Baskin Robbins ran background checks that turned those kinds of things up.

He got a polite "no thank you," at a lot of places. A handful of "I wish I could hire you but...." A half-dozen responses of "there's no way in hell."

He was living in a place that let him pay cash down, in advance. A crappy little apartment in a crappy part of town. Not dangerous, really, but everything about the street he lived on screamed "no prospects."

He ended up at a job assistance place run by a local church – the folks in Idaho all had religion, it seemed – and after three weeks of no joy, one of the thousand-year-old people who volunteered at the place asked for his story. Solomon told as much as he thought he could without being kicked out or brought up on charges somewhere. The old dude nodded and said, "You should be a motivational speaker."

"Nah. Shit – I mean, stuff – ain't for me."

The dude shrugged. He wore a nice suit and a watch that probably cost half of what Solomon still had in cash. "I knew a guy who made it work. Internet." Another shrug, and he added, "Though I have to confess the only thing I do online is FaceTime my grandkids and play Candy Crush."

Solomon spent another day at the job search place. Then he bought a computer – another thousand gone! – and set up a YouTube site. He worried about it at first, wondering if there was any way that Two-Teeth could find out about him. Then he figured if it wasn't a rap video with at least one chick in a thong, the chances were slim Two-Teeth or any of the rest of the crew would bother with it.

He recorded himself, just talking about his thoughts. He put makeup on – that was humiliating, going into the WalGreens and asking for that shit – to cover the tats on his cheeks, but other than that it was just sit down, turn on the computer, and start recording. Talking about growing up near Skid Row, talking about the gangs.

The video gathered a grand total of three views.

Solomon did it again the next night. And the next. He didn't expect much, but what else was he going to do? Get drunk at one of the five or six bars in the area and then get tossed in the slam for drunk and disorderly? He was still a black man, and now he was a black man in a city that seemed like it was one hundred percent white religious folk, so his chances of avoiding jail while going to a bar seemed slim.

No, it was just the videos. Just the computer and his thoughts going into the nowhere of the internet.

The fourth night he recorded, he signed off with a murmured, "Gangs eat you up. They shit you out."

It was an angry sign-off, given in a dark apartment where he felt more alone than ever in his life. The girl with the blue eyes seemed a bit farther away, a bit less real with every passing day, and Solomon knew if it wasn't for the fact that he'd stolen from Two-Teeth, he probably would have gone back.

The next day, when he signed on to his video feed, he saw that the last video had fifty views. Ten comments, half of which commented on his "eat you up and shit you out" sign-off. "Great catchphrase, brother!" one shouted.

Three more videos. Now they were getting hundreds of views each. A few more, and they were picking up ten thousand and more. Which, of course, made barely enough in advertising on YouTube to buy a package of Ramen noodles or Mac and Cheese, but… damn, could he do this? Could he warn people away from the traps he'd fallen into, and also make a living at it?

Seemed like the answer was yes, when a few days later he got an email from a teacher in Kuna, a little school a few miles away. She'd seen his videos and knew he was local, and asked if he could come speak at her school. "We can't pay much," said the email. "But maybe if you would be willing to accept a $100 honorific you could come out for an hour."

A hundred dollars? For an *hour*?

Solomon Black was dialing her number before he finished reading the email.

A few more gigs followed. One of his videos hit a hundred thousand views. A prep school in New Hampshire flew him out to talk about his life, which made him laugh 'cause the kids he saw there were about the farthest thing from "at risk" he'd ever seen. But they paid for his airfare, a hotel, and five hundred dollars as a speaking fee.

Six weeks after that, he started Wise Words, LLC – a company that billed itself as providing "a real look at real life to at-risk youth."

The videos got more popular. And then more popular still. Solomon found himself speaking all over the United States. He had a manager for his speaking gigs, and a few years in there was talk of a book deal. It never happened, but Solomon didn't care. He'd never been a books kinda guy.

Five years. Six. Living in an actual house now, and wondering if he should buy one instead of renting.

And he met Ramona.

He was out walking that Saturday night. The nightlife in Boise was pretty nonexistent after eleven o'clock, and Solomon still worried about getting grabbed by some cop for the crime of being too black in a white state, so when he was out on a Saturday night it was usually just a walk around his neighborhood. Nothing past eleven, and nothing in the downtown area where the few bars could be found.

This particular night, he was walkin' in the park.

Just a walk in the park. Livin' the dream.

He knew most of the people who were there; mostly late-night joggers or dog walkers who he'd seen enough times that they weren't much scared of him anymore, and a few even nodded and smiled when they saw him.

The one person he hadn't seen before was a tiny gal in yoga pants and a crop top which showed off a fine body, and when she turned her gaze on him he saw that the whole package was topped by a face so beautiful it literally stopped him in his tracks.

"What you want?" she said. "I got mace."

That made Solomon smile, mostly because he couldn't think of a single place where she'd have the room to stash mace. She frowned at that, and he held out his hands. "Nothin', nothin'," he said. "Don't want nothin'. Just out taking in the breeze." He cocked an eyebrow at her. "What about you?"

She looked surprised and a little confused. "What *about* me?"

"What do *you* want?"

She looked even more confused for a moment, then apparently realized that Solomon was turning her own question back on her. "You being a smart-ass?"

He grinned. "Only when I'm talking."

She laughed at that. "You're funny."

"Only when I'm talking."

That was good for another laugh. A few more jokes earned him the right to walk with her. The walk earned him a first date – a meet-up at a place where she said there were free electro-swing classes. Solomon had no clue what electro-swing was, but the girl – "My name's Ramona Mirada, but you can call me Ramona," she'd said with just the right mix of attitude and flirting – was going to be there, so he was in.

Turned out that electro-swing was some kinda oldie-style music with a house beat under it, and that the people learning it were mostly gawky teen boys dressed like Mafia dudes from the 1920s. Solomon watched *The Untouchables* once, and thought that was pretty legit – Al Capone was an original street king, and the dude who took him down was a badass, if a bit straight-arrow for Solomon – but these kids looked like they'd have lasted about ten minutes on the streets of Chicago.

Damn, but they knew how to dance, though.

Solomon expected to just laugh when they started moving. But those skinny teenage boys knew how to make the most of long legs and stick-thin arms. They did some stuff that Solomon had seen before – a lot of electro-swing was variations on pop-and-lock moves that Solomon knew well – but some of what they did was just this side of magic.

He tried to mimic some of it. He failed miserably. Ramona laughed at him, and he laughed back at her when she fell on her ass after trying a high-kick move.

They moved in together six weeks later. Solomon had enjoyed something of "normal" life for years now – work, taxes, eat, sleep, repeat. He'd settled into life in his neighborhood, in his work, and in his own skin. But now, with Ramona in his life and waiting when he came home after a trip or a local gig, he started to think maybe he actually *belonged* in this place, and in his life.

That was the beginning of the end, and had he been Big Wise he would have seen the writing on the wall. Only took four months for it to happen. Four months of domestic bliss, four months of work at something he loved, then coming home to the woman he loved even more. Four months of being in love – he'd even started learning Spanish, for no other reason than because he wanted to please her – and then a month more of happiness when he found out Ramona was pregnant.

At the end of that month he found her in their bathroom, weeping. He tried to comfort her and couldn't. It wasn't until he'd been in there with her for over two hours that she finally admitted why she was so upset.

"I don't believe in abortions," she sobbed. "I'm *Catholic*, dammit."

More weeping. "It's okay, baby," Solomon said. "Not like we was planning on a kid, but it's okay. Gonna be a mix of a hot momma and a bad-ass dad, so I figure –"

Whatever else he was going to say was drowned by even louder sobs. He couldn't figure why at first. He was making enough to pay for a family. And Ramona definitely *was* a hot momma, and he was sure as shit a bad-ass –

He froze. He was holding her in his arms, but what had once been a loving, hopeful embrace now became as rigid and cold as if Ramona had had a statue carved around her.

"I don't believe in abortions," she said.

And then she cried even harder when I said the baby would have a bad-ass dad.

"It ain't mine," he said.

Ramona stopped crying. He hoped she would scream at him, would shriek "How *dare* you say something like that?" and then make him sleep on the couch for a month of Sundays.

She didn't, though. Just stared. Just started crying again, but quiet this time. Looking at him like she was full of hope and fear and wasn't sure which one was going to be in charge of the moment.

The only voice he heard was that of Big Wise. *Bitch be crazy. Bitch be a loser. Bitch just lost the best thing she never really had.*

Solomon nodded, and didn't know if he was nodding at the situation, or nodding because he agreed with that part of him that had suddenly surfaced after so many years.

He knew what Big Wise would have done in this situation. Big Wise would have knocked her around, maybe even put her in the hospital. Then Big Wise would have found out who it was knocked her up and put that unlucky soul in the ground.

But he wasn't Big Wise.

Big Wise never woulda been cheated on in the first place. Big Wise was the shit, and no one cheats on the shit.

For a moment he missed it again. Missed the brothers, missed Two-Teeth. The little girl in a suitcase didn't matter in that moment. All that mattered was the hurt he felt, and the knowledge that, bad or good, such hurts had never come to him in his time as a Five-Deuce.

He wanted back in. So much, he wanted back in.

He stood up. Walked out of the bathroom.

"Solomon, please, just –"

He didn't hear the rest. He was out and away. Running from Ramona, from their apartment. From the life he'd dared to hope for, and the life that he knew had been nothing but a short-lived illusion.

Big Wise could have told him it was going to happen. If only Solomon Black had listened.

He moved out of the house. Left it paid for through the next month, but that was it. Ramona was on the lease with him – they'd cosigned when his lease renewal came up, and he figured that she could deal with it or take the hit to her credit. He sure as shit didn't care about it one way or another.

Let the cocksucker who knocked her up take care of that shit.

Even if she didn't pay, and the landlord tried to come after *him*, too. He would deal with that when it came. He even thought maybe – just maybe – Big Wise would show up on that day. Would maybe give the landlord a bit of a *talkin'-to*. Big Wise's *talkin'-to*s generally ended up with the other party bruised, bleeding, and more than willing to listen to any requests that Big Wise might send their way.

No. That ain't me.

But when he looked in the bathroom mirror of his new place – the first place, the crappy little pay-as-you-go place he had started in – he saw little of Solomon Black looking back at him. Big Wise was the man on the other side of the glass. Big Wise's dark eyes, his need to commit violence.

"Livin' the dream," said Solomon, and on the other side of the mirror, Big Wise mouthed the words as well, and smiled the white smile of a shark.

Within three weeks of moving, Wise Words, LLC, was no longer booking gigs. A month after that, the manager dropped him via a curtly-worded email. No more offers for Solomon Black to speak. He tried to tell himself it was just a slump, but knew that was a lie. The reality was that Solomon Black had died. He was gone, and no one wanted to pay Big Wise to talk about the dangers of gang life, because the reality was that Big Wise *liked* the gang. He *missed* the gang.

Big Wise wanted back in.

11

Wanting in was one thing, though. Feeling the past reach out for him was something else. And it terrified him.

He was sitting in his apartment when the call came. A *buzzzzz* that continued on forever, which was good because anything shorter than forever wouldn't have penetrated the haze he was operating in pretty much twenty-four/seven. He fished the phone out of his back pocket and stared at the screen. He expected it was Ramona. She kept calling, at first to ask forgiveness, then to plead with him to come back. "It's over," she said. "It was a one-time thing. I knew him forever, and you were gone and we –"

Big Wise never got past that part of the call or the voicemail. He clicked disconnect and drank some more from the bottle of Colt 45 malt that had become his best friend in the past few weeks. He figured he'd do the same this time, or maybe ask her what the dude's name was who so easily slid into his place –

(Who showed up in my territory, poached on my turf!*)*

– and then tell her he was going to beat the guy to pieces, and then maybe give her a black eye or two as well. Only…

… it wasn't her.

The screen lit up, and there was no name to go with the number, but there didn't have to be one. He knew that number, just like he knew his social security number and the amount of money he'd stolen all those years back. Numbers he would never forget.

The number on the phone belonged to Two-Teeth.

He didn't want to take it. No way the dude was going to call in order to say, "Hey, how you doing?" and then welcome him back to the fold. No, this was something bad. Had to be. 'Cause that's all life had to give: bad and more bad, and the only way to get anything other than that badness was to reach out and *take* what you wanted.

Only now, Two-Teeth was reaching out for *him*.

Solomon Black wanted to hang up the phone. To run again. But that part of him was small, and getting smaller every day.

"What?" he said into the phone

"Who is this?" demanded the voice on the other end of the line.

Solomon cocked his head. "Who is *this*?"

"I asked you a question, asshole. You better –"

Solomon looked at the phone. Realized that the number wasn't in his incoming calls list, but his *outgoing* calls.

How the hell could that possibly happen?

He didn't know.

Another sound came. *Buzzzzz…*

Again, his alcohol-sotted brain didn't pick up on the sound. And that was fine, because even if it had it wouldn't have made a difference, because in the next moment Solomon felt himself fold over like –

(a little girl in a suitcase)

– a lawn chair. He didn't know why or how, but he knew in that last moment that he had lost control. Of his career, of his love life, and now of his own body.

He closed his eyes, and went into the darkness.

Then he opened them again, and found himself in a white room. A crazy dude in a cardboard mask of a happy face on the iPad bolted to the wall. A watch on his arm and a collar rigged with explosives around his neck.

Then running.

And the worst thing was that he was back home. Back to Skid Row and Five-Deuce territory.

Was Two-Teeth still here? Did people still remember Big Wise? Was anyone looking for him?

He didn't know. He couldn't even be sure if the person who answered the phone when he called that number belonged to Two-Teeth or just someone who'd inherited the number after Two-Teeth got done with it.

The latter had to be the case. No way Two-Teeth was still around. That was something that Solomon Black had learned over the years: no one really got ahead in the gangs. Not long term. A few people ascended to the height of gang life, but they always ended up in prison or in the ground. Two-Teeth wasn't any different, and at this point, the better part of a decade after Solomon had fled the hood, there was no way he was going to be anywhere but in a permanent bunk in a max-security prison somewhere or an even more permanent bunk six feet under.

Still, it wasn't good being here. Wasn't right. His tats were easily visible, and no way they'd go unnoticed, even in the middle of the night. Sooner or later someone would see them, and would let the Five-Deuce in the area know that someone sporting their tag on his face was in play. They'd act – they'd have to. Either it was a pretender, in which case they'd deal most harshly with the offender, or it was an old member come home after prison, and who'd need to be given at least token respect on his return.

No one had seen so far. But they'd been running a while. Something both Big Wise and Solomon Black had in common: they both hated running. He wasn't good at it, and his body always seemed to find the least efficient way to put one leg in front of the other. He would have worried that the others would leave him behind, only Do-Good said they had to stay together. That worried him. Sooner or later, he figured that someone would fall behind – or get left behind. That was the way of things. That was the world he lived in: a world where women cheated, little girls got sold to a life in the sex trade, and where anyone who couldn't keep up got left behind for the wolves to take down.

At least he was the only one who knew this area well enough to get them where they had to go. 1514 Chambers Street. No one would ditch him if he was their only hope at getting to where they needed to be before Do-Good exploded them from the neck up.

They got a fifteen-minute countdown. With barely a minute left, Solomon stopped in front of the house that Do-Good wanted them at.

He couldn't say a word when he saw it. He knew the area well. He knew this *street* well, because he'd come here often in the old days. This street had a special place in his heart. A special place in his history.

But he'd never known the number of the house. Or, if he had, he'd forgotten it. Why bother with numbers when everyone you spoke to probably knew where it was?

"What now?" said the skinny kid. Clint.

Noelle shoved her hands in her pockets and shivered. She was cute enough, Solomon supposed, though she had a pretty typical white-girl-lack-of-ass, and he really didn't know what he could have done with that thing, push came to shove.

"What could we possibly find here?" she said.

Naked fear shone in her eyes. But Solomon knew that it was nothing compared to the terror in his own eyes.

Not here. Not here. Not HERE.

Something beeped. For a moment he thought it was the old days. When he'd started, some of the guys still used beepers, and coded messages would come in occasionally. The beepers disappeared in favor of phones, but Solomon still knew the sound. *Beeeeep.*

Only this wasn't a beeper. No coded message. It was the watch Do-Good had stuck on him. As when they left the white room, Do-Good's voice came over the watches.

"Do-Good says, *GET READY FOR MORE!* Your challenge: steal something inside the house and get out again. Must be worth two-hundred and fifty-thousand or more... and for an extra challenge, only *Elena* can handle the merchandise! You have five minutes, so scoot!"

Solomon heard a few people gasp. He felt like gasping, too, though he knew his reasons were different than those of the others.

"Two hundred and fifty grand?" murmured Clint.

"There's no way –" began Elena, the dumpy-looking chick who Solomon told himself Ramona'd probably look like in ten years, even though he knew that was a straight-up lie.

"This whole *place* isn't worth that much," said Noelle. "How –"

Then Solomon was talking. "Oh, no, please, no, this ain't happening, it can't be –"

Chong walked up to the door and hammered a big, meaty fist on it. He waited a breath, then slammed his shoulder into the door. It didn't give. Solomon knew it wouldn't, and would have told Chong that if the big guy had let him.

Or maybe not. The guy was a dick. Thought he knew better, thought he was tougher than everyone else. Solomon knew that wasn't true – 'specially not here. Chong might *be* tough. But he wasn't street, and street was what you had to be when you walked this part of the world.

Solomon watched him for a moment, then felt himself start moving up the stairs to the porch. Chong hit the door again, *thud,* and again the door didn't budge.

"Help me," spat Chong.

Solomon ignored him. He went to the edge of the porch. Reached up. Felt around.

"This isn't a good time for gardening," said Chong, slamming into the door yet again.

"Shut up, man," Solomon muttered.

"Get your ass over here and –"

Chong shut up as Solomon pulled out the key from inside the planter he'd been feeling around in. Still there, just as it had been all those years ago. Still part of the place where he became Big Wise.

He went to the door and pushed the key into the lock. Turned it. Chong's mouth sagged open.

"How did you know that would be in there?" asked Noelle.

Solomon didn't answer. Not until he was inside. Not until he saw the sofas, the porn mags, the drug paraphernalia, the tags. Until that moment, he could try to convince himself it wasn't the place. Even finding the key didn't convince him, because maybe the place was just a house now. Just a normal house with a normal owner who hadn't bothered to change the locks – or the plants – since purchasing the house away from its last owners.

But it was all there. All the signs, just like it had been all those years ago.

"How did you know about this place?" asked Elena, echoing Noelle's question.

Solomon shrugged. "It's where I got jumped in."

12

"No kidding?" said Chong, eyeing Solomon as though he was a totally different person. "You were really Five-Deuce?"

Solomon's eyes narrowed. He gestured at his cheeks. "What the hell you think these were? Birthmarks?"

Chong shrugged. "I guess I figured you got them to prove you weren't lying." He eyed Solomon, a strange, sideways glance that had something unknown in it. Something Solomon didn't like. "What was your name again?"

"You know my name, asshole."

"No, your gang name."

Solomon almost answered. Then his mouth clamped shut.

What if this guy knows Big Wise? What if he's looking for me?

Stupid. Ridiculous and stupid. What would a dude like him want with Big Wise? Or any member of the 52s, for that matter?

Solomon had no answers to any of those questions, so he did what he tended to do whenever faced with a question whose answer he didn't know: he ignored it.

He pointed at the far end of the room, where stairs led up to the second floor. "We should look up there."

Elena was staring at her watch. "Only four minutes."

Solomon didn't answer. Just started up the stairs.

"Where we going, *bro*?" asked Chong, close behind him.

Again, Solomon didn't answer. He just led the group down the hall. Past one room, then he turned to face a closed door midway down the hall. He tried the doorknob, knowing it would be locked but figuring it was worth a try just the same.

It didn't turn. Just rattled back and forth and stayed closed. Solomon made as if to smash in the door with his shoulder, then eyed Chong and nodded to the empty air beside him. "Help a guy out, *bro?*" he asked, putting the same sarcastic edge on the last word as Chong had done a few moments before.

Chong laughed as though Solomon had just told a great joke, and took up position beside him. "One, two...," he began.

"... *three!*" shouted Solomon.

Both men hit the door at once. The cheap wood splintered, surprisingly lightweight. Solomon tumbled forward, driven to the ground first by gravity and then by Chong's weight as the big man pitched forward and drove Solomon down under him.

Solomon grimaced and shoved Chong away. "Easy, dude," said Chong.

"You call me *dude* or *bro* one more time and I'll –" Solomon cut himself off before completing the threat. He didn't know what he would have said, but knew none of them had time for threats. Not now, and especially not here.

He knew Two-Teeth couldn't be around anymore. There was no way. But whoever *was* in charge, they wouldn't react happily to a bunch of people sneaking in and ransacking the place.

He stood, brushing splinters off his pants. "Anything valuable here is gonna be... in...."

Solomon's voice disappeared as he saw the bed. The rickety table set up beside it. And the money on the table.

Piles of tens, twenties, and hundreds. And not just the penny-ante stuff that so often parked itself in this place before being distributed to the members of the gang or – more often – passed up the chain of command.

"Two hundred and fifty thousand dollars," murmured Noelle, her white-trash accent still noticeable even in whispered awe. "Think that's two hundred and fifty thousand dollars?"

"Yeah," said Clint. The black kid looked around like he expected something to jump out of the walls, while Elena crossed herself and whispered something under her breath.

Chong recovered from his surprise first. He rushed to the bed. "Eyes on the prize, guys!" he shouted, and reached for a pile of the money, obviously planning on just grabbing as much of it as he could and pocketing it all.

"Stop!" shouted Noelle. Surprisingly, Chong stopped moving, and looked back at the petite girl. "'Only Elena handles the merchandise,' remember?" she said, pointing at her watch.

Solomon glanced at his own watch. Two minutes.

Elena did the same thing, frowning at the timer that counted down to death. Then she looked around. She spotted a backpack on the floor – probably the same thing the money had arrived here in – and began stuffing wads of bills into it.

"That is more money than I ever saw in my life," whispered Clint.

"What does Mr. Do-Good want with it?" asked Elena, still shoveling handfuls of money into the bag. "He had to know it would be here."

Solomon only listened with half an ear. He looked around, glancing at the shattered door and the splintered frame. No hiding what had happened here. That meant that when the homies got here, there'd be instant response. Whoever the O.G. was...

He looked away from the doorframe. His gaze moved to the wall. There was a picture there. He hadn't noticed it until now, preoccupied with getting into the room, then getting off the floor, then the money on the bed.

Now, he had a moment to look at the image on the wall.

Two-Teeth was standing there in the picture, tossing a pair of gang signs: one of them a crude "H" for the Hoover in 52 Hoover Crips, the other a sign that meant he was a cop killer. For an instant, Solomon hoped that the image was one kept in memory of a fallen brother. That Two-Teeth was dead and whatever O.G. was operating outta this place now had his picture up there as a gesture of respect.

But the background was recent. The car he leaned on was a model from this year.

Two-Teeth was alive. He was still here. And that meant that this money was his.

"Oh, no," Solomon breathed. He turned to Elena. "Hurry, lady. *Hurry!*"

Elena paused from pushing bills off the table into the bag, obviously confused.

"What's wrong?" asked Clint.

"What's *wrong*?" repeated Noelle. "Everything about this is wrong!"

Solomon wasn't listening to her. He was too busy shouting, "We gotta move!"

Chong shook his head. "Duh. I doubt your homies would just slap our wrists if they found us here."

Solomon felt his hands open and close frantically, like he wasn't sure whether to make a fist or try and wave his hands fast enough to fly away. "No, we gotta *hurry*," he said, disturbed to hear how close the words were to coming out as a moan. He pointed to the picture on the wall. "We don't get out of here before that guy shows, we're gonna *pray* Do-Good kills us first."

"And you didn't think to mention –" began Chong.

Solomon turned to him. His fists bunched – at last, and the anger that flowed through him was a relief compared to the terror that still threatened to overwhelm him – and he shouted, "I thought he woulda died or been busted by now."

Elena must have finally caught onto his terror, and something inside her must have warned that Solomon wasn't exagerrating, because she suddenly looked just as terrified as he was. She began shoveling the money into the backpack even faster. Some bills fluttered to the ground and Clint made as if to grab them, but Noelle stopped him.

Then Solomon heard a sound that froze him and everyone else in the room. The screech of a car pulling up in front of the house. The sound of a car door slamming.

"He's here," said Solomon, and now the words *were* a moan. He wasn't ashamed of it either. Not at all.

An image filled his head. Early on – he was Big Wise already, but hadn't been that for long, and was still getting used to his role as a lower-rung member of the 52s. SFD had brought him to a crack house on eighth. Big Wise knew the place by sight, but had never been inside. He expected it to be trashed – places like that weren't famous for hygiene – but hadn't expected the smell.

Piss and shit were the first smells that hit him. But they weren't the worst. The worst ones were the smell of rotting meat and, below it, a tangy odor that Big Wise recognized but couldn't quite place. Not until he'd seen what SFD had brought him to see.

"You in now, little brother. Be sure you don't make no stupid mistakes."

Big Wise stared at the body on the floor, and knew that the acrid odor under it all was the blood that had run thick and deep from the man's body. Big Wise *thought* it was a man, at least. He couldn't be totally sure, since every one of the body's limbs was so bent and broken it was impossible to tell whether they had been muscular, flabby, thin, or much of anything else. The chest didn't reveal much, neither, since it had been flattened to a grotesque point, probably by heavy blows from the crowbar that still lay across the body.

The face itself was gone. Just a thick mix of bone and blood.

Man? Woman? For some reason it bothered Big Wise less to think of it as a dude. But it could have been either, and that was the truth.

On the wall nearest the body, in long letters that must have been red but had faded and dried to sickly browns and blacks, was the simple message: "Tr8r."

"Two-Teeth made you a brother," said SFD. "Make sure you don't do nothing that'll bring your family down. Two-Teeth don't like it."

Big Wise wanted to laugh. He had no intention of doing anything to bring the 52s down. But no laughter was possible when looking at this. "Two-Teeth do this?" he said.

"Does it matter? It happened. That shit's enough," said SFD. But something in his eyes screamed the answer. Two-Teeth *had* done this. And something else in SFD's eyes told Big Wise that Two-Teeth had enjoyed it.

Tr8r, he thought now. That's me.

Two-Teeth made traitors suffer. And Two-Teeth was here.

Elena had finished packing the last of the money. She walked toward the door to the hall, but stopped when she heard the front door open.

The house filled with silence, so heavy it made Solomon want to claw at the air. It felt like he was drowning.

"Someone in here?" came Two-Teeth's voice.

Noelle clapped a hand over her mouth.

A moment later, Solomon heard the heavy clomp of someone huge walking up the stairs. He smelled the tangy scent of his memory, and cringed, already feeling the blows raining down.

Elena took a step toward the door. But that was no good, was it? No way to get out – the stairs were the only way down from the second floor, and that was where Two-Teeth was. Between them and the door.

13

Solomon did the only thing he could think to do: he ran. Not for the stairs, but for the other end of the hall. He didn't look to see if the others followed. They either would or they wouldn't. They would either make noise or they wouldn't. Two-Teeth would hear them or...

His mind stalled at that thought. He knew they had maybe two seconds to get out of sight before Two-Teeth got close enough to see over the low wall that separated the stairs from the hall; to see *him*.

He flitted down the hall, trying to step as light as he could. The final door was just ahead. He grabbed it, opened it, then slid inside.

The rest of the group was behind him. He hadn't heard them, which was good since it meant that Two-Teeth –

Clomp! Clomp! Clomp!

– wouldn't have heard them either. But it was almost their undoing, too, since when Solomon turned once he got out of the hall, he almost slammed into Noelle, who was so close behind him he should have felt her breath on his neck. She collided with him, and they almost fell.

Two-Teeth would have heard that. He would have *had* to.

But a hand darted out. Chong. The big dude's arm corded with thick muscle, and he let out a small *whoof* of air as he struggled to keep either Solomon or Noelle from falling.

Clomp.

Then Solomon was upright. Moving aside to let Clint and Elena join them in the tiny space. It was a bathroom, dingy and reeking of long-unwashed surfaces. The sink was a chipped mockery of itself, the mirror above it broken out to reveal the mildewed wall behind. It was a close fit for *one* person, let alone five.

It would have to do.

Elena had barely entered before Solomon pushed the door shut, stopping at the last second to keep the latch from clicking. He turned the knob slowly, edging the door home.

He had to do it slow, because he had to do it quiet... because there was no more sound coming from the stairs. Two-Teeth was in the hall.

A few more thuds. Lighter, these, the sounds of someone walking carelessly toward a place he expected to find silent and closed. Then there was a roar. A shriek.

Noelle yanked a hand free of her pockets long enough to clap it over her mouth, to silence the cry that Solomon could see struggling to free itself from within her.

"We have to go," whispered Elena, even as there was another roar, and a heavy noise that Solomon figured was what it sounded like when a beast of a dude grabbed a bed and flipped it over one-handed.

"We can't go, you dumb –" began Chong in a harsh whisper. But he didn't finish the thought, because he saw Elena pointing at her watch.

Solomon looked, too.

0:42...

0:41...

Elena took half a step toward the door. Solomon grabbed the handle to the door, covering it with his big hand. He shook his head. "We go, we're worse than dead," he whispered. But he looked at his watch again.

0:39…

Two-Teeth started screaming over and over, a wordless rant that Solomon thought was probably the last thing that nameless, faceless body had heard before the pain began.

Footsteps sounded as Two-Teeth ran into the hall. Coming closer.

Solomon still held the doorknob in his hands. So he felt the tiny tremor as it was gripped by a hand on the other side. He thought about holding onto it, trying to stop Two-Teeth from turning it. But what would that accomplish?

The knob turned under his palm.

Then, outside the door, a cell phone rang, sounding the opening scratches and beats of N.W.A's "Gangsta Gangsta." The sounds ended as Two-Teeth apparently picked up and shouted, "What is it?" A moment of silence, then, "What. The. FUCK?"

More footsteps sounded, this time moving away as Two-Teeth ran down the hall. Down the stairs, sounding like he was taking them two at a time.

Clint reached for the doorknob. Solomon grabbed his hand and shook his head. Clint looked at his watch. "We aren't going to get out in time."

Solomon hesitated. He didn't want to get his head blown off. But Two-Teeth… if he found them here, that would be infinitely worse.

So he waited. Waited.

Below them, they heard more crashing as Two-Teeth upended more furniture on his way out of the house. Solomon nodded. Waited for another crash.

When it came, he turned the knob and led the others out. Not downstairs – if Two-Teeth spotted them before he left, they'd all be dead, one way or another. Either Mr. Do-Good would kill them or, if they *weren't* lucky, then Two-Teeth would.

No, Solomon and the others had to wait until he was gone, and even then couldn't leave by the front door, which was easily visible for at least a block up and down the street. Two-Teeth had the attention and instinct of any apex predator, and might easily spot movement at the house, even in his rearview mirror.

So he didn't go for the stairs. He led them, instead, back to Two-Teeth's room.

14

They all followed him, moving silently as possible. Even after the front door opened and shut, they still moved on cat's feet. Noelle was the only one who broke the silence.

"Fifteen seconds! We won't make it!"

Solomon ignored her, leading a concerted rush to the window in Two-Teeth's room. They had to swerve around the remains of the table that had held the cash, and the bed that looked like it had been flipped as easily as a piece of paper.

Clint ran to the window and began yanking on it, trying to open it as Noelle said, "Ten seconds!"

"Move, dammit," shouted Chong.

Outside, they heard the squeal of tires as Two-Teeth burned rubber down the street. That was what Solomon had been waiting for. He had known that the window wouldn't open, but hadn't wanted to risk what came next. It was the side of the house, and from the sound of the car he figured it was on the back of the place from Two-Teeth's perspective. Even so, he'd waited until the last possible second.

Do-Good's message just said they had to leave the house before the five minutes was up, not that they had to leave the property, so Solomon hoped they'd have time.

"Four!" Noelle had abandoned silence in favor of a panicked screaming.

Solomon grabbed the table off the floor. It was a lightweight, rickety thing, and even as he swung it, the leg he'd been holding separated from the rest of it. That was fine. Better, even.

He swung the leg at the window, smashing it out, then quickly running the leg around the edges to clear away the dangerously jagged shards of glass that remained.

Then he was over and out, pitching himself through the now-open window, rolling onto the eave that circled the house, rolling away barely in time to miss being crushed yet again by Chong's weight as the big dude tossed himself out as well.

An *oof!* as Noelle followed, landing on top of Chong. Then Clint. Then Elena.

"Did we make it?" she was screaming even as she landed. "Are we out? Did it count?"

The watches everyone wore beeped. Solomon went rigid, his jaw locking as though if he clenched it hard enough he might block the collar's impending blast. Might save his head from splashing all over the eave.

The blast didn't come.

Chong levered himself out from under the people who'd followed him out the window. He jerked his way free, sending Elena tumbling to the side. She almost rolled right off the eave, saved only by Clint snagging her with a viper-quick grab.

Chong didn't notice or care. He was still crawling, moving toward Solomon as he growled, "Why'd you wait? You coulda killed us!"

Before Solomon could answer – could explain why he'd waited, and exactly what Two-Teeth could have and *would* have done to them if they were seen – Chong threw himself forward. Solomon felt the big man hit him, and felt a few shingles slide loose of their moorings below him at the same time. Then he felt nothing at all – no weight, no sense of self. Just the air rushing past as Chong and he both went right over the side of the eave.

He vaguely heard the sounds of the others making their way down, but only as a dim, faraway recognition. The rest of his attention was taken up by pain as his body hit the hard-packed dirt below the eave.

He heard Chong groan beside him.

Good. Maybe he's dead.

But he wasn't dead. Far from it. In fact, Solomon realized that the big man had fallen partly on *him*, which probably shielded him from some of the pain of falling on the brick-hard ground. That was why Chong was up first. Hands and knees, then standing, then he was down again as he threw himself on top of Solomon.

Solomon was a good fighter – a *dirty* fighter. He was tall and wiry and he knew from experience that he was much stronger than he looked. But Chong was less hurt by the fall, and had at least twenty pounds on him, not to mention the advantage of gravity since he started the fight on top of Solomon.

Solomon punched automatically, and felt his right hand connect with Chong's head. The swing was wild, though, so instead of hitting the bigger man in the temple or jaw – either of which would have rocked him away and maybe knocked him cold – he hit the man in the back of the head. Chong grunted and reeled back, but only a bit. Only the shortest moment of dizziness and then he was back on the attack – and Solomon was pretty sure he'd broken a

couple of fingers. That wasn't unusual in a fight, he knew –
just as he knew that he could still make a fist and use it in a
pinch – but it hurt like hell, and cut the force of all his attacks
on that side in half.

Chong rocked back forward. Solomon tried to meet
him with a left jab to the nose, but turned out the other man
had a bit of fight experience, too. He didn't try to lean away
from the punch, which would have been useless
considering Solomon's reach. He just bunched up his
shoulders around his ears, slid to his left, ducking the blow.

Chong peppered Solomon back with a quick one-two
combination. The blows didn't hurt him much, but they sent
the back of his head pounding into the dirt.

That seemed to give Chong an idea, and he switched
away from punching. He grabbed Solomon's shirt in one
hand, his hair in the other, and raised the upper half of
Solomon's body, then slammed it backward.

Solomon's vision simultaneously clouded and slid to
the side as the back of his head slammed into the dirt. He
barely had time to gasp in pain before Chong repeated the
action, and Solomon could see – barely – bloodlust creating
a kind of insanity in the other man's eyes.

This fight wouldn't end in defeat. It would end in
Solomon's death unless he did something fast.

His left hand scrabbled, trying to find something.
Anything. He came on a rounded form, cold and hard, that
his body recognized must be one of the lawn ornaments that
lay scattered about the outside of the house. They'd been
there forever, remnants of the last owner of the place before
the Five-Deuce moved in, and which the gang had never
bothered to remove.

He lifted the thing, and his heart plummeted. It was so light – obviously hollow. Even hitting Chong on the side of the head with it wouldn't make a difference. It might cut him, might make him dizzy, but wouldn't stop him.

Chong rocked backward, then forward again, and again Solomon's head impacted the unforgiving ground. He couldn't take much more of this.

"Stop! Don't do this," shouted Elena.

Something about her scream penetrated the mist of rage and pain that had all but destroyed his rational thought.

What am I doing? How does this help anything – help me?

Chong actually paused with Solomon's upper body held at a forty-five degree angle, preparatory to the blow that would signal the end to any resistance and then the end of his life.

Solomon used the moment. Acting seemingly of its own accord, his wrist flicked to the side. There was a strangely bright-sounding crackle of breaking clay. He felt blood in his hand – he must have cut himself – but didn't even feel the pain. He just clenched his fist around the same jagged shard that had cut him, then sent it sideways.

Chong shouted as the shard went into his side, just under his ribs. More wetness on Solomon's hand as blood gushed. Chong rolled away, tumbling back to the ground as pain and the shock that sometimes accompanied sudden blood loss drove the strength from his body.

Solomon followed him over, rolling with him. The shard was gone from his hand – must have fallen out after he sliced Chong with it – but he swept up another one and when he rolled over on top of Chong, he jammed it against

141

the other man's throat. Didn't slice him open, though a part of him –

(The Big Wise part.)

– screamed that he should do just that.

He pushed hard enough to break the skin. A red line down the side of Chong's neck.

Chong froze, and didn't move even when Solomon leaned in close enough to whisper in his ear, "If Two-Teeth had found us... believe me, getting our heads blown off would have been a mercy."

He waited. Chong glared at him with hatred and fear, the two so intense they melted into each other.

Their watches beeped. He heard Do-Good speak from them, his strange, shaky-giddy voice warbling out, "Do-Good says, *PHEW!* That was close. Next challenge: go to 1089 Heart Street. Time: 20 minutes."

"Where's Heart Street?" said Noelle.

"Knowing Do-Good, it's probably two or three miles away," said Elena, her voice a mix of weariness and disgust.

Solomon glanced at them, then looked back at Chong. "We done?"

Chong nodded, slowly since the shard still bit lightly into his neck. "For now," he said.

Solomon considered this. He nodded, then gave Chong one last jab with the shard. A bit more blood welled. "All good," said Chong.

Solomon stood. He kept holding the shard in his hand. Glanced at it and saw it was a curved piece of a lawn gnome's head, shattered into pieces.

Just like our heads are gonna be.

He turned to the others in the group as Chong huffed his way to his feet. "Twenty minutes." said Solomon. "Lotta time."

"You know the place?" asked Elena.

Solomon nodded. "Yeah. First break we've had: it's not even a mile away, so twenty minutes'll be easy."

He gestured for everyone else to leave, a bit worried that he'd have more trouble with Chong and not wanting the rest of them to get any ideas about jumping in to help one or the other of them if it happened. He was pretty sure everyone hated Chong, but not at all sure what they felt of him. Normally he didn't care about such things –

(*Be honest,* Solomon *definitely cares... but Big Wise don't give a shit.*)

– but their feelings mattered if they liked Chong better than him. Their allegiances were unknown, so having them around in a fight wasn't a good idea.

Chong slowly got to his feet, groaning. When he got up, he felt at his side and that was when Solomon realized what had happened to the clay he'd stabbed Chong with. It still jutted out an inch from his side, blood drooling around it.

Ignoring Solomon, Chong took hold of the shard with a pair of trembling fingers.

"I wouldn't do that," said Solomon.

"Who asked you?" snarled Chong.

Solomon shrugged. "Just there's no telling how much is in there, and it's clay so it could break into pieces inside you. Plus I seen plenty of guys pull knives from them and then bleed out." He leaned close to Chong. *Big Wise* leaned close to him. "I don't give two shits whether you die or not, but you start bleedin' too bad and you're likely to slow me down."

He turned on his heel and walked to the front of the property.

He heard a scuffing behind him, and knew that Chong had fallen into line. He grinned at that.

15

The good feeling started to fade quickly. And for some reason, when Elena said, "Isn't this nice? I feel almost like I'm out for a stroll," Solomon felt even worse. Every minute that passed made him realize more and more how badly screwed he was.

He had to figure out a way to get out of here. Not just out of whatever game Do-Good was playing, but out of this area. He kept seeing Five-Deuce tags, and every one he saw drove his despair a bit deeper. Big Wise, for once, had no answers. Both Solomon and his gang alter-ego were in agreement on this one thing, if nothing else: staying here was suicide.

Chong snorted at Elena. "Yeah, it's great. Just on our way to a tea party with the queen."

Elena swung around, shaking a finger at him. "Why do you always –" Her mouth slammed shut as she noticed the blood on Chong's side. "You're hurt!"

She moved toward him as though to help. Chong waved her away, but didn't look at her. He was glaring at Solomon. "Don't touch me!" he belted. Then, softer but with no less anger: "I'm fine."

"You're not," said Elena. She sounded like Solomon's mom had sounded when she thought he was doing something extra dumb. But her next words surprised him. He would have expected her to coo something like, "You poor man, you must be in such pain! Let me help you!" That was the type of vibe she gave off sometimes – someone whose life was taking care of people.

But she didn't say that. Instead, she got a strangely hard look on her face. "What happens if you fall behind? Then we *all* have to fall behind. And then we die." She gestured at his side. "Let me look at it."

"I thought you said you didn't work at a hospital," said Chong.

"I don't. But I know how –"

"No!" shouted Noelle, loudly enough that everyone jumped a bit. "There's no time to take care of that," she said. "He'll just have to push through it."

"Noelle," said Clint softly. "We have time." He looked at Solomon. "Right?" Solomon nodded grudgingly, and Clint turned back to Noelle. He spoke in low tones, trying to convince her away from whatever hysteria was on the verge of grabbing her. "See? We're close. Better we take a minute and –"

"No!" shouted Noelle. "Don't you see? Mr. Do-Good isn't going to make *any* of this easy on us, and he won't have given us extra time." She paused. "So there's something that will happen if we don't hurry. I know it."

"Like what?" asked Clint, still using his "come on now let's be reasonable" voice.

"I don't know," said Noelle. She looked away. Shoved hands in pockets. "But something." She looked back at him, then at Elena, then Chong, and last at Solomon. "You know it's true. You can feel it."

Her eyes spooked Solomon. He felt himself nodding, but had no sensation of doing it himself. "I think she's –"

"She's right," Chong said. He started walking, but only made it a few steps before pausing and wincing, his hand at his side.

For a moment, the group wavered. Solomon could see them looking at each other, asking what to do. Elena and Clint, at least. Noelle was so scared she was practically dancing in place. Chong looked like he was wavering, too, maybe on the verge of asking for help.

But Noelle's eyes... so intense, so very scared. That fear was something both Solomon and Big Wise understood. She sensed something. She wasn't street royalty, maybe not street at all, but Solomon got the impression that she'd had it tough. That she'd faced pain and come through it. That honed a person's senses, and made them someone you listened to.

But the others were going to stay behind. He could tell. So he took matters into his own hands. He started walking, tossing a derisive, "You fall behind, I ain't waiting for you," at Chong.

"Then you'll die when you get too far."

Solomon stopped then. Turned and grinned his most dangerous grin at Chong. "Not if I take you outta the game." He paused a moment before adding, "Eyes on the prize, isn't that what you said?"

He kept walking. Noelle fell in step with him instantly. Clint and Elena followed a moment later, the Latina tossing a look at Chong that was half regret and half encouragement.

It was a small victory for Solomon: he had moved people. That had been his job for years, as a motivational speaker, and before that, in a rougher, more violent way as an up-and-coming 52. But that victory faded the next time he saw one of his old crew's tags, and thought of Two-Teeth. The dude wasn't just going to forget that two hundred and fifty grand had disappeared. He'd be diving into his own crew, using fist and blade and threat and pain to convince them to tell the truth.

And when they didn't tell him shit, he'd turn to the streets at large. Word would go out, and if Solomon was still in the area he'd be found and brought to stand a quick trial before a man who would serve as judge and executioner.

He saw the bloody man in his mind. The letters and single number on the wall: *Tr8r.*

He walked faster, not sure whether he was more worried about what Noelle had said – that their "extra time" would turn out to be part of Do-Good's plan, and something they would need to have – or worried about being found out here on the street.

A few more blocks, and something started to nibble at Solomon's consciousness. Something bad was happening around him, but he couldn't place it. He felt like he'd seen something – but only with part of his brain, a section cut off from the rest of his conscious thought.

What is it?

He looked around. Something was there. But what?

When did it start?

That was easier: it had started out on this street. When they turned the corner and began walking this direction. They weren't far from Heart Street, so maybe it was just that they were getting closer to whatever Do-Good wanted from them when they got to number 1089.

No. It's something else. Something –

And in that moment, he realized what it was. Realized that he'd seen it instantly, but enough time had passed that it had changed. Grown older, more rundown.

"Still the same car," he whispered.

"What?" said Noelle.

"What the hell kind of nonsense –" began Chong.

"It's the same damn car!" Solomon repeated. He backed away a step.

No way. Not possible. Can't be.

But it was. The same puke-green car. Years later, and it looked like it hadn't been washed in all that time, but it *was* the same car.

He's got to have sold it. It showed up here after the new owner drove it away. There's no way –

"The *hell*? Big Wise?"

Solomon turned slowly, stiffening as he saw the man emerge from an alley where he must have been taking a piss, still fumbling at his zipper as he lunged forward and then screamed, "Where's my *money*, you asshole?

Solomon turned to run, all thoughts of the game fled from his mind. But the man from the alley reached into his coat and pulled out his gun and growled, "Move and I'll shoot you in the back, Wise. Swear to God I will."

Big Wise didn't move. He only glanced at his watch.

Glad we have the extra time. Just out for a stroll? No chance. Not in this neighborhood.

He raised his hands. "Hey, Pat," he said, as Detective Patrick "Pat" Pattinson strode up to him.

149

16

Pattinson buried the gun in Solomon's gut. The hard end of the muzzle concentrated all the power of the guy's punch into a square inch, and Solomon suddenly felt like he'd had his guts yanked out. He bent double as his breath exploded from him, trying to scream in pain and managing only a whispy, *hrk, hrk, hrk* sound.

Pattinson leaned in close. "Who said you could call me Pat, Wise? We ain't friends. We're just a pair of guys on the street, and one of them owes the other a helluva lot of dough."

He backhanded Solomon, knocking him down. Solomon looked around, trying to find some way out of this. His gaze settled on the backpack Elena still wore. "We've got money!" he screamed just as Pattinson kicked him in the side. Another explosion in his stomach.

"Really? Really?" Another kick. "About ten years too late, man." Pattinson went to kick Solomon again, but stopped as he seemed to become aware of the others for the first time. His eyes widened as he saw the strange group, and the collars they all wore. "The hell is this, some kind of fetish team? Or are these new recruits? You trolling for some other crew? The Six Pacs?"

His eyes moved from Clint to Noelle. "Nah. Wrong color," he said. He pulled a badge from his belt and waved at them. "Get outta here. Me and Big Wise are going to have a chat, then I'll probably bust him. So unless you want to spend the night in a holding cell...."

Solomon felt cold inside. No way was Pattinson going to "bust" him. No way was he going to see the inside of a cell. If Solomon was lucky, Pattinson would wait until the others left, then shoot him for "resisting arrest" as soon as they were gone.

If he was unlucky, Pattinson would turn him over to Two-Teeth.

But Pattinson didn't know what Solomon did: that the others couldn't leave. That they were in this mess together. That gave him hope, but also made it that much harder for him to figure any way out of this – certainly not in the time they had left before Do-Good popped all their heads off.

"I made you a lot of money, Pattinson. You owe me."

He knew the second he said it that he'd made a mistake. Even before Pattinson kicked him again, before he felt the rib crack inside his chest.

"You *stole from me*, Wise."

"Bullshit. You were shaking us down, and that meant you were involved in something and needed to get paid to shut up. And you're still here, so you *did* get paid eventually, and the only one who lost money was probably Two-Teeth himself."

Pattinson looked sharply at the others, then back at Solomon. "I don't know what the hell you're talking about, Wise."

But Solomon knew different. He saw in Pattinson's eyes that he was right. "You do. And you gotta know that if you turn me over, I'm gonna let Two-Teeth know you was tryin' to shake me down for more cash, on his turf."

"Like he'd believe you."

Solomon climbed to his feet. He smiled tightly. "He would," he said. He put a hand on Pattinson's shoulder, knowing the cop would be doubting his standing with Two-Teeth.

"You're a dirty cop," said Solomon. He would have said more, but there was a sharp gasp and he turned to see Elena clap her hands to her cheeks. "What?" he demanded.

"I just realized," managed Elena. "Do-Good's rules."

Clint's eyes widened. He backed a few steps away. Chong, too. Noelle had her hands deep in her pockets, hunched over like she was worried about getting hit with something. "We aren't allowed to talk to the police," said the girl. "Do-Good said –"

Solomon didn't hear her finish.

17

There was a crashing sound, then silence, then a ringing. That was okay. Peaceful, almost. Solomon could have just flowed into that ringing noise, like a river of sound he could float through forever.

The ringing ebbed, replaced by a deep bass drum that pounded through him and shook him worse than when he rolled with SFD and the dude cranked up his tunes so loud the woofers in the back seat felt like they were hammering into Solomon's spine.

Bam-*bam*, bam-*bam*, bam-*bam*.

The bass drum beat away the ringing. Took its place and smothered it in a sound that brought pain with every touch. A moment later he realized the pain was coming in time with his heartbeat –

(*bam*-bam, *bam*-bam)

– and a moment after that realized that he wasn't dead. Nothing dead could hurt this bad. A tiny part of his brain marveled. *Shouldn't* he be dead? Something had exploded, he knew that. So his head was gone, it had to be. Gone like a mannequin's head, the remainder melting and dripping sizzling bits across what was left of his chest.

(*bam*-bam, *bam*-bam)

The pain/sound drew his attention, and it was only then that Solomon realized he hadn't been seeing anything for a few seconds. Nothing but black and then red and now more red, red pumping out of the ragged stump that ended six inches below his elbow.

He started to scream as he understood what had happened: the device on his wrist had exploded. Not just a timer, not just a way for Do-Good to communicate. A bomb, just like the collar.

His head lolled to the right, coming face to... *what*? Not face to face, because there was nothing left of Pattinson's face to look at. The blast that had torn Solomon's hand and wrist away had also blown all the meat from the front of Pattinson's skull. Nothing was left there but a few hanging bits of flesh, a few ragged strips of skin. The nose bones jutted out, strangely angular against the softness of the pulped matter that had melted to the skull.

The jaw was missing.

No, not missing. Right there. Right there next to me right there on the ground and what are those things those things everywhere are those his teeth dear God dear Jesus are those his teeth?

Solomon started screaming.

"Leave him!" shouted Chong, looking at his watch – not exploded, but whole. Because he hadn't talked to the cops. He hadn't broken Do-Good's rules. "We only got four minutes."

Then he seemed to realize that he was looking at a bomb on his *own* wrist. He shrieked and began yanking at it, trying to tear it away from himself. There was no give, and he turned and ran, but only got fifty feet before his collar blinked red and started to beep. He stopped. Not sure what to do. Rigid, terrified. Unmoving.

Noelle was shouting, whimpering as she looked down at Solomon. "We can't help him," she said. "We have to –"

"No!" barked Elena, also looking at Solomon. She was reaching for him – it seemed like she was reaching for something a thousand miles away – grabbing for his stump. She caught it. Pressed it tightly, trying to stop the bleeding. Solomon screamed as again fresh waves of agony burst against him. "We can't leave him. He's the *only one who knows where we're going.*"

Clint went to Pattinson. Flinched, but still reached down and pulled the cop's –

(Ex-*cop's.*)

– belt away from his pants. He wrapped it quickly around Solomon's arm, using it as a tourniquet. "Besides, Do-Good said we have to stay together," said Clint as he pulled on the leather strap. "That includes him." He glanced at Pattinson. "You shouldn't have talked to him."

"Scolding later," said Elena.

Clint yanked on the belt one more time. Then wrapped it around and around. Solomon screamed the whole time.

Clint turned to Chong. "Some help?" he asked, even as he thrust one arm under Solomon's back and started to lever him up.

"I ain't helping him," said Chong.

"Well we're not leaving him behind to die," said Clint, his eyes flashing. "So you can either help or run ahead. But I don't think you'll like that very much."

Noelle mimed a head exploding, which made Solomon cough out a spat of hysterical laughter. He didn't know why. He was still screaming, still hurting, still maybe *dying*, even though he saw that the blood from his arm had slowed from a gush to a stream.

Chong cursed under his breath. He helped Clint pull Solomon to his feet, wringing another set of screams from him.

Solomon felt like Clint and Chong were punching him with razor-studded hands as they lifted him off the ground, jostling him to get him into position.

Then they ran.

Not running. No. Slogging. Tripping. Killing me. Killing me.

He became aware that someone was shouting at him. Asking him a question. Pointing.

Solomon looked up. He could barely make out what he was seeing. Two green blurs.

What's happening?

The green blurs swam in and out of focus, and it took him an eternity of seconds to realize that they were the crossed arms of a street sign; that someone was shouting, "Which way?" into his ear.

Where are we going?

Heart. Beating heart. Blood out of me. Blood on the ground.

He gestured with his chin, not even sure if he was telling them to go the right way. They had to be somewhere. Had to find a heart. Heart Street. Street royalty.

His thoughts started to dissolve. Solomon was leading the group, the bleeding leading the blind into a night that grew darker around him with every passing step.

I'm dying.

Maybe. Probably.

He stumbled forward. He had no choice – he was being dragged along by Chong and Clint and, ahead of them both, he thought he saw a flickering image. It winked out a moment after he saw it, and a retreating part of his mind whispered that it hadn't been real. Just a hallucination.

But Solomon knew different. He knew what he'd seen: his daddy. Zeke "Face" Washington, gesturing for him to come closer, come faster… and wearing a smiley face mask all the while.

Solomon stumbled forward.

The night deepened.

Interlude

1

Thaddeus Sterling heard the doctors. That is to say, he heard a general *buzz-buzz-buzz* that something in his mind told him was words. But he didn't register anything of it, other than the times.

"… a month…."

"… less…."

"… maybe days…."

Thaddeus nodded at the right times, his brain figuring out when the pauses were, when to nod, even as it retreated farther and farther into itself.

Then the doctors were gone, and Thaddeus had no idea how long he had been sitting there. Had no idea how the phone had gotten into his hand, and no recollection of what he had been doing with it.

Then it buzzed – again – and Thaddeus realized that was what had dragged his mind out of the fog, out of the darkness. The phone's screen lit up, showing a text notification.

Thaddeus looked at the texts. Realized that he had sent half of them without even knowing it. What *did* he know?

"… a month…."

"… less…."

"… maybe days…."

He looked at the texts, realizing now – fully and completely – what he had been doing when the doctors arrived.

Thaddeus, "Tad to my friends," Sterling was a very rich man. And very rich men rarely got that way, and certainly did not *stay* that way, without planning for the future. Without taking decisive action. Even as his conscious mind disappeared, the primal parts of his subconscious had taken over. Had done what had to be done.

Thaddeus looked at the texts. The last one was incoming. Asking a question.

Tad tapped out the response:

> **TAD: It's worse than I feared.**
> **Make it happen.**

The answer came quickly. Anonymously, as always, but that was to be expected.

> **X: when?**
> **TAD: 24 hours.**
> **X: it'll cost**
> **double 4 rush**

Tad tapped out one more sentence. Three little words. For a long time, his thumb hovered over the button that would send the message. It stayed there for a full minute as Thaddeus thought about what he was about to do. He was careful. That was another thing that kept him wealthy, kept his businesses stable, and had until now kept his life as close to perfection as any mortal could hope to enjoy.

He came to a conclusion – the one he had always known he would reach, even as he pretended to consider for one last moment.

His thumb touched the glass of the phone. The message sent.

TAD: Just do it.

2

FBI REPORT FILE FA2017R2

Appendix B

Reproduction of YouTube comments on pertinent videos – see Appendix AA for list of videos, both active and since archived, Appendix AB for list of videos no longer available, and report sections 18 through 20 in re actions taken to recover videos that disappeared during hours following incident.

See also Appendix AC list of known commenters as matched to YouTube designations, and Appendix AD for list of YouTube designations belonging to persons still unknown.

For list of known homicides attributable to YouTube commenters, please see report for File FA 2018R2.

*** NOTE: FILE FA 2018R2 HAS ADDITIONAL APPENDIX – FURTHER HOMICIDES CONTINUE, AND HAVE BEEN NOTED (WHERE KNOWN)***

See also Appendix AD and files referred therein to list of Portobello Road videos, comments, and homicides. N.B.: Hard copies of the files must be relied upon, as *all electronic*

files are subject to corruption by parties unknown. See Internal
Report FA 2019R43.

Comments to YouTube video designated A14

---

3 COMMENTS   SORT BY

Crying0nTheInsid3
Anyone going to do this???   O.o?
👍 👎 REPLY

HansomeMuthah92
Dunno. Maybe.
👍 👎 REPLY

MyL0ssHisGain!
WHAT ARE YOU PUSSIES TALKING ABOUT?
HELL YES. *I'M* GOING TO DO IT.

We ALL should do it.

I'm leaving now. Get off your shit train of doubt – you
know why we're all watching this – and get moving.
👍 👎 REPLY

THREE

1

Chong wasn't his real name. That hadn't been okay at first, but it turned out fine for him in the end.

The kids at his school started calling him that when he was eight. Didn't matter that he was third-generation American, or that his name was easy as any, and easier than most. They called him Chong because he looked Chinese, because they were assholes, and because – most of all – they could already tell he was smarter at the age of eight than any of them could hope to be at fifty.

Chong was a genius. He realized *that* when he was two. Plinking out notes on a piano in his parents' house was one of his earliest memories. He remembered the white and black keys, his tiny fingers moving slowly over them. Slowly – but still faster than any other child with arms too short to wipe his own butt *should* be able to do.

He remembered staring at crotches. Not that he was a pervert or anything. But a two-year-old sitting on a piano bench would see mostly that level when adults hovered nearby. *Lots* of them did. *Lots* of them *oohed* and *aahed* and said words like "precious" and "prodigy" and "unbelievable."

A few asked his parents to let them have him. To let them take him away to places where he "would realize his full potential."

Dad was a banker. Mom had once been a painter of some note, before she retired to make babies and then found out she would only ever have one and spent the rest of her life pretending that one was enough – though Chong knew that was a lie.

But both had caring hearts. The kind of hearts that doomed people. "He needs his mother," Dad had said. "He needs to be around other kids his age," Mom said.

That was the beginning of Hell for Chong. A world that he wished every day would just *end*.

It did, eventually. He got out of grade school early. That was partly because he was so smart his teachers were having trouble answering his questions; and partly because he had finally gotten sick of the teasing and made an example of the worst of them.

Erin Westmoreland's head hadn't exactly exploded when Chong hit him in the back of the skull with the brick, but it had definitely shifted. Gone concave where it should have been convex, and the boy fell and twitched a bit and then was quiet.

No one ever *really* thought Chong did it. Not *really*.

That was what they said. But he knew otherwise. The teachers only looked at him indirectly, out of the corners of eyes that remained vigilant to him.

The other kids looked at him even less, and spoke to him not at all.

Only Mom and Dad actually said they believed that Chong had nothing to do with "that poor, poor boy." And they *did* believe he was innocent, Chong knew. They couldn't *not* believe it. They were good-hearted, both going to church regularly, both giving a full fifteen percent of their earnings to various charities.

That was stupid, and the day he found out about it he called a meeting. He was only twelve at the time, so he was still a junior in college. Twelve, and what surprise his parents' faces showed when he sat them down and explained the economic realities of their donations. He called up the spreadsheet he'd prepared and took them carefully through the reverse pyramid of earnings, showing how much they would likely lose in interest and investment returns over the course of the next twenty years should they continue their nonsense "charity work."

They looked at him with the same delight they always showed when he did something they felt validated their life choices. "Look how *smart* he is," he could practically hear them thinking. "Look how *well* we did by him."

Out loud, his father said, "Of course I know all that, son. I'm a banker, after all." His eyes softened even further than usual, going from cowlike to positively vapid. "But we're fine. We have enough, and others have a bit as well. We have plenty to live on, and your mother and I have been careful. We won't want, and we'll be able to retire just fine." He clapped a soft hand on Chong's shoulder. "You don't have to worry about us."

"You're a good, good boy," breathed his mother, her own expression the empty mirror of her husband's.

Chong almost screamed at them. Almost shouted what he was thinking, which was, "I'm not worried about *you*. Who gives a shit about *you*? It's *my money you're spending!*"

But he didn't. He just did as he always did when they said something blaringly stupid under the twin guises of kindness and/or wisdom. He smiled back just as vacantly as they were smiling at him, said, "Gee, I guess I didn't think of it that way!" and then went back to quietly thinking about the best way to murder them.

The answer came quickly after that, and a few days later his parents' car went off the side of Latigo Canyon Road. They'd been on the way to the beach. Chong had demurred ("Gee, I'd *love* to, you know how much I *love* the beach with you guys, but, gee, I have so much homework!") and not three hours later got the visit.

It was just as he'd expected; as he'd imagined for years. A mournful cop. The priest from his parents' congregation.

There were a lot of words. "Poor boy," and "Your parents were wonderful people" were the most oft-repeated. Chong just nodded, barely hearing them. He always had trouble pretending he was interested in other people – they were all so *stupid* – and now he had a wonderful excuse to not even try.

Grief.

His eyes filled with tears. He let out a ragged sob or two at random intervals.

And tried not to let on that he was dancing cartwheels inside.

The cartwheels stopped, though, when he discovered that his parents' money was all left to him in trust. He couldn't touch it before he was eighteen, and then would have access only to monthly payments until he was twenty-one.

Nine years. Intolerable. Unthinkable.

Chong petitioned for emancipation, and after the judge told him he'd represented himself with vigor and nerve and was by far the most accomplished pre-teen he'd ever met, shook his head and denied Chong's motion and told him to come back in a few years.

Intolerable. Unthinkable.

The judge died. No one ever figured out why.

Chong still didn't have access to his money, though. That was why he started seriously studying computers. He was living with his grandmother, a senile old bag who didn't even notice when he used her credit card to buy a laptop, or ask where he'd gotten it when she finally realized he was spending hours on the thing in his room.

He learned quickly, as always, but this time found that he actually *enjoyed* what he was learning. Everything from the construction of the hardware to the coding of the software.

By the time he was fourteen, he was confident he could hack into the bank that held his money and take what he wanted. Six months later he was confident he could do it and no one would even know.

But of course he didn't. Why bother? By that time, he was already rich.

2

Finding the deep web was easy. Unlike what most people thought, the deep web was just the unindexed stuff that was available on the internet. A lot of it was personal records, everything from dental visits to bank accounts. Some of it was just low-level data repositories by companies that wanted to keep a record of everything they'd ever done in their online presences. All mundane and boring.

Some of it *could* be useful, and Chong accessed it quickly enough. Hacking into governmental databases and even those of most financial institutions was too big a risk – at least at first – but he could get into a *lot* of useful stuff without going that big.

In fact, the smaller places were even better in a lot of ways. Wells Fargo might keep accounts of every single penny, NORAD might have entire teams of people monitoring for hacks. But the mom-and-pop gun range a few miles away?

Easy.

Chong carved his way into one of them, not even bothering to mask his tracks – because he left only the smallest of them. He was an ant on a cookie. Who would notice if he carried off a crumb or two?

He grabbed a birthday, which was there in plain sight. A guy named Jerrod Hall. A nice anonymous name with a nice, boring record at the gun range. But the nice thing about gun ranges was that they required people to sign in and provide a bit of information that Chong wanted, like drivers license records and social security numbers.

The last was encrypted, of course. All but the last four digits.

Chong used the drivers license info, along with the last four numbers of the SSN, to contact Mr. Hall's bank.

The way he found *which* bank to call was easy, and surprisingly low-tech: along with the birthday and drivers license info, the range also had a listing for Hall's next reservation, so Chong just waited outside the gun range until he saw Hall drive up and go in.

Another nice thing about gun ranges and the shops that most had appended to them: few windows. There *were* cameras, but those were easy to spot, and easier to avoid.

Chong went to Hall's ride: a 1989 Ford pickup truck with no alarm. Chong popped the door open with a slimjim he'd made himself after watching a few YouTube videos.

He got in and opened the glove box and flipped through the papers there. Lots of vehicle maintenance records. Oil changes, filters, and everything else a good, conscientious vehicle owner might use. Most of them had been paid for with a bank debit card.

Chong called the bank. Pretended to be a harried Jerrod Hall, who had just had his bank card stolen and wanted to cancel it and lock his account. It was over and done in five minutes.

No harm, no foul. Just a bit of inconvenience, to see if the information he had found would yield results. Most people thought of hacking as what they saw in movies and TV shows: some good-looking actor slamming away at the keys (Chong refused to call it typing, since most of their fingers never left the home keys and they looked more like epileptic baboons than people with computer skills), while saying things like, "into the mainframe" and "breaching their security" and "I'm in!"

Hacking was more than that. There was computer work, sure, but it was also low-tech stuff like breaking into cars to see what bank a person used or finding their birthday since most people never bothered to use anything other than some variation of that to lock their phones or their computers.

So Chong had just hacked Jerrod Hall. At the end of his time in the range he would find out that his account wasn't working. He'd call the bank and sort it all out in an hour or two, and the bank might well look into it. Not much help there, since Chong made the call from a burner phone he paid for in cash and then, after the call, had broken into pieces and tossed those pieces in various trash cans throughout the city.

Chong had hacked someone.

It felt delicious.

He did more and more, and soon his bank account had enough cash in it he had to change accounts to an out-of-country account. The Caymans were easy to work with, and more than happy to take his money into a secure account that they would not reveal without the force of an entire government leaning on them – and maybe not even then.

A hundred grand. Two. Three. He never siphoned off more than a few hundred from any one person – never more than a crumb here and a crumb there – but the money built up quickly.

It was exciting at first, but as with everything else, it became boring after a time. Chong started looking for something new. Something more.

That was when he ventured into the dark web.

The deep web was just the unindexed material on the internet. The *dark* web was just that: darker, more swollen with dangerous, *exciting* possibility.

Getting into the dark web was even easier than jacking Jerrod Hall's social and birthdate. Chong just downloaded a TOR browser, and he was in. Not that that allowed him access to what he was looking for. He was in the dark web the same way a newcomer might be in a city. He had stepped over the border from the surface web to the dark web, but stood just inside the city limits. He wasn't actually to Main Street, and couldn't even see any buildings in the distance.

But he got deeper in. A few dark web search engines came next. A bit more digging.

And then Chong found Nirvana. He created Portobello Road.

3

One of his parents' more annoying tendencies had been an appreciation of Disney movies. Not just the new ones, not just the animated classics, but old crap like *Mary Poppins* and *Escape From Witch Mountain*.

One of their favorites had been *Bedknobs and Broomsticks*, which Chong came to dread almost as much as he dreaded having actual conversations with his mom and dad. In the Disney movie, David Tomlinson sang a song called "Portobello Road," which he extolled as the place where you could find anything and everything in his trademark upper-crust English accent.

It was nonsense, of course. The real Portobello Road *did* exist, but it was just a street market full of t-shirts and trinkets.

So Chong created a Portobello Road that was the real deal. A place in the deepest part of the dark web where you *could* buy or sell anything. T-shirts? Check. Trinkets? Check.

And a few other things, too. A night with a guaranteed virgin would cost only a few thousand dollars, if you knew where to look and were willing to fly to whatever country hosted the kidnapper who had taken her.

If you knew how to get to the Portobello Road of the dark web, you could rent, lease, or buy anything from random Disney memorabilia that Chong's parents would have loved, all the way up and through things like endangered animals, explosions, and even human beings.

Chong created the place, and it quickly became the Amazon of the dark web. He administered it, but he also dove into the fray, and soon had set himself up as a go-between for several immoral but highly enterprising groups. He brokered deals for three percent, which was a deep undercut on every other broker for illegal goods and services, and as a result he got more business than he could handle.

The only other place that challenged Portobello Road's dominance as the place to go for anything and everything was another dark web marketplace called Silk Road. But the FBI closed it down in 2013, and its founder, Ross Ulbright was taken into custody. Silk Road 2.0 came on almost immediately, but it lasted all of a year before suffering the same fate.

Chong barely noticed. As soon as Silk Road came down he had two items of business that took all his attention. The first was to make sure he reached out to all his clients on both sides of his deals and assure them that they would all be satisfied; that Portobello Road would continue. That was critical, because he knew that the kind of people he was dealing with would not take kindly to their money disappearing or their goods not arriving as promised.

The second was to make sure the FBI broom wouldn't sweep him up along with Ulbright and other Silk Road admins. He felt like his balls crawled into his stomach and continued heading north until they were about to pop out through the top of his skull, because he was about to do something *really* dangerous: hacking into the FBI databases to see if his name appeared anywhere.

He felt like puking the whole time.

He also felt truly alive.

He found his name nowhere. He was clean – at least so far as the FBI was concerned.

He turned back to the deals he had made.

Silk Road 2.0 fell. Agora fell, as did Amazon Dark, Blackbank, and Middle Earth. Alphabay was shit from the beginning, and by the time it appeared it was nothing but a mosquito compared to the dominance of Portobello Road.

His happiest moments were always when he was making his own way. Making *his* own money, taking what *he* wanted, killing *his* own parents with *his* hands and *his* mind. And Portobello Road was the ultimate extension of that, because he had created a world there, and that made him a god.

The name *was* still a lie – you couldn't buy *everything*, not even in Chong's wild playground of wish fulfillment. But you could buy a lot, and all of it was illegal. Nothing small, either. No orders less than fifty thousand *ever* went through Portobello Road. That was the rule. It wasn't a place for dilettantes.

The money streamed in - Chong still took three percent of any deal he personally brokered, and half of one percent of *all* deals routed through Portobello Road – but Chong barely noticed. That hadn't been the point for years. Now it was just the rush that came with the knowledge of his superiority. He lived in a two-room apartment in West Hills. Not particularly nice, not particularly seedy. Right in the middle. He flew under the radar that way, and the only real signs of what he was doing on the multiple computers and servers he ran in the second bedroom were unusually high levels of power consumption and a lot of internet data. But he paid the LA Department of Water and Power on time every month, and made his payments to the telecom company that supplied his internet, and no one said anything.

Good times.

Not the best times, though. The best times were the ones where Chong went out "into the field." He lived for Portobello Road, but recognized that even that thrill would pale after time, unless he kept things fresh. So whenever there was a big enough client, or an interesting enough transaction, he saw to it personally.

He personally oversaw transit and delivery of two tons of meth from the Seo-bong Faction, a Korean organized crime group, to the Camorra, an American crime family that had been a power in New York City for over a century and had decided to extend its business across North America. Once, he logged a seven-million-dollar deal that consisted of him taking a helicopter to deliver three coolers full of body parts, a gurney, and an aquarium that held a variety of tropical fish to an uninhabited island in the middle of the Pacific Ocean. He even oversaw the transfer of six young girls that were taken out of various bedrooms in various middle-America states and were now bound via chopper to a place far enough into international waters that the laws against various types of sexual conduct were nothing but vague rumor.

It was all so fun.

He'd known – vaguely – that it couldn't last forever, but he told that part of his brain to shut up, and kept playing in the make-believe land of Portobello Road. He was king, dictator, secret agent, banker, economist, hacker... he was *everything*.

Then came the white room. Then came Mr. Do-Good.

Chong was sitting on his chair in the front room. One of his few nods to his ever-bloating offshore accounts was that chair. It cost ten thousand dollars, and it sat in kingly majesty across from his one other major purchase (not counting the computers that hummed merrily in the next room): an eighty-inch UHD TV.

On the huge screen, the Broncos were getting killed. Chong had fifty bucks on the game, betting the guy in the apartment across the hall that his team would come out ahead. The fifty bucks was nothing, but Chong loved winning.

Unfortunately, the Broncos apparently didn't feel the same way. After the second fumble, Chong pulled out a cigarette and yanked the lighter from his jeans. He looked nothing like a stereotypical hacker, he knew. He didn't wear Coke-bottle lenses in black-rimmed glasses, he wasn't thin enough to shatter in a heavy breeze, and he despised both Hot Pockets and Monster energy drinks. Instead, Chong had thick muscles honed under the merciless gaze of a personal trainer who also tutored him in Krav Maga, and he stood at a few inches over six feet.

Usually Chong liked those facts; liked that on the rare occasions when he felt like hitting up a bar, he turned more than a few heads with his size and bearing.

But sometimes – like now, trying to work his cigarette lighter out of the pocket of his shorts while cradled in a chair whose soft body had form-fitted to his own bulky form – he hated his size and his muscles.

In the time it took him to get out the lighter and put the flame to a cigarette, the Broncos threw a pass that was intercepted and run to the fifty-yard line by the other team.

"No, no, no!" Chong shouted. "Eyes on the prize, guys! Eyes on –"

His cell phone buzzed. Chong cursed and worked *it* out of his pocket, albeit with a bit more speed and urgency than he had pulled the lighter out. He looked at the screen of the phone. Not many people had this number, and no one who was not rich or powerful.

He read the message, then stood and, with one last muttered curse at the team that was going to cost him fifty bucks, headed out of the room. He went down the short hall, past his bedroom, and into the back room – the "office" where he kept the hardware that let him operate Portobello Road.

He had consciously designed it to look like a junkheap to anyone who didn't know better. Anyone who *did* know better would see a collection of the top computers money could buy. And those were the cheap ones. The better stuff was all hardware that Chong had custom-built himself, and he figured he had enough computing power in this small space to not only topple more than a few countries, but to then step in and keep them running smoothly afterward.

A few – a very, very few – might also note that he had designed the layout to look like the super-hacker Neo's operating area in *The Matrix*. No green lines of alien-like code appeared on these screens, however. Instead, each one held a matching image of David Tomlinson, crooning soundlessly as he danced through Disney's idealized version of WWII Portobello Road.

As soon as Chong entered the room, sensors located in the walls and on the computers themselves picked him up. Nothing changed visibly, but Chong knew that inside the computers a series of very fast calculations were occurring. Measuring his facial features, body temperature, and a host of other variables. They matched themselves to Chong's profile, and then David Tomlinson stopped dancing and instead turned to say, "A spoonful of sugar...." The phrase repeated three times, and midway through the fourth Chong cut in to say, "Isn't quite as fun as killing a baby seal."

It was a rotating passcode, that shifted based on the day of the week, month of the year, and several other variables that only someone with Chong's mind could keep straight. Maybe fifty people in the United States. If either the passcode or Chong's face and body measurements didn't match up to what the computer required, a lockdown sequence would initiate, followed swiftly by the computer wiping itself clean of everything but a shell that would refuse to do anything but feed lines of David Tomlinson trivia to every wireless printer in a five-block radius.

But Chong answered the password, and his face still belonged to him, so instead of becoming that idiot shell, David Tomlinson grinned out of all the screens, said, "Deee-*lighted*" in that accent of his, and the screens switched to the many businesses and deals going down on Chong's definitely *less* idealized version of Portobello Road.

Military-grade armaments, drugs, human flesh... it all made its way here, brought by enterprising souls who would hook up with buyers in need of just such "particular" merchandise. There was even a community bulletin board – Chong's version of a Craigslist ad – where people could request anything from an illegal pet to a dead spouse... and where other people could post their willingness to provide just such things.

Six screens were devoted to deals Chong himself was handling. All showed what looked like eBay screens, though eBay generally did not accept postings of or bids for Stinger missiles, high-quality opium, or dead children.

Chong loved seeing the entire office, but those six screens were his favorite. They were *his* jobs. Portobello Road produced an insane amount of cash for him on a daily basis, just as passive income that came in as a result of the tiny commission it siphoned off after every sale. So much so, in fact, that no deal Chong oversaw himself would ever be more than a drop in the bucket.

But those deals – and the computer screens that showed them – were what he lived for. He had been surprised by a lot of things in his life. By how easy it had been to kill Erin Westmoreland, then his parents. How easy it had been to teach himself to dance between the electrons of the internet, and then among the frantic, circuslike stylings of the dark web. How easy it had been to set himself up as first a broker of deals, then a participant, then an overseer of countless of them.

But more than anything, he was constantly surprised that he didn't really need most of it. Not the money, not the memories of murder – though those did have better replay value and more action than any Marvel movie – but the *rush*.

So those screens – they existed as the moments where he rolled the dice. Where he played whatever cards found their way into his hands. And though he *could* have cheated often, he never did. He always played fair. Always scored the bid himself, never tried to lock out a competitor.

Where was the fun in cheating? Where was the fun if you always knew you'd win?

Now, though, as always, the temptation to do just that rose as he saw that one of the jobs he was bidding was going against him.

But that was part of the fun, too, wasn't it? The temptation to cheat, to lock everyone but himself out of the deal. The *overcoming* of temptation, and winning with nothing but his wits and his willingness to do whatever it took.

One more murder came to mind, as always. There had actually been a lot of them, but the one he warmed himself with most often was that of Jerrod Hall, owner of, among other things, a bank account, a Ford truck, and a gun. When Chong was bored one day – bored bored *boooored* – after Silk Road closed, he had seen Jerrod Hall on the street.

The man might be armed – even in gun-shy California, there were people who carried concealed weapons permits. The man might even be a gun *nut*; might carry enough deadly hardware to make Rambo think twice.

Chong had grown surprisingly large, true. His muscles were hard and strong. He was a black belt in Krav Maga. But still, the odds were against him.

He pretended to need help, calling out in faux pain as Hall walked past an alley that Chong hid in. The guy walked into the alley. And Chong killed him.

He didn't use a brick or the long-distance method of cutting brake lines and programming failures into a car's electronics. He used his hands.

Jerrod *was* armed. He tried to draw a gun, and Chong knocked it out of his hands and then squeezed and squeezed and squeezed until Hall wasn't moving anymore. Then Chong cut off the man's fingers – no good for the police to find bits of Chong's skin under the man's fingernails, which had raked his face a time or two during the fight. He buried them in different parks, shoved them into the knotholes of half a dozen trees. No one would ever find them – not without a helluva lot of time, a very concentrated and specific hunt, and a metric crap-ton of luck.

He was terrified. He was *in* it. He was… alive.

He went home and logged onto Portobello Road. Knowing he would make money hand over fist, and knowing he wouldn't care about that at all. Just about the rush.

4

The possibility of losing, he knew, was the main part of the rush. But that didn't mean he actually wanted to lose. No, he wanted – *needed* – to win in the end. That was why he went not to the computer that represented the call he had received while watching the Broncos, and what the caller wanted. He went to one of his smaller screens. The thumbnail on the Portobello Road sales page showed a series of small cannisters. Chong didn't know what they held, and didn't care. He only knew that he had a buyer interested in it, and one of the assholes bidding on it had just outbid him.

Maybe the bidder was a private purchaser. Maybe a broker like Chong. Didn't matter. The guy was going *down*.

Chong entered a number a full ten percent higher than the highest bid. His client had been very explicit about the amount of money he would pay for the mystery product, and Chong had just exceeded it. But not by much, and he knew he would make up the difference out of his own account if it came to that.

His client might be angry. That was okay. Chong would either be able to deal with it, or would have to take measures to ensure his safety – which would mean his client's *lack* of safety; his death. But that was okay, too. That was all part of the rush.

Another bid came in. "Stop outbidding me, you shit," said Chong. He frowned, then entered another amount. So high no one could possibly meet it.

This is definitely getting fun.

He watched the screen. Mr. Moneypants on the other side of the bidding was quiet. Chong watched the bid timer countdown. It hit zero.

"I win," he said aloud.

And inside, he said, *Again.*

Only then did he turn to the other screen. Not much time had passed since his call, but he knew it was a high-value client on the other end of the phone. That was the only kind who had Chong's number. And the dude was connected enough and rich enough that he might actually be able to *do* something about Chong screwing him over, if he felt like that was happening.

So Chong got to it. He withdrew his phone again, then tapped a link. Several faces appeared on the phone. Kids' faces. He grinned again.

Good selection today.

He turned to a third screen. This one had a list of payments, each assigned a code name that belonged to one of Chong's personal clients. They were buyers or suppliers, each one either supplying goods or supplying to Chong the funds to purchase them. The funds were in bitcoin, which would be paid upon or before delivery. Each of the orders had a payment, and each was marked either, "Order pending," "Order in transit," or "Order fulfilled."

As he watched, the screen flickered. Chong frowned. That did happen from time to time, because even though he had battery backups, if the power went out in the world around him, those backups could not possibly maintain the same high levels of power as the good ol' electric company.

Still, the flickers made him nervous. He was a hacker. He knew what could happen if the computers failed – or seemed to. He'd run a diagnostic as soon as he could. He should probably do it now, but his client was waiting. His important client. His *dangerous* client.

And not checking his computer now would just add that much more excitement.

The computer did it again. Now Chong's danger radar, only pinging once at the first glitch, went into a long, sustained *beeeeeeeep* that sounded like an internal flatline in his head.

Then the sound in his mind disappeared as a new sound appeared. Louder than the imaginary tone in his mind, and much lower. Not a *beeeeeeeep* but a *buzzzzz*.

Pain arced through him. Pain, then a strange, disjointed sensation. He felt his forehead hit the side of the desk he had been sitting on – how had that happened? – and then he felt himself laying on the floor.

Then... nothing. And the final thought:

What... a... ru...

5

The thought that had sent him to dreamland was the same one sounding in his mind when he came out of it.

... uuuush...

What a...

What...

What a... rush...

The feeling lasted as he sat up. As he saw that he was on a hospital bed. His first thought was that he'd had a heart attack. People who sat at desks did that, right? They had heart attacks. That was even kind of an exciting moment.

Then he saw where he was. The bed, the other beds, the other *people*. The white room.

The rush grew and grew and grew as he looked around, and suddenly it was a rush no more. It transitioned, as painful and shocking as anything Chong had ever experienced, to a new feeling. Panic.

He was stuck in a white room with a buncha losers, and the only person with whom he'd come into contact since then was Mr. Do-Good. Which was bad, considering that Do-Good was definitely on the other side of whatever game Chong had suddenly discovered himself in.

The panic scared him senseless. For a while literally; he hadn't even been able to talk when he woke. The older gal woke him, which was a shame given that he'd much rather have opened his eyes to see the other chick's face. Noelle was low-rent, trashy – and that would have put her squarely in a category that Chong dug on.

But no... just his luck.

The older woman – Elena – had spoken to him for a while, but the words were just a continuous *wa-wa-wa* that Chong could not understand.

Eventually his pain- and panic-fogged mind cleared enough to hear her. But he didn't care what she was saying. When she asked his name, he used the name he'd adopted all those years back as a vengeful reminder that sticks and stones might break his bones, but call Chong a name and that name will be the last thing you think of as a brick pounds through your skull.

So Chong spoke little.

Mr. Do-Good, though… that dude said a lot. Not just with his strange, jerky, disjointed words, but with the *way* he said them. Odd stutters in his speech, breaks in the middle of sentences like he had lost the track of his sentence and had to look at cue cards to figure out where he was again.

Crazier than a bag of schizophrenic cats.

Chong did what the dude said, though. He followed to the house that looked like the set of a gangsta rap video. He ran from a dude that looked like he'd been tossed *off* a gangsta rap video for looking too tough for that kind of music.

He ran, and ran, and ran.

The panic pulsed inside him. But still there was also that sensation.

What a rush.

What a rush.

WHAT. A. RUSH.

The rush sharpened when that idiot Black –

(What a name! If there's anything worse than a Chinese guy called Chong, it has to be a black dude actually named Black.)

– almost got them killed while they waited at Two-Teeth's place. Chong didn't even think about attacking him on the roof. It just happened. They rolled off, fell. Chong on top in an instant, just like always, and that fought the panic back. He was winning, just like always. He'd killed a lot of people, but not by strangling them. No one but Jerrod Hall had ever had their throat crushed by Chong's big hands.

Grabbing Black like that felt like a replay of a favorite memory.

Rush, a rush, what a rush-rush-RUSH!

Then the bastard stabbed him. Shoved a goddam piece of a goddam gnome into him, and every time Chong moved the thing sent shocks of pain running up and down his entire frame.

They had to run, and the piece was still in him. Chong knew it might well be cutting him to pieces inside, but at least as long as the bit of clay or ceramic or whatever it was remained there, no blood gouted. He knew it was only a matter of time, but what else could he do?

He ran with others – literally and figuratively – for the first time in his entire life. They were bound to him, and he to them.

He hated it.

Hated it more when he saw the idiot Black –

– running toward what turned out to be an off-duty cop. Chong didn't give two farts in a bottle that the dude got his hand blown off, though he was more than a little irritated when something stung him an instant later and he pried it out of his cheek and realized he was looking at one of the cop's teeth.

What a rush became, *Is this really happening?*

And he knew the answer. The horrible answer.

Now, more running. Holding Black's nearly-dead weight, dragging the man along as they ran to Do-Good's next assignment. Clint was under Black's other arm – the one that ended in an oozing stump, thank Heaven; Chong figured he'd rather actually die than have to be holding that thing.

"We gotta ditch him," he panted.

"You know we can't," Clint answered, his voice also coming in gasps.

And there it was. The biggest panic in this whole thing: *Chong wasn't in charge.* Do-Good was, and that was no big news. But worse than that, Chong sensed he wasn't even the most important person among the strangers who had found themselves in a deranged scavenger hunt.

Even Solomon Black was more important than him right now. Because Black was the only one who knew where they had to be in only…

Chong glanced at the smartwatch/explosive on his wrist. A tiny corner of his brain noted what it looked like. When he got out of this, he'd start something new. Something grand. He'd key off what he'd seen of Do-Good's operation, hunting through the dark web until he found the stuff. No way was it legal, so the only way it could be here was via a place like Portobello Road. Chong would hack everything he could find. He'd tear apart the base code of the entire *world* to find Do-Good. And then he'd make him pay.

But not now. Because that death-switch on his arm showed they had only a bit over five minutes left to get where they were going. 1089 Heart Street. They'd had twenty minutes to get there, but dealing with Black's stupidity had cost them more minutes than they could afford.

And Do-Good knew it would happen.

That was obvious. Why else would he give them twenty minutes to take a walk that Black had told them all would be much shorter than that?

He knew. Knew.

Again the panic surged. The danger-radar was still sounding its long, flatline tone in his mind. Chong worried that soon it would be an actual flatline. Because when he was up against someone as prepared as Do-Good, what could *he* do but die?

No. I can survive. Then... something worse than Jerrod Hall, worse than Erin Westmoreland. Do-Good's gonna die, and it's gonna take a good long time. Then who's gonna be wearing the smile, huh?

He said none of it. He just ran. Stopped a moment when they got to another intersection. Just like every time it had happened since Black got himself exploded, Clint jostled the sagging man and pointed at the green cross-panels that showed the names of the intersecting streets.

Each time, Black took a bit longer to respond. This time was the longest yet. His voice slurred. "It'sh... it'sh...." Clint jostled him again as his voice faded. Black jerked upright, pain obviously chasing away some of the cloud of darkness that must be enveloping his mind.

Why does everything bad always happen to me?

"Uhhh... right... righ...."

Black faded again. Clint started pulling them to the right, Elena and Noelle already heading that way. Chong resisted. "We don't know that's the right way."

"He said it was," murmured Clint.

"He's out of it. We gotta leave him."

"We stay together or we die."

"How do you know? Maybe we don't. Mine was the only one that lit up when I tried to run off. Maybe it's just the person who leaves the group – or gets left behind. Or maybe...." Chong licked his lips. They were dry, parched with the dehydration caused by all the running and all the panic. He wished for a moment he'd drunk more water back at the white room. "Maybe we just kill him. Then we're not leaving a player behind. We're just leaving a body."

"No," said Clint. His eyes were suddenly hard. Harder than Chong's, even when he was killing people with his bare hands. Chong wondered what the kid's story was.

Nothing good.

"We're taking him. We're taking *everyone*," said Clint.

Beyond them, Elena and Noelle had stopped. They were tethered to the group, just as Chong was. "Come *on*," shouted Noelle, her voice shrill with terror.

Chong sighed. He started dragging Black's dead weight. Another glance at his watch.

Two minutes left. Two minutes, and who knew how far left to run?

6

A bad moment where they ran into a bum who looked like he wanted to chat with them about the benefits of tinfoil hats, another when they had to run past a fire station and Chong's heart began to pound, fearful someone would come in or out of the place and spot the suspicious group running along in the middle of the night. But they ran past the bum, and no one came out of the fire station.

Still, they weren't going very fast, and every step shaved precious seconds from their time, and Chong felt every one of those seconds like a knife, hacking away at the edges of the only life that really mattered in all this: his.

They stopped at another intersection. "Which way?" said Clint.

Black didn't answer, so Chong hollered, "Which way, asshole?" in Black's ear.

Black mumbled something Chong couldn't make out. Partly because it was low and muddled, partly because at the same time, Clint said, "Right. We go right."

"How do you –" snarled Chong, cutting off when he realized that Clint's eyes had gone from the street signs to a house across the deserted street. It finally registered that one of the street signs said the most beautiful set of words he'd ever seen: Heart St. And just across, kitty-corner from them, stood 1089.

They slogged across the street, and as they did Chong's confidence returned. They'd be all right. They'd make it through the scavenger hunt, and then Chong would be the one to make the rules of the game. A game only Do-Good would play, and only Do-Good would lose.

The confidence fell away while he and Clint were still in the street. The mind-beep, solid and sustained, was replaced by the *beep-beep-beep* of the collars around Chong's, Clint's, and Black's collars.

Elena and Noelle were already across the street, already standing in front of the house. Chong could see the question in their eyes: should they go, and risk being blown up with Chong and the others, or should they stay where they were in the hopes that Do-Good let them keep playing?

Neither woman spoke, but both appeared to come to the same decision at once. They hurried back to Chong and the others. Which was stupid, because it wasn't like they could help him or Clint drag Black any faster.

Beep-beep-bee –

The sound cut off.

Made it.

But of course there was no celebration, no cheering, and *definitely* no rush. Even if anyone had been inclined to shout in joy or do a cartwheel, there was no time. The collars stopped making noise, but the watches all blinked. They all looked at their watches even as Do-Good spoke.

All but Black. Bruthah gots no watch to look at, yo!

The thought, ridiculous as it was, made Chong want to giggle. He didn't. If he started, he thought he probably wouldn't stop.

He focused on the watch, on Do-Good's voice, his hysteria gradually swallowed in anger and confusion.

"Do-Good says, *WAY TO GO!* But no rest for the wicked. Next challenge: get inside the house. Time: sixty seconds!"

The countdown started. Before "60" had shifted to "59," Elena was already moving. She walked toward the house that Do-Good had directed them to. Like most of the others in the neighborhoods they had passed through, the place was a shitheap. Sagging eaves, scrub-ridden dirt all around it. Graffiti on a few of the walls, one "window" broken out and replaced with a haphazardly-bolted patchwork of plywood sheets, the others covered by black iron bars.

"P... please...," murmured Black.

Elena was on the porch now, the backpack full of all the money they'd taken from Two-Teeth's crib bouncing on her shoulders as she leaped toward the front door.

She knocked. Chong felt like panic no longer just gripped him. Now it was squeezing the life out of him. He wouldn't have been surprised to feel his head pop like an overripe zit.

"Hey!" shouted Noelle. "That's not allowed! We –"

"We're allowed to talk if they talk first. We just have to wait until they say, 'Hello.'" Elena's response came out crisp and calm, and Chong couldn't help but admire her poise. She was someone he'd like to work with, to face on opposite ends of a Portobello Road deal.

She was also likely to get them killed, which dampened a lot of his admiration of her.

"Noelle's right," Chong said. "We don't know –"

Elena cut him off with a gesture, then pointed at Black. "Mr. Do-Good helped us with this one."

"Helped!" barked Clint.

Elena kept talking, still cool as ice. "They'll let us in when they see him. They say, 'What happened?' and we respond and ask to come in and they let us." She pointed at her watch. "Mission accomplished."

"They might not let us in," Noelle said. Her hands wrung together, then shoved into her pockets. "Not in this neighborhood."

At the same time Clint, his voice laden with disgust, said, "Is that all you see here? An opportunity to game the system? Damn, lady, this guy's dying and all you can see is –"

Before he could finish, Noelle pulled one hand out of her pocket and glanced at her watch. She suddenly bounded to the door herself and knocked again.

Chong laughed quietly. Elena had already done that. What more did Noelle expect.

And sure enough, nothing happened.

"Come on," Noelle muttered, knocking harder. "Come on!"

"Hold him," Chong said, letting Black's arm slide off his shoulder. Clint grunted as he suddenly took the full weight of the other man.

"What –"

Chong ignored him. He hurried to the porch, looking at his watch as he did. Twenty-five seconds.

As he ran to the door, he glanced automatically into the room. A light was on inside, a bulb that hung naked from the ceiling, flickering due to a loose filament or just crappy wiring in the entire house. The dim glow it cast allowed Chong to see a view he suspected was typical for this area: junky chair, couch with stuffing leaking from several tears, all oriented toward a large tube-style TV that hunkered on a stand at least two sizes too small for it.

The glance showed him little else, and nothing at all he cared about. The time was counting down, and whether Elena's "please help us" theory was right or wrong, they didn't have time to be subtle.

Chong reared back on one foot, kicking out with the other. He half expected his foot to bounce off a steel core held to a reinforced frame, given the crime-ridden neighborhood they had operated in all night. But the door just crackled, splintered, and opened. Half the frame came off around it, leaning to the side and then falling to the floor inside the room with a dry clatter.

Chong looked back. "Move!" he shouted. They did. Noelle had already run back and now struggled with Clint, the both of them bearing the full weight of Black. The 'banger's head lolled from side to side as they lurched inside.

Elena made it before them, of course, and she and Chong counted the seconds on their watches as Noelle and Clint tried to move fast and fast and faster still.

They made it with a full three seconds to spare. Chong stared at his watch as the countdown halted, expecting new instructions. Do-Good's smiley face avatar spun and winked in the corner, but nothing else appeared.

"Made it," said Noelle.

"Yeah," said Chong, turning to take a better look at the room and hopefully figure out what they were going to do here. He would be a good dog for now. He didn't have a choice.

But sooner or later, me and Do-Good are coming face to face. I won't strangle him. He'll just wish for something that easy.

A deeper look at the place revealed little more than Chong had already seen through the window. Only one thing of note, in fact. But that thing caused him to freeze.

They weren't alone in the room.

7

"Why isn't she moving?" asked Elena, echoing the question that was ringing through Chong's mind.

He hadn't seen the woman on the couch when he looked in the window. Part of that, he knew, was that panic and adrenaline had done a real one-two punch on his mental status. But the other part was that the woman was so thin, so motionless, so…

Gray.

Even in the flickering twilight of the room, Chong could see that her color was off. She slumped on the couch, almost off it. Her legs had jammed up against the chair that was the room's only other furniture, and Chong suspected that was the only reason she hadn't slid right onto the floor.

"What's wrong with her? Why didn't she –" began Noelle.

"Drugs," whispered Black.

Chong jerked, surprised to hear the man's voice.

Shouldn't he be dead by now?

Shouldn't we all *be dead by now?*

(And in his mind he heard Do-Good's madly jittering voice saying, "Don't worry, give it time!")

The thoughts were unwelcome, and Chong covered them with a kind of intentional disgust. "Shit, man," he said to Black, not even knowing if the guy could hear him. "You're jonesing at a time like this? You're a *junkie* on top of everything –"

"No," said Elena. "He meant the girl's on drugs. Dee-Dee."

Again, Chong didn't understand. Again, that fact frightened him. He was a genius. One of the smartest people in the United States, probably.

And he was missing things. He had missed the drug paraphernalia on the floor – a few lighters, some crinkled tinfoil, bent spoons, syringes. He had missed the tube around the arm of the woman on the couch, the needle tracks clustered like a dark nebula around the inner crook of her elbow. The trashy, obviously fake-gold chain around her neck that had the words "Dee-Dee" in ridiculous cursive letters in the middle.

"Dee-Dee," he said. He sounded empty, but again couldn't help it. His mind wasn't doing the right things.

Flatlining. Everything's flatlining.

(Death is coming, and it'll be the ultimate rush… and it won't be fun at all.)

"Is she alive?" asked Clint.

Noelle looked at him, obviously asking if she could let go of Black, which Chong found hilarious. She could probably let him fall and then kick him in the face and he wouldn't even notice.

But he noticed more than you did. He noticed the drugs.

Chong hated the guy even more at that moment. His side, where the piece of lawn gnome felt like it was chewing its way through not just his body but his very *soul*, added an extra shard of agony, as though happy to remind Chong that Black had gotten the best of him.

Gonna get him, too. Do-Good, Black, all of them.

Clint was nodding now, and Noelle flashed a quick smile, then let go of Black. Clint groaned a bit as the weight fell onto him, and flicked a look Chong's way.

Chong crossed his arms. The motion made his side hurt more, but he wanted Clint to get the message: *I got my own problems, bub.*

Noelle felt at Dee-Dee's neck. "She's alive," she said.

Clint nodded like this was good news. "Okay, so what now?"

The question had no answer. Chong's mind, usually such a fertile field, lay silent and fallow. "Dammit!" he shouted. "I'm so sick of this!" He kicked the couch, the only thing in reach. The room was small, so the kick moved it enough that it hit the TV stand, sending both it and the TV into a rickety wobble.

Everything in here was on the verge of breaking, he realized. Even him. Maybe *especially* him.

"Easy," Elena said, trying to soothe him – which only made him angrier. "We –"

A sound slashed her words, killing them in her throat. It was a scream, but high-pitched and airy. Chong thought for a moment that it must be someone dying in the back room. But again, someone else – someone *less* – guessed what it was before him.

"That's a baby," breathed Noelle. Her face was white, and she had her hands shoved so far in her pockets that Chong thought she might very well break through them and keep going, her whole body folding into her pockets and then disappearing into a singularity with nothing but a comic *blip* sound to mark her departure.

Clint eased Black to the floor. "Guys, Solomon's not doing well."

"Who gives a shit?" demanded Chong.

Elena began walking toward the back of the house, where a small hallway obviously led to the place's bedrooms and bathroom. She halted mid-stride when everyone's watches beeped.

Chong didn't want to look. None of them did, he knew. But they looked anyway. The night still belonged to Do-Good, and perhaps it was Chong's imagination, but Do-Good's voice seemed to reflect that now. He sounded almost hysterical; mad with the power of life and death.

"Do-Good says, *GREAT JOB!* Your next challenge is to find out who's in the back room. An easy one, so you only get thirty seconds."

Chong stared at the watch, mind teetering on total numbness as he saw Do-Good's words mirrored there. Clint sighed almost comically, then began levering Black back to his feet – or his shins, since the guy still didn't have even enough strength to support his own weight. Black screamed, but even the scream was weak.

Noelle stepped forward. "I got it," said Clint. Noelle nodded and fell back.

"How chivalrous," muttered Chong. Then he followed as they trailed Elena down the hall.

Noelle moved slowly, obviously working off mental fumes. The thought made Chong happy, even as it enraged him. Maybe he was doing better than she was. But what did that make him, really?

Second dumbest in the room. Not top one percent of one percent... just barely ahead of some trashy chick who probably faked a GED to get a job at the worst bar in the worst part of town.

It made him mad enough that he shouldered her aside so hard she gasped in pain. He liked it.

Elena was already at the end of the hall, Clint lurching along after her, dragging Black with him. Stumpy must have found a bit of a second wind, because he was actually trying to step forward on his own. He wasn't that great at it – he looked like someone who'd just suffered a serious stroke and been roofied at the same time – but maybe he wouldn't slow them down so far that he'd get them all killed.

Elena went into the room at the end of the hall. So did the Clint/Black dynamic duo, and Chong heard Clint mutter something under his breath as he followed them into the room.

The baby's cries had faded a bit, but as Chong entered the room they dialed back up to full force. "Same to you, kid," Chong muttered. A giggle escaped his lips.

Don't start laughing.

Or do. Just laugh and smile and maybe you can have a Do-Good face right before that madman blows off your head or your hand or both.

The bedroom he found himself in was just as crappy and dirty as the rest of the place. A bed that leaned hard to one side and looked like it had only heard of clean sheets as a rumor on par with Bigfoot. Another TV, which didn't surprise Chong; his experience was that the most impoverished person would rather part with food than their intake of media.

As in the front room, drug paraphernalia littered the floor, along with clothing and food wrappers. The stench of the place had an almost physical weight to it.

And there, in the corner: a crib. Movement inside as the baby who was now howling his or her little brains out grappled with a thin blue blanket.

8

"We can't possibly…." Chong didn't turn to look at the speaker, knowing that he would see only Noelle, hands in pockets, shoulders hunched up around her ears. He wanted to kill her, too, he realized.

All of them.

Chong looked at Elena as she lifted the baby from the crib.

"What, are you going to burp it?" demanded Chong. "Play patty-cake?"

Elena shifted the baby expertly to her arms, and Chong saw that it was definitely a girl. Easy enough to deduce when the baby was naked.

He looked away. He didn't care that the baby was naked, but she was also filthy, and Chong felt suddenly nauseous.

He flinched as Do-Good spoke, the voice cutting into his discomfort and turning it to near-panic. "Do-Good says, *KEEP IT UP!* Your next challenge is to *take* one baby out of the house, and *leave* one dead body behind! Two minutes, chop-chop!"

That made the vomit come hurtling upward. Chong clenched his jaw and forced it down, the acid burning all the way to his stomach. *"Dammit!"* he shrieked. He knew he didn't have time for this, but it was either let off some steam or start giggling and puking and crying all at once. He looked around as though he might spot Do-Good, right there in the room with them all. "I *will* kick your ass!" he shrieked. "You hear me? I know people!"

Movement as Noelle flinched away from him, hands in her pockets. Chong reached for her, suddenly sure that he could do this task easily. Just take the baby out, and leave the quivering, cowardly bitch behind with a broken neck and her hands shoved up her own *ass* instead of her pockets.

Beeeep.

"Do-Good says, *TAKE IT EASY!* Eyes on the prize, guys."

Chong flinched. He remembered speaking the words, right before he heard a buzzing noise and woke up in the white room.

How long has he been watching all of us? Watching me?

Before that moment, Chong would have guessed such surveillance was impossible. He was too smart not to notice someone tailing him, and though he knew it was possible to take over others' computers and watch them out of their own webcams, such a thing could never happen to him. Not to one of the world's greatest hackers, on a par with lucky12345, petr0vich, the Shadow Brokers, M0rningGl0ry, UCry2... Chong would have bet that no one but maybe the entirety of Bureau 121, North Korea's elite team of hackers, could possibly spy on him.

But someone had.

Someone had heard him.

The prospect of getting his head or hand blown off had terrified him. But this... he had to concentrate to literally keep from pissing himself.

Elena had the baby securely in her arms now, and she hurried past. Noelle took the opportunity to shrink away from Chong, hurrying after her.

"Wait!" shouted Clint. "We can't! I mean, we just –"

Elena turned. The baby's cries had dwindled as she expertly bounced the child in her arms. "I'm good with kids," she said quietly, as though that were an answer to Clint's protestations. Then she turned and left the room. Noelle did, too, and Chong followed.

They all waited in the front room, none of them daring to go far from Clint as he lurched his way down the hall, still dragging Black.

Chong figured Black was the body they'd have to leave. Only what if he didn't die in time? Would the rules be broken if they killed someone on the "team"?

He didn't know.

Maybe he wouldn't have to, either. Elena was staring at Dee-Dee, who was still splayed across the couch and floor. Her eyes were open now, but whatever she had taken had not let go of her beyond that. She breathed shallowly, her body a pale shadow – almost a mockery – of life.

"We have to leave a body behind," murmured Elena, still bouncing the baby in her arms, sounding as calm as though she were going through a grocery list at the store.

Carrots, check. Bread, check. Body? Isn't that in aisle five, where they keep the junkies?

Chong giggled again, while Noelle squeaked a horrified, "No!" and Clint said, "You can't be serious!"

"Eyes on the prize, guys," Chong managed, the words coming out between the gasping giggles that still held him.

But he wasn't giggling as he turned and kicked, putting even more oomph behind it than when he'd kicked in the door to the house.

The kick caught Clint square in the stomach. Chong expected that would be it for him, but the kid surprised him. He exhaled hard, the kick driving all the air from his lungs, and fell – that was to be expected – but instead of just laying on the floor, he dropped into a weird half-roll that ended with him in a crouch, ready to take whatever Chong might bring his way.

Chong couldn't have cared less. He wasn't going to take on Clint. Not with a piece of clay jutting from his side, not when there was easier fruit to pick.

Unlike Clint, Black *had* fallen and stayed down. He had fallen backward, somehow twisting as he did so that he splayed out parallel to the couch. Dee-Dee's feet were only a foot from Black's head. Not that he cared. He was staring sightlessly at the ceiling. But as far gone as he was, he seemed to know what was coming, at least on an animal level, for his legs kicked weakly, his feet driving as much as they could against the refuse-littered floor. He actually managed to push himself an extra, useless inch away from Chong.

Too little, too late. Not that there was ever a possibility of any other outcome.

Chong fell onto the guy. He wrapped his hands around Black's neck. Black choked, and for a moment Chong thought the guy's face wavered. Melted. It was Jerrod Hall, dying beneath him in an alley where no one watched and no one cared. It was Erin Westmoreland, feet beating a jitterbug dance against the floor as his crushed brain tried for a few last instructions before it gave in to the darkness.

Something hit Chong from behind. It drove him face-forward, almost laying him flat against Black. He let go of the man's throat with one hand, his own hand flattening against the floor to keep him from falling to the side.

"Don't, don't, don't!" shouted Noelle. She was what had hit him, jumping on his back to keep him from killing Black.

Chong's free hand lashed backward. He caught her with the back of his hand across her jaw. The angle was bad, but it punched her back all the same. "It has to be done, you dumb bitch!" he screamed. Then he put his hands back around Black's throat and stared into the man's face as he squeezed and said, "And you were always gonna die anyway, right?"

Black made no sound. The fingers of his remaining hand scrabbled weakly against Chong's arm. Chong felt like laughing – and finally for a *good* reason.

The laughter never came, though. Instead there was a dull, meaty *splut!* and Black's eyes no longer stared up at him in dread. Chong's hands still clasped the man's throat, but now they were drenched in gore. Splashback.

He looked at the huge tube TV. No longer on its stand, now it was on the floor, taking up the space where Black's head had been. A spray of red – some of which was what had wetted Chong's own hands and arms – dyed the carpet around Black's body in a near-perfect triangle.

The TV had fallen. And Black's head had just *popped*.

Chong looked to the side. Elena still bounced the baby girl in one hand, the other still extended after pushing the TV over onto Black's upraised face.

"Shit, lady!" Chong wanted to shout. It came out as a muddled croak.

Elena turned her gaze on Chong, and now it was not just calm, it was *cold*. "You were taking too long," she said.

9

Chong should have said something. *Wanted* to. Couldn't.

Clint muttered, "Why would you…?"

Elena walked past Clint, who stared, stunned, at Black – or at least, at Black from mid-neck down. Then past Noelle, who shrank away from her.

Elena sighed. "We didn't need him anymore, and he was dying anyway. Would you rather have killed *her*?" she asked, pointing at Dee-Dee. "A choice had to be made, and I made it." Then she was out the door.

Chong stood, rubbing his hands absently on his shorts as he followed her out. He barely registered that Noelle and Clint followed as well.

Outside, Clint looked slowly from Chong to Elena to the house. "We coulda figured something out. Coulda –"

"Maybe they were right," interrupted Noelle.

Clint turned to her, face showing disbelief. She leaned away from him, hands in pockets, face showing shame… but also agreement with what Chong had started and Elena had so ruthlessly finished.

"We *killed* –" began Clint, then checked himself. He turned to Elena. "*You* killed a man. And we just kidnapped a baby!"

Elena shrugged. "Whoever that woman is, she isn't exactly a great mother. Social services would have taken the little girl away if we didn't," she said. Then she stared at the baby in her arms with eyes that were cold as long-banked coals. "Trust me, I know."

Clint was actually *shaking*. Whether with rage or fear, Chong couldn't tell, but he worried that the kid was going to break apart, and take the rest of the survivors down by doing something stupid.

"Oh, okay," Clint managed through gritted teeth. "You *know*. Well that makes it all right. So we just – where are you going?"

Elena had begun walking back to the house. "I'm not an idiot, Clint. And I have no reason to keep the baby, which I would have told you in a moment if you hadn't started spouting stupidity." She was back on the porch now, and headed toward the still-open door as she said, "Mr. Do-Good said we had to take the baby. He didn't say we had to keep her."

Of course.

The thought came not in response to Elena's words, but to what came after. He looked at his watch before it had stopped beeping, before Do-Good started speaking.

"Do-Good says, *DON'T STOP NOW!* Next challenge: *leave the baby in the street* – at least three blocks away. Two minutes to get 'er done, so get moving, folks!"

Noelle murmured what sounded like a prayer. Then, surprisingly, Clint lurched away. He started walking down the street, turning after ten feet to gesture that the others could follow him.

Apparently Noelle, who had been signed onto Black's death, now found a line she didn't want to cross. "We can't just leave the baby in the –"

"Yeah we can," Clint answered tersely. For a moment his eyes were every bit as hard and dark as Elena's had been. It was only a moment, though; an expression that had come and gone so fast Chong couldn't really be sure he had seen it at all. Then they softened as Clint added, "Trust me."

Chong could see Noelle considering it. Then, slowly, she nodded. Clint turned and started walking again. Noelle hurried until she was walking abreast of him, and Elena did the same a moment later.

Chong was alone. Not far behind the group, but so alone. Discounted. Unnecessary.

"You were taking too long," Elena had said. And the way her eyes looked right then... Chong suspected that if it had been necessary – or even convenient – she would have dropped another TV on *his* head.

Who are *these people?*

Just one more question he would have to answer later. For now, he hurried after the group. Two minutes to go three blocks. Easy.

But what was Clint planning to do when they got to wherever he was leading them? No matter how tough a spirit the kid might be hiding inside himself, Chong doubted he had the balls to drop a baby in the street.

Elena did, though. So the job would be done, of that he was sure.

But it turned out Clint *did* have the balls to drop a baby in the street.

One minute and thirty seconds into the walk, Clint turned and held out his hands. Elena handed the baby over with a quiet nod of approval, which Chong didn't understand. What was going on? They were going to be seen, standing here like this. And they weren't up to answering any questions should anyone come out and ask what they were up to.

Clint put the baby on the street, next to the curb. He unwrapped the baby's blanket, and as he did he said, "Give me your lighter."

Chong's brain, still firing at maybe one percent of its normal speed, didn't cough up the little factoid that Clint was talking to *him* until the kid glared at him and said, "Now."

Chong nodded, stupefied. He handed over the lighter, wondering for a mad moment if Clint planned to set the baby on fire – and an even madder moment where he wondered if it would be beautiful.

Clint flicked the lighter, then held it to the baby's blanket. The baby screamed as it started to realize it was on a hard, unyielding patch of asphalt. Chong cringed, not wanting anyone to hear, then – finally – realizing that was exactly what Clint wanted. The fire he had just set was just another bit of insurance.

Clint tossed the flaming blanket about ten feet away. Flames leaped high, the blanket curling into a black mass on the driveway where Clint had chosen to toss the cloth. Then Clint darted off. Chong followed as Clint and the others ducked behind a car across the street, waiting.

The baby kept crying.

Chong looked at his watch. The countdown was gone: they had done what Do-Good asked, and appeared to be safe. As he did, he heard Clint exhale in relief. Chong peeked with the others around the side of the car, watching as a man came out of the building nearest to where they had left the baby.

"Shit!" he shouted when he saw the fire – no fear at the flames, just annoyance as he stamped them out with his heavy boots. He looked around, and Chong flinched, worried the man might see them.

He didn't. Instead, the guy finally heard the baby yowling. He rushed to her, picking up the naked girl and checking her with expert hands. He glanced around once, then went back into the building he had come from.

"Smart," said Elena. She eyed the building. "Fire stations are a safe surrender site."

Chong stared at the sign on the side of the building, a red-lettered thing that said, "LAFD – Los Angeles Fire Department," along with the station number. "I didn't know that," he said, interested in spite of himself. The sight of the fire station had terrified him – both when they ran past it the first time and when they returned to leave the baby there – but now the fear transformed to cool calculation. "So you can just leave a baby here?"

Noelle stared at him, the first time she had really met his gaze. Again, the world shifted as he realized now *her* eyes were dead, black, fearless. "Why are you interested?"

Chong almost laughed again. Worse, he almost *told* her. Almost said, "You never know when it'll be handy to know where people drop valuable things in the street." But he choked the words back, and tried to hold her gaze. Felt himself losing a staring match with the least assertive person he'd ever met in the strange, slipstream version of the world he had fallen into.

Things shifted back a moment later as Noelle shrank away again, huddling low against the car.

"I never would have thought of that," said Elena admiringly. She looked at Clint. "Good job."

Clint nodded.

"What will happen to her?" asked Noelle.

"She'll go into the system," said Elena.

Noelle gasped. "Will the mom be able to find her or –"

Elena chuckled, low and humorless. "Given what we saw in that house, the baby is better off anywhere but there."

"Maybe," said Clint. The single word was loaded with meaning. Chong didn't know what that meaning *was*, but he could tell Clint was thinking of nothing good.

Noelle put a hand on the young man's arm. Chong felt a stab in his side and for a moment couldn't be sure if it was the piece of clay digging in for a long night, or just jealousy.

He looked away from the tender moment. Stared at his watch. It was blank, not even the Do-Good smiley face avatar looking back at him. "Was that it? We done?" he said.

Everyone else looked as well. A long, long moment. Long enough that Chong dared to hope that it *was* over. That he could be done with this, and go back to his office and start bidding on half his screens while he devoted everything else he had to finding Do-Good. Maybe he'd use Portobello Road to hire a killer. Or five. Or ten.

But the night wasn't over. Not by a long shot.

10

"Do-Good says, *WAY TO THINK OUTSIDE THE BOX!* For this next challenge, remember: home is where the heart is! So go back to the house on Heart Street, then hide outside and *watch*. Two minutes to get yourself there and hidey-hidey-ho!"

As Do-Good said the words, Chong heard Noelle give out a low, pitiful moan that he probably would have found hilarious in any other situation.

Only he felt like moaning himself, and that wasn't hilarious at all.

With one last glance at the fire station, Clint stood and headed back to where they had just come from. Mr. Do-Good was whipsawing them now, pulling them back and forth like an insane puppet master.

As they walked up to Dee-Dee's house – still a dump, only now with the added feature of a door hanging half off its hinges and a frame that lay like a tumble of pick-up-sticks just inside the doorway – Noelle asked, "We're supposed to hide?"

She looked around, and Chong could tell she'd seen what he had already noticed: there was nowhere to hide. Not without actually going *inside* the house, and Chong definitely didn't want to do that. He didn't know what Do-Good had planned, but he suspected the idea of going into a little box of a place and hoping for the best was not in his best interests.

"Out back?" he said.

They moved as a group, skirting the edge of the house, passing a side door that Chong assumed led into whatever joke of a kitchen the little place boasted, then into the back "yard." Just as nasty and rundown as the rest of the property – a ten-foot by twenty-foot space bounded on all sides by a wood fence that looked like it had probably been built sometime in the 1800s.

Still, it was better than just waiting in front. Do-Good had told them to hide, so this would have to do. "I guess this is our best bet," he told the others. Or maybe just told himself.

"You sure?" asked Noelle. "This doesn't look like the kind of neighborhood where people react nicely to uninvited guests in their backyards."

"You think the Beverly Hills crowd would be more lenient?" asked Chong absently.

Noelle bristled a bit. "How would I know?"

Chong grinned at her. His side hurt, his brain felt packed full of mud. But it felt nice to argue with someone who wasn't as big as he was, trying to stab him, or trying to blow him up. "I don't know," he said. "I assumed the best clients for hookers would –"

"Give it a rest," said Clint.

Chong probably would have turned his ire on the kid now, but Clint didn't sound demanding. Just tired. He leaned against the back wall of the rickety fence, then let himself slide down until he was sitting in the dirt at its base.

Noelle glanced at Chong, a bit of steel still glinting in her eyes, then went and sat beside Clint. "This has not been my best night," she said quietly. Then she glanced at Clint and added quietly, "I guess your day was worse, though."

"What makes you say that?" Clint asked in guarded tones.

Noelle shrugged. "You said you were in the cemetery when...," she gestured around, "... all this started. People don't go to the cemetery for a party."

Clint's shoulders slumped, as though he had successfully avoided thinking about this fact until now. "No," he said.

Chong, interested in spite of himself, glanced at his watch – still nothing there – before saying, "So spill. Why were you there?"

Clint's gaze jerked up for a moment. Chong expected him to look angry, or to tell him to butt out. Neither happened. Matter-of-factly, Clint said, "My sister died. Ten years ago today – that's why I was there. At the cemetery." His gaze shifted to Noelle and he smiled sadly. "You kinda remind me of her. She was nice, like you. Quiet and sad sometimes. But nice."

"What about your parents?" asked Noelle. "They'll be worried –"

"No parents," said Clint. "I got left outside a fire department."

Chong laughed at that. Not loud – he didn't want anyone wondering what was going on in the back of 1089 Shit Street – but it *was* funny.

Not to anyone else, though. And Chong realized – again, last to the party – that Clint hadn't been joking. "That's how you thought of that," said Noelle. He nodded. She exhaled loudly, then said, "Sorry. My parents are gone, too."

"That sucks," said Clint. "When?"

Noelle shrugged. "My mom died when I was little. My dad... it was recent."

No one spoke. Even Chong felt no urge to break the silence.

Finally, Noelle asked, "Did you ever finally get adopted? Anyone take care of you?"

Clint shook his head. "Nah. Just bounced around. Foster care, a few government places."

"At least you had your sister," said Noelle. She sounded hopeful, like this was the one fact that would carry her through the night. Then her eyes narrowed as she said, "Or did they try to split you guys before... what happened to her?"

Clint's expression clouded when she mentioned his sister. "They tried to split us up, all the time. We just acted out until we got sent back."

"Must've been hard," said Noelle. Her brassy trash-accent softened a bit as she said it, and Chong thought in that moment she could have passed for a girl who grew up *near* a trailer park, instead of in one.

Clint shrugged. "It was mostly okay. One hellhole, though."

"What happened there?" asked Noelle.

Chong was starting to feel purposefully left out. He didn't like the feeling. One thing to refuse to mingle with others, but another thing entirely to be left out, so he said, "Nosy kid, aren't you?"

Noelle ignored him, but did say, "Sorry if I'm butting in," to Clint.

"'Sokay," said Clint. "That place... it's where my sister died. Or at least, disappeared. They never found her."

"Then maybe she's still alive. Or –"

Clint shook his head. "No. Something happened. She was taken from the home in the middle of the night, and never came back." His expression hardened. "I knew she was gone. Dead. She would have found me, or I would have found her otherwise."

Noelle's hand went over her mouth. "I'm so sorry," she said. "Was it their fault she was taken? The people at the orphanage? Is that why it was a hellhole?"

"I think so," said Clint, his voice almost machine-like now. A dead thing just reporting data. "I got transferred to another orphanage and I heard Eighth Street Children closed a while later."

"That was the name of it? Eighth Street Children?" asked Noelle.

"Yeah," said Clint. "No idea why they –" he broke off, staring at Elena. "What?"

Chong looked at the older woman, who had been standing nearby but curiously silent throughout the whole conversation. She shrugged, but he saw something flit across her eyes. A moment of –

A veil seemed to fall across her gaze. "It's nothing," she said.

Clint squinted at her. "Nothing?" he repeated, his tone making it clear he didn't believe that at all. "Why –"

A car revved nearby, the sound followed quickly by the squeal of brakes and the high whine of locked wheels sliding across asphalt.

"Shut up, all of you!" said Chong. The sound of the car had been familiar. He had to –

The watches beeped. Chong flinched, wondering what new task they would be given. But when Do-Good spoke, he said only, "Do-Good says, *PAY CLOSE ATTENTION.*"

Chong looked at the others, but they were already creeping toward the house. Peeking into one of the barred windows. The house was about the size of a shoebox, so the bedroom they had taken the baby out of was visible, and beyond that they could see a large slice of the front room where Dee-Dee still lay in her drug-induced slumber.

Chong had figured out what they were about to see. Apparently he *was* still the smartest guy around, because the only person who didn't gasp when Two-Teeth walked in through the still-fractured door was Chong. No one else had recognized the sound of the man's car, the deep rumble of an engine designed to make noise that would announce the coming of a VIP.

But Chong had.

He had known, but that didn't stop him from quaking a bit as the guy walked in. Even peeking over the back of a window, through bars, through another room… even then, Two-Teeth was a terrifying sight. He'd seen him in the picture back at the 52s safehouse, but seeing him in a picture didn't do the man justice, anymore than taking a picture of Everest could capture the terrifying enormity and coldness of that place.

A gun stuck out of his waistband, but Chong doubted he'd require its assistance for any mayhem that needed doing. Indeed, blood stained his hands and shirt, along with other smudges and smears that made it look like he'd been rolling around in a mud-pile.

"Dee-Dee!" the man shouted, striding to the couch, huge feet crunching over a fast food wrapper, a discarded paper cup, drug paraphernalia. None of it registered. He was staring at a spot on the floor, and though it was hidden from Chong's view, he knew that the guy had to be wondering what happened here. How a man literally lost his head to a television set.

Two-Teeth skirted the gory area as best he could, then reached down and lifted Dee-Dee by the front of her shirt as easily as Chong might pick up a Chihuahua.

Dee-Dee hung bonelessly. Two-Teeth shook her. "Wake up! Wake up, bitch! What happened here?" Another shake. "Where's my money? You take my money?"

Dee-Dee moaned. She tried to lift her head but couldn't. It hung weirdly behind her, lolling back so far that Chong could have sworn she was looking behind herself and straight at the huddled group watching the whole thing through the window.

"Money?" Dee-Dee finally managed. She shuddered. "You... you got some money for me? For the kid?"

Two-Teeth shook her again, this time in disgust. "Sonofa...." Another shake. "Someone *took the money*, Dee-Dee."

Dee-Dee giggled at that, and finally managed to stiffen her neck enough to look at Two-Teeth. "Boss is gonna be piiiisssssed," she said in a dreamy singsong.

"Who was it?" demanded Two-Teeth. "Who took it?" He gestured at the floor. "Who did all this?"

Dee-Dee shook her head. The movement was so slow Chong felt oddly like he was watching a movie played in slow motion. "Maybe SFD? He always comes 'round, pawin' at me –"

Two-Teeth shut her up by shaking her so hard Chong swore he heard the woman's teeth clack together. "SFD didn't do it. And he won't paw you no more – or anyone else. Neither will Zonker or Mako. And you don't come up with some good damn answers and you might join them at –"

Dee-Dee cut him off. She laughed, loud and hard. Not at what Two-Teeth was saying, though. Chong could tell that whatever she was laughing at, it was nothing anyone but her could see.

Two-Teeth's mouth curled in sudden concern. Not for Dee-Dee, not even for the man whose remains he was all but standing in. "Where's the kid?" he demanded.

"The same place as always," she said.

"You dumb –"

Two-Teeth moved as fast as lightning, slamming a huge fist into the side of Dee-Dee's face. She went from giggling to sobbing in the space of half a second, but Two-Teeth was already gone, stomping toward the back of the house.

Chong dropped to the ground along with the others, hoping that the gangster hadn't seen them.

He didn't. If he had, he wouldn't be heading to the back of the house, he'd be heading around to kill us.

He remembered the look on Black's face when he realized that Two-Teeth might be coming to the Five-Deuce safehouse. Sheer, unadulterated terror.

Chong had no wish to find out – especially not firsthand – what kind of person could induce that level of panic.

He heard Two-Teeth slam into the bedroom. A roar heaved itself through the bars, into the backyard, and Chong knew the gangster had discovered the empty crib. Another roar, then the sound of plastic and wood sheering apart, and Chong guessed the big man was just beating the crib to pieces.

A moment after that, Chong *knew* that was what Two-Teeth was doing, because there was a sudden *chunk* and then he was staring at one of the crib's slats. Two-Teeth had thrown it against the wall so hard it speared right through the drywall and halfway through the cheap siding of the outer wall itself.

The wood had jabbed through not five inches from Elena's face, and she gasped. She clapped her hands against her mouth to stifle the sound – too late. Inside the house, all was suddenly, deathly silent.

Two-Teeth heard.

11

Chong held himself as still as he'd ever been in his life. Beside him, the others were equally rigid statues, all of them hugging the wall in the hopes that Two-Teeth hadn't heard Elena, hadn't heard something out back, wasn't –

The sound of the window sliding open was deafening to Chong. Clint and Noelle had slid to the side when they first ducked away from the window, but he and Elena had just dropped straight down – which meant they were directly under the window that Two-Teeth had opened. Chong could imagine the man up there, peering through the bars, craning to see what had made the sound.

He didn't think Two-Teeth could see directly below the window. The bars were fairly flush with the window itself. Just straight lines bolted to the wall, no curve that would allow Two-Teeth to lean out at all, maybe glance down, maybe see...

Shut up, Chong. Just shut UP!

He hadn't said anything, but somehow the thoughts seemed totally legitimate, like if he didn't *think* quieter, Two-Teeth would just sense him there.

So he thought quiet thoughts. He didn't even look at Elena, so close to him that he could smell her sweat and the barest hint of whatever cheap perfume she wore when she went to work before all this started. Didn't look, because he was worried that even shifting his eyes would make a sound that would alert Two-Teeth of what hid only inches below him.

Chong and the others remained there, motionless, for a period that was likely only a few seconds but which nevertheless felt like an *eternity.*

But eternity finally ended: Two-Teeth muttered something, then Chong heard the thud-crackle of the big man stomping over trash as he went back to the front room.

Chong started to edge back to the window. He didn't want to watch, but Do-Good had told them to do it, hadn't he? What would happen if he just cowered down below the window instead of watching?

Besides, he had to admit, he was curious. He *wanted* to see what would happen next, just like he had *wanted* to watch Erin Westmoreland's blood pooling around his head; just like he had *wanted* to sit beside Jerrod Hall's body while it cooled in the alley.

Elena grabbed his arm, trying to stop him. He shook her off, and wasn't at all surprised when she joined him at the window a moment later. Noelle and Clint, too, all of them peeking into the house. The call of curiosity was too persuasive to resist long.

Chong saw Dee-Dee, holding one hand to the nose that Two-Teeth must have flattened when he hit her. Blood gushed out of her clenched fingers, and when she spoke it was with a wet, painfully nasal tone totally devoid of the dreamlike quality it had previously held. Pain had sobered her. "What'd you – the hell did you –"

Another slap sent her reeling, screaming. "Where is she?" demanded Two-Teeth. "That baby's *mine!*"

"She's... she's back there. Two-Teeth, I swear, I –"

Two-Teeth forewent the subtlety of a slap, opting instead for a closed fist that turned Dee-Dee's right cheek from convex to concave.

Just like Erin Westmoreland's head.

"She ain't there!" screamed Two-Teeth. "I got no money, I got no product for what the man paid for, Dee!" He hit her again. "Where is she?" Dee-Dee cried out, but before she had any chance to answer, Two-Teeth began screaming, punctuating every few words with a punch. "Where is she?" (punch) "What..." (punch) "... happened to..." (punch) "... the baby?"

Chong didn't know how Dee-Dee could have answered, even if she knew what to say. Her mouth had dissolved under Two-Teeth's fist. Her lower jaw sagged, obviously dislocated, probably shattered. She made a few *nnn, nnng, nnn* sounds.

Two-Teeth dropped her. She slid below the level of the couch, but there was no mystery about what was happening down there. Two-Teeth began kicking, then the kicks turned to stomps. The sounds changed, too, from muffled thumps to sharp cracks to moist, sucking noises.

Two-Teeth stomped down one last time. Chong heard a sickening *splut.*

"What happened to the kid?" Two-Teeth demanded. But the words were spoken in an offhand way that neither demanded nor expected a reply.

Chong wondered what he would see if he could be a fly on the wall. He suspected that there would now be *two* headless corpses in the room: one whose skull had been squashed under the weight of circa-1980 electronics, the other whose head had been flattened under size-sixteen Nikes.

Movement caught his attention. Chong looked down, seeing Noelle. She was quivering, one hand dug into her pocket, the other clamped over her mouth as she stifled the screams that so obviously wanted to come.

Chong's eyes narrowed. He put a finger over his lips, then moved it ninety degrees to slide it across his throat, putting every remaining shred of confidence and threat into his expression as he wordlessly let the silly little girl know that if she made a sound, Two-Teeth wouldn't even *have* a chance to come after her.

If you blow us... if that guy comes after us... we might be in trouble, but I promise promise promise *you that you will be the first person to pay.*

Noelle nodded. She looked like she was gagging back vomit, but no sound came.

Clint, white-faced and terrified as well, reached out and grabbed her arm. He squeezed it reassuringly, and that seemed to help.

A moment later, though, any reassurance was lost again as a new sound tore through the night.

Sirens.

Police.

And then, in between the rise and fall sound of the sirens, a beep that Chong felt as a physical blow. He tensed, not even looking at his watch for a moment, sure that Two-Teeth must have heard it.

Maybe he did. But whether he did nor not, apparently he decided that he didn't want to be found inside a house full of dead bodies – at least one of which likely had his footprints etched into what remained of her.

Two-Teeth started cursing under his breath, a low roll of obscenities that could have killed small animals, but at least the curses started to move away from the window.

Chong released a breath he hadn't known he was holding and looked at his watch. Words scrolled across, and Do-Good whispered, in an almost pained voice, "Do-Good says, *DON'T GET CAUGHT.*"

Chong abruptly realized that he was alone. The others had deduced what the message meant before he did: that the cops were coming here, that it was part of Do-Good's plan, and that they had to abandon ship fast.

Noelle was the farthest away, dragging Clint behind her as she ran around the side of the house, keeping low in case Two-Teeth looked out any of the windows. Elena was fast on their heels.

Chong cursed.

Not second-dumbest in the pack. The *dumbest now.*

His collar beeped, warning him that he had to catch up with the rest of the scavenger hunt's contestants.

He ran for the corner of the house, wanting to call out to the others to slow down but not daring to do so. He wanted to call out, to ask what they thought would happen if they came around the front of the house at the same time Two-Teeth came out of it. But yelling would just hasten any meeting between the group and the homicidal maniac in the house.

All he could do was run, staying low as well as he passed under a window. Around the corner. Passing the side door –

– and in the instant he did, the door seemed to explode.

Two-Teeth was coming out.

Two-Teeth was *here, now.*

Even as he realized it, Chong felt the solid thud of someone barreling into him. Actually, it was more like being hit by a car. He felt no give the way he would have expected to when flesh hit flesh. He just felt a solid block as Two-Teeth knocked into him, then fell on top of him.

Chong would have guessed the gangster weighed in at upward of three hundred pounds. When he hit the hard ground and felt the other man's full weight on him, he upped that to at least three-fifty. He looked up, reeling from the twin impact of the ground and the man on top of him, not sure which was harder or less forgiving.

Two-Teeth stared down at him. Anger settled into his features, replaced by a burning rage as he glanced to his left. Chong followed his gaze, realized what the gangster was looking at, and suddenly knew without a doubt that he was in the last moments of his life.

Two-Teeth saw Elena. Saw the backpack she wore. The backpack they had taken from Two-Teeth's own room.

"YOU STOLE FROM ME!" he roared. Absently, almost idly, he put one of his big hands around Chong's throat. The world immediately began to spin around him, and Chong wondered if he was about to have done to him what he had done to Jerrod Hall.

He's going to kill me. Kill me, then kill the others.

Who gives a shit *what comes after? He's going... to... kill... me... and...*

Chong's thoughts began to drift. He was losing consciousness.

No. You're a winner… always… winning…

Two-Teeth didn't stop choking him, but apparently wasn't content with simply crushing his enemy's throat. He pulled, and Chong felt his head lifted away from the ground, then Two-Teeth shoved violently, bouncing Chong's skull off the ground.

"You stole!" screamed Two-Teeth. He slammed Chong's head against the ground again. Again. "Stole from *me*!"

Chong heard something break. It sounded like it happened in the middle of his brain, the sound an explosion that ricocheted through his body and mind.

Something broken. Broken…

Dancing. I'm dancing. Two-Teeth is killing me like I tried to kill that pecker Black and now I'm dancing like Erin Westmoreland.

That was the thing that made him act. The lizard brain part of himself knew he was dying, knew it was over… but knew, also, that it didn't want to go out alone.

Chong barely registered what he was doing. The world had stopped swimming and was now dark. His hands felt far away and he could no longer feel his feet or legs at all.

Paralyzed.

(Then how will I dance with Erin Westmoreland?)

His thoughts fell apart, but that lizard part of him still managed to do what it wanted. Still reached to his side, still pulled the sharp piece of clay from inside him. He felt the blood gout, felt warmth on his hands – again, only unlike when he felt it after Elena dropped a TV on Black's head, this time the blood seemed not just warm but *burning* and Chong knew it was because it was his blood not some nobody's it was his and there was no way that it could be his blood he was dying but he couldn't be dying and...

His thoughts fell away. But not before he curled his hand tightly around the clay and punched up and to the side with it.

For a moment. Two-Teeth's hands slackened. For a moment, Chong's vision returned – at least enough to see the huge man's hand clamped to the side of his throat, trying hopelessly to staunch the flood of red spurting around the rough edges of a clay shard.

"What about... my money?" Two-Teeth managed, even though the blood burbled out of his mouth, too, making him sound as though he was drowning.

He sagged.

Chong grinned.

Killed you, Erin Westmoreland. No one gonna call me Chong unless I want them to. You don't get to. Not you or Jerrod Hall or Mommy or Daddy or David Tomlinson and the spoon full of sugar that I hate so much playing in the background and... and...

Chong's thoughts went away. The lizard closed its eyes and did not open them again.

Interlude

1

Hope opened her eyes, then closed them, then opened them again.

That was how it went for hours and days and weeks and... forever. That was how it seemed, anyway: a forever time where she opened her eyes and saw/sensed something, then closed them, and when they reopened there was a new sight, a new feel.

Blink, blink, blink, and times and places passed by with a strangeness she had never known and could never hope to understand.

She did know this, though: she hurt.

First the hurt was deep inside her, curled in her heart and her stomach. It felt like there was a heavy weight, a piano or an elephant that sat directly upon her.

Then the pain moved. It flashed like lightning, pulsing through her arms and hands, then her legs and feet. Each burst of electric pain made her scream, even though the screams went no farther than the outer edges of her mind. She made no sound.

Blink, blink, blink; pain, pain, pain.

She opened her eyes and saw Daddy looking at her, his kind eyes kinder than she had ever seen them before. "... all right, sweetie," he was saying. He smiled, and she knew that he saw her open her eyes. Then the smile faded, and the world faded with it –

(blink)

– and when she opened her eyes again, she saw gray with a bright spot. A ceiling? She heard the *wah-wah-wah* of a siren, but it sounded far away. She heard people murmuring, but could not tell what they were saying. Then –

(blink)

– she opened her eyes once more, and the gray was gone. Instead she saw only blue, blue sky. She heard a sound, too, a *whop-whop-whop* that she knew she had heard before, but did not know where or when. She heard a voice she didn't know, partially drowned-out by that strange *whop-whop-whop*.

"… be nice being rich… nything happen, can't…."

(blink)

The darkness this time was longer. There were vague sensations inside it, but none pierced the blackness. She felt things pulling, pushing. Hands all over her, rubbing parts of her. She felt the pain grow stronger, then fall away to nothing. Then the pain came back, but it didn't hurt, exactly. More like she was floating over it, as though the pain were a river and she was floating down it on a raft the way she did that one time with Daddy when they both went to Hawaii.

The darkness wavered. Colors sparked behind her eyes, and when she opened them she stared once more at a bright spot on gray. Different than before, though: the gray she saw was darker, the light brighter. She stared at it for a long time, then did something she felt like she had not done in a million years: she moved her head.

She saw white now, instead of the gray. She didn't understand what the white was, though – not until it moved. She heard the low *swish* of fabric, and smelled a dry, acidic smell as the person wearing the white coat moved past her.

Another person took the place of the first. Another white coat. A pair of hands dropped into her sight, and she felt something touch her arm.

(blink)

She woke again, and again turned her head. She saw white, but not a coat. She saw a bed. Someone was in the bed, but she could not see who it was. No one she knew, she thought. A man? Probably. Probably old, because his arms were thin and gray and covered in fine white hairs.

She closed her eyes.

This time, the blink was different. This time she saw something in the darkness: a face. Small like hers, and strangely familiar. The face's eyes were closed. Then they opened, and again Hope screamed inside herself. She screamed and screamed and screamed, because the face *had* no eyes. There was just a dark field, a blackness so complete that Hope knew it wasn't just blackness, it was nothing at all.

She was looking at infinity, though she did not understand the term as such. She knew only that she was looking at something so dark and so perfect that she could not understand it beyond knowing that it was unnatural. It was *wrong*.

She tried to close her eyes, to shut herself away from the dreadful sight of the two dark pits that stared at her with nothing behind them, nothing inside them. But of course, she could not shut her eyes, because they were already shut. She floated in a dream, then drowned in a nightmare.

Then she woke up, one last time. She stayed awake.
And the *real* nightmare began in earnest.

2

FBI REPORT FILE FA2017R2

Appendix C

Reproduction of comments on partial videos recovered from designate Portobello Road – see Appendix AC for list of videos recovered from Portobello Road, and report sections 21 through 22 in re actions taken to recover videos and reconstruct corrupted files where applicable.

See also Appendix AD list of possible Portobello Road users who may have commented on applicable videos

For list of known homicides possibly attributable to Portobello Road users, please see report for File FA 2018R2.

See also Appendix AD and files referred therein to list of Portobello Road videos, comments, and homicides. N.B.: Hard copies of the files must be relied upon, as *all electronic files are subject to corruption by parties unknown*. See Internal Report FA 2019R43.

Comments to Portobello Road video designated PR9

---

5 COMMENTS   SORT BY

Name: XXXXXXXXXX

Comment: I checked the names. Legit. This happened. IS happening.

Name: XXXXXXXXXX

Comment: Bullshit. Stinks of a sting.

Name: XXXXXXXXXX

Comment: Can't be. Would be entrapment.

Name: XXXXXXXXXX

Comment: Not worth it.

Name: XXXXXXXXXX

Comment: I DID IT. NOT THE VIDEO, I DID WHAT THE VIDS SAID AND IT WORKED GUYS HOLY SHIT DO YOU KNOW WHAT THIS MEANS WE CAN MAKE IT RIGHT WE CAN STOP IT ALL AND MAKE IT RIGHT

FOUR

1

Elena heard nothing but ringing at first. Then she became aware – slowly – that the ringing had dissolved to a series of short, sharp tones. *Beep-beep-beep…*

She looked down. Tried to find the communicator on her wrist, but for some reason couldn't see it. She couldn't see much of anything, for that matter; the world had dissolved into a white so bright the memory alone made her eyes water anew.

The tears helped, though. She blinked them away, trying to find the source of the beeping, to find out what Mr. Do-Good wanted before he got fed up and –

Sight and understanding rushed into her mind.

Chong. Chong he died. Then…

Then he'd exploded. Nothing small like when Solomon had his hand blown off, not even the larger blasts from when Mr. Do-Good demonstrated the punishment for refusing to play by blasting the heads off the mannequins in the white room. The explosion this time started with the collar, no doubt, but whatever was packed into the devices around their necks must be much more powerful than Mr. Do-Good had let on. A bright flash, then a shockwave knocked Elena right off her feet, and when she managed to sit up –

(beep-beep-beep)

– there was nothing left of Chong or the gangster who had attacked him but a dark patch on the ground, and a larger ring of red and gray.

She blinked again. Looked at her wrist, trying to find the communicator. She still couldn't see it, and had to blink more until she realized why, and wiped away the thick layer of soot and soft matter that covered it.

Bits of Chong. This is all that's left of him, just a sludge to be wiped away.

She tried not to think of that. It wasn't hard, because a moment later she read the words on Mr. Do-Good's communicator and realized she had been hearing another sound for a few minutes. Sirens. Getting louder, coming closer.

Not good.

Worse than not good, in fact. The cops were coming, and Mr. Do-Good did not like that fact. Or at least, he didn't want any of the remaining players of his game to meet up with the newcomers. That was the message she saw on the communicator, and heard Do-Good saying.

"Do-Good says, *DON'T GET CAUGHT!* Run, run, *RUN!*"

A moment later, Elena felt something grab her. She screamed and tried to hit it, but the swing was unpracticed and wild and she felt only air.

Whoever was holding her grunted and said, "Elena, we have to go."

She punched again, her mind still fighting the shock of the explosion that had knocked her off her feet. This time she connected with something, and was rewarded by the *ooof* of someone in pain.

Oddly, she placed the tone and timbre of the sound and matched it to a face and name even though she had not been able to do so with the actual words of the speaker only a moment before.

"Clint?" said Elena, and barely recognized her *own* voice. High-pitched, pinched with terror and confusion and pain. She sounded like a little girl version of herself. Like the children she saw every day, coming in and out of her office in a never-ending train of misery.

"Time to go, Elena," said Clint, and she felt herself lifted to her feet. She wobbled for a moment, and another set of hands steadied her.

"Easy," said Noelle.

The world finally focused – or came as close to focusing as anything could on a night where madness ruled.

"What…?" managed Elena.

"No time," said Clint. He snapped his fingers an inch in front of her nose, obviously trying to draw her out of the shock he feared would incapacitate her. "We gotta *go,* Elena."

She nodded. "'Kay," she said. Then firmed her mouth and said, "O-kay," consciously over-enunciating the first syllable, as though doing so would bring her mind back into focus.

It worked, at least enough to get her moving. She took a few stumbling steps, realizing as she did that Noelle had pushed herself under Elena's arm, and now partially supported her as they tripped their way out of the yard where Chong had –

Don't think of that.

Wise words. There was enough to think of without focusing on something that was over and done and couldn't be helped.

She took a few more lurching steps before her gait firmed. Noelle let go of her, obviously sensing that Elena could move of her own accord and that trying to bear her weight would likely only result in both of them tripping over each other.

Elena spared one more look behind her. She saw she was wrong in her previous appraisal: the explosion hadn't completely disintegrated Chong or the gang-banger who had beaten him to death's door. There were still pieces of them. A smear of gore on the singed siding of the house. Something hanging off one of the chain-links that fenced in the yard. A leg bone, denuded of all but a few strips of blackened flesh, jutted out of the ground like a sapling in a madman's garden.

She turned away.

Nothing I could do. Nothing to do but what I did. But what we *did. But what we're doing.*

The words were a familiar refrain. Not a welcome one, but at least comforting in that familiarity. They were words she had heard in her mind hundreds, thousands, *tens* of thousands of times.

She ran, and the words bounced with her steps, and when she and Clint and Noelle all dove behind a parked car in order to avoid being seen by a police cruiser roaring down the street, the words followed her still.

Nothing I could do. Nothing to do but what I did.

2

Elena was the one who came up with the idea, all those years ago. It hurt, but there was nothing else that could be done. Not and keep the home operating. That was the most important thing, and the thing she had to remember: it was all for the greater good, and the only thing that mattered was the children. Not one specific *child*, but all of the kids as a group.

It didn't even matter that Higgins took the idea and ran with it, or that he pocketed so much off the top of each deal. Though when she finally confronted him about *that* she realized she had severely underestimated how much he was stealing. She pushed him – not physically, but emotionally. It worked, too.

Higgins liked to think of himself as some kind of supreme power. But it was just a dream, and easily burst when Elena broke into his computer and saw the ledger. Not the one that he showed to the government or to the donors, the *real* ledger sheet. A list of offshore accounts and balances that Higgins no doubt thought he'd kept well out of the range of mortal eyes.

But he wasn't as smart as he thought. Not very smart at all, in fact. It was an easy matter to figure out his passwords, and an even easier one to arrange transfer of half the funds in his accounts to new accounts that she opened – some of them in the very same banks he was using.

He found out, of course. Higgins might have overestimated his importance in the grand scheme of things, and *certainly* overestimated his intellect in comparison with others, but he was not a complete fool. He saw the dip in his accounts, and easily figured out that Elena was the one behind it – just as she had known he would.

"Where's my *money*?" he demanded.

It was early. No one was in earshot, and probably no one else in the building was even awake. That was, no doubt, why he had chosen to come in and challengef her like this. Higgins was a "roll in at the crack of noon" kind of guy, but he knew that Elena often showed up well before official work hours started. She cared. She thought what she was doing mattered.

So of course she would come in early. Of course she would work hard. And of course he would storm in like this, full of what he undoubtedly thought of as thunder and fury, but which more resembled whining and bitching.

"Well?" he demanded when Elena did not respond to the first shouted question.

She continued to ignore him. She entered the final tally on the business ledger that she had been keeping since she started here, saved the work, and only then looked at Higgins.

"Your money?" she said quietly.

She was only twenty-two at the time. Fresh out of college, only a few months into this job. But she had sized Higgins up early and well, and knew that he would react to bluster with bluster. But the quiet tones of someone who held real power... *that* he wouldn't know how to deal with.

Just as predicted, he looked away from her as soon as she spoke the words. Still, the fire wasn't completely gone from his spirit. "My *money*," he said again. "Where did you put my money?"

"Nowhere."

"Nowhere? Did you give my money away or something? What do you mean 'nothing,' and where do you get off –"

Elena held up a hand. Higgins clamped his jaw shut, obviously trying to convince himself it was because he was a good, benevolent deity, and not because he was just afraid of what she might do next. He glared, but the glare was weak.

Elena smiled her sweetest smile. "I didn't do a thing with your money," she said.

He slashed a knife hand through the air. "Don't give me that," he said. "Half the money –"

"You're not listening, David," she continued sweetly. "I said I didn't do anything with *your* money. But some of the money in those accounts wasn't yours. So I took it and put it somewhere safe, until it's needed."

Higgins' eyes grew so wide he looked more like a caricature than an actual man. "You... you *what?*"

She steepled her fingers and looked squarely at him. "I. Took. The. Money. That. You. Stole."

"How *dare* you –" he began.

She cut him off with a gesture. "Cut the crap, David. What are you going to do about it? Tell the police? What would that do to this place?" she said, gesturing around her.

"I don't give a *shit* what it would do to this place," he snarled.

"I know that," she said. "But it's good to finally hear you admit it. So how about this: you get half. I could have taken more. I could have taken *all* of it. But as bad as you are, you're a convenient face for what we have to do. So do your jobs – both of them – and leave me alone to do mine."

David's eyes bulged so far out of their sockets that Elena suspected he would either explode or just die of a heart attack. He did neither. Instead, he visibly deflated. "I'm going to change the accounts," he muttered.

"Fine. But I know how much to expect from each transaction, David. And though you *could* steal it all, you won't."

"Why not?" he said. A bit of the snarl returned to his voice – but only a bit.

"Because I didn't just take the half of the money that you stole, David. I gathered information about the accounts, and about where the money went after that. I have enough dirt on you to ensure you go to jail for a very long time."

"And you, too."

Elena spread her hands wide and put on an innocent expression. "For what, David? There's no proof of anything but you taking money that has no explanation. There's no proof that I ever had anything to do with what's going on here. Just you, David."

He looked like he was trying to figure out something to say. Finally, he settled on, "Be careful, Elena," before sweeping out of the room and slamming the door behind him.

That was fine. Let him posture. Let him bluster all he wanted. Elena didn't care. She only cared about getting the money to keep this place going. For the children.

3

She hadn't been lying about what she said: David *was* a convenient face for what she came to think of as "funding." She certainly didn't want to be the person showing up for the drops, or the one who was contacted for the supply lists that needed filling.

But "convenient" was different than "necessary," and she suspected after their little meeting that David would probably outlive his usefulness in either department. She had thought him a fool based solely on how easy it was to guess his passwords; now she *knew* he was a fool based on how easy it was to guess them even after he changed them. They were all names of his dogs, and even though she'd told him she broke into his computer, he kept right on using his pets' names as passwords. The names themselves were easy to find, since David kept a list of them taped under his desk.

Idiot.

And she thought him an even bigger idiot when she realized he was *still* skimming off the top of each deal. Elena was still living in a one-room apartment in a part of the city almost as rundown and ramshackle as the place she worked, and she was fine with that fact. She had decided long ago that being rich wasn't a goal.

But if she was sacrificing comfort and security, why should she have to watch David flaunting his excesses and his expenditures? Worse, sooner or later someone would have to realize that he was spending far more than he made. An IRS investigation would not harm her directly – she'd been telling the truth when she said that any evidence of wrongdoing would only link to David – but she didn't need the attention.

Neither did the children.

And it was all for them, wasn't it? All for the children she had grown to know and love? Wasn't everything she did meant to keep them sheltered and fed and protected?

And David… David was going to ruin it all.

The final nail came when he showed the thug into the home. When he allowed that monster to come in and take what he wanted.

Elena wasn't there when it happened. She was home, sleeping the sleep of the just and the merciful. But she noted that one of the hall motion sensors registered movement in the night, and checked the CCTV footage of the hall. The images were grainy, but enough to make out that David was one of the people who had walked through the hall. The other was clearly some kind of gangbanger, with a hat whose brim was pulled low enough she could not make out his face. But she could tell the look well enough – the basketball jersey, the high-tops, the jeans slung so low she thought they had to fall off at any moment.

She followed David and his guest through the place, cueing up different feeds each time they left one camera's field of vision and entered another one.

And finally she came to the moment where David gestured at one of the children. When the other man packed the little girl in a *suitcase* like she was nothing more than a pair of socks or a t-shirt.

David entered the office while she was still watching the feed. He tossed a pile of bills on her desk – an even stupider move than usual, given that the secretary that helped her and the three other case worker/social worker/everything elses that the center needed to operate was sitting right outside her open door.

Elena slid the money quickly into a drawer. Locked it. Then she went to the door and shut it before returning to her desk and saying, "What did you do, David?" She kept her voice low. The alternative would be to start screaming.

"What are you talking about?"

"Don't, David," she said. Her words came out sharper than she intended, and much louder. She calmed herself, willing the secretary to keep on working and not stick her nose in – there was enough for Elena to deal with as it was.

Especially with one of the kids missing.

She waited a moment. The door didn't open, and Elena spat, "Did you think I wouldn't notice what you did?"

"Cash was low," David said with a shrug. "You know that as well as I do."

"I do. And I also know that you care very little about the kids, and very much about yourself. So don't pretend that what happened over the weekend was about anything but you."

"Look –"

"How are you explaining the fact that we're missing a child?"

He waved her off. "Same as always. Papers have already been prepared and filed. Officially, the girl is at a foster home. Someone who has been paid – out of my cut, thank-you-very-much – to wait a few weeks, then file a missing persons report." He shrugged. "So sad when they run away."

"You didn't check any of this with me."

"Why should I?" snarled David. Now he was in her space, pushing his gray, forgettable face up close enough that she could smell his breath, boozy and heavy and sour. "I'm in charge, Elena. You are the newest of new hires, and not someone I have to keep around." He seemed to realize as soon as he said this how untrue it was, because he sighed – another blast of cheap whiskey fumes – and his expression softened. Not his eyes, though. They remained hard and quietly angry. "I know your heart's in the right place. Isn't that why we started all this in the first place?"

"Maybe it's time for a change," she said.

He snorted. "Sure. And we go back to serving crap food and providing cots that barely hold the kids up without breaking. We go back to wondering where the next month's rent comes from, and where the next meal for the kids comes from." He pointed at her computer, where the feed had frozen on the moment where the man folded the little girl into the luggage.

In the image, it looked like David was looking at the camera. And *smirking*.

"I left that there for you," he said, his expression a mirror of the one she saw on her computer. "I wanted you to find it."

"Another stupid move. What if someone else had seen it?"

"No one else looks at the footage. No one else cares." David sighed again. "And even if someone else wanted to, they couldn't have seen the footage. I password protected it." The sigh turned to a grin, the grin turned to a leer. "And I didn't use one of my dogs' names, either." The leer widened. "I had to come up with a whole new system."

"Let me guess – birthdays?"

David's smile hitched a little. He covered with a laugh. "You got me." He spread his fingers. "But I can take care of that. You, however, have something else you should be watching out for."

"What's that, David?"

The grin disappeared. "Mr. Higgins."

"What?"

"My friends and peers call me David. You are neither."

Elena didn't like the way this conversation was going. She felt a sudden thrill of fear, which was totally new to her. She had been creeped out, irritated, and bored by David Higgins, but never afraid of him.

This won't do. It won't do at all.

She covered with an eyeroll, but could tell from David's expression that he bought it about as much as she bought his pretense at nonchalance over his continuing password gaffes. "What exactly is it that I should be worrying about?" She nodded at the drawer holding the money. "This money from an 'anonymous donor' will cover Eighth Street Children for a good long time, and since that's the only thing I care about, I can't see anything to worry about, other than your bringing people into the home rather than sticking to procedure and having the kids grabbed in their foster homes or at school."

He shrugged. "It was a rush job. No time to wait. They had a specific need, and we had something that would fill it." He leaned in again, placing curled fists on the edge of her desk. "He needed something to take her away in. That surprised me a bit – kid looked plenty strong to me. But I realized I had just the thing. I knew you'd love my choice, too. It had your name *all over it*."

Elena felt her brows come together. She looked back at the image on her computer. The man putting a small bundle of flesh and bone into a suitcase. She clicked the mouse, zooming in close. She had been furious when she saw the girl being packed in that way. The children that disappeared were sacrifices to the greater good. That didn't mean they had no value, and that thought was all that had pounded through Elena's mind. It had crowded out everything else – everything but rage at what had happened, and how the little girl had been treated.

It had even crowded out the recognition of her own property. "You used my bag," she said dully.

"Your fault, when you think about it. You come in late to work from a long weekend, trailing that bag with you like some kind of prize, showing everyone that you think you're so much better, Miss World Traveler –"

"I was visiting my mother in Phoenix. Hardly world travel, hardly –"

"– and you just left it here –"

"I just kept forgetting –"

"– for weeks and weeks –"

"I just –"

"– even though I kept telling you to take it home."

She stared at David. He was still grinning. She felt fear, and knew that the game had changed.

"Did you empty it out first?" she asked.

David nodded. "Mostly. I may have forgotten a thing or two. Some panties." He chuckled. "I was pretty surprised at some of them. Naughty, naughty." His eyebrows gave a sadistic, sexual up-and-down.

"Where is it?"

"Your underwear?"

"The bag, you shit."

"Now, now," said David. He sounded totally at ease all of a sudden. Not a good sign, Elena knew, because a man like David could only possibly be at ease when he knew he was holding not just a winning hand, but the *only* hand. "Language, Elena."

"The. *Bag.*"

He shrugged. "Honestly? I have no idea. The buyers probably ditched it somewhere. Maybe tossed it out of a plane over the Pacific Ocean. Maybe fed it to a furnace." He leaned in closer than ever. So close that David Higgins was all she could see. "Maybe I asked them to bring it back. Full of hairs and maybe some skin." He shook his head, mock-sadness lengthening his features. "Shame if the police realized a little girl was missing, and realized that traces of her were in a suitcase. *Your* suitcase."

"They would never be able to match her up with –"

"I have a brush full of hairs. Can you picture it?" David opened his eyes wide as he acted out a scene with an invisible second player. "Why, no, officer, I have no idea where she might have gone." He snapped his fingers. "But

I seem to recall... why look at this! Her brush wasn't reassigned to another child. See, here it is! I don't know how DNA would help in the search, but...." He shrugged. "Hope springs eternal, officer. Whatever I can do to help. I'll even pray, and maybe you'll find something that will tell you where she is." He pretended to wipe away a tear. "Hopefully she's just run away. I know that's what happens with most orphans who disappear. But I do fear...."

Elena shook her head. The fear was still there, but she did her best to cover it with a snarl. "You think that scares me, you dumbass? You think they'll find something like that and come for me? Or that if somehow they pinned something on me that I wouldn't tell them about your part in it? About the fact that *you* were the guy who did all the deals; that *you* were the only person who ever touched one of the children –"

"- and about the fact that I signed all the paperwork that sent them to foster homes before they disappeared?" he finished. He shrugged. "I know you can pin that all on me. But I'll just tell on *you*, and I guarantee that the luggage, the DNA, and a few pictures I've taken will ensure you sit right beside me in any trial. Maybe I'll even cut a deal and you'll end up being the only person in jail. I'm good at deals." He finally moved away from her, sprawling in the chair on the other side of her desk. "I have no interest in telling what I know," he said. "But I need you to understand that your hands aren't clean. They never have been, and now I have proof of that. So whatever happens to me...." He shrugged and flicked a bit of imaginary lint from his lapel. "We're in this together, Elena. We're partners. You take half the money, you get half the risk right along with it."

"You'll 'tell on me'?" Elena repeated. She laughed. It wasn't funny, and she knew that was the least important part of what David had just said, but for some reason it was the only thing she kept hearing. "You'll *'tell on me'*?" She laughed again. Harder and longer this time, with a thread of hysteria running through the sound. "You sound like one of the kids. Like a damn *child*."

David shrugged. "Maybe so. Regardless, *you* better act like a grownup. Make a smart choice." He pointed at the drawer where she had put the cash. "You tell yourself you're doing this because one kid dying is better than dozens suffering –"

"We don't know they die," she said.

He gaped. "What the hell do you think happens when they leave here? You think they go to Disneyland and then live the rest of their life in a house made of candy?"

"We don't know they die."

"We do. *You* do. You always have." He stood. "So tell yourself whatever you want. Do what you want with the money – donate it to the home, or buy a boat with it. I don't care. But you *will* stop acting holier-than-thou, and you *will* stop threatening me. Got it?"

She tried to think of some way around what he had done. Tried to think of something to say that would take back the power she had until now enjoyed. She came up with no solutions to the problems that had arisen, and only one word: "Yes."

David didn't move. He raised his eyebrows as though expecting more. "I get it," she said. David still didn't move. He just stared at her for long seconds, and suddenly she realized what he was waiting for. She realized what he expected, and realized also that doing it was somehow the worst thing that would happen today. "I get it... *Mr. Higgins.*"

He nodded and walked to the door, opening it and taking a step out. Then he turned back to her. "And I expect you to get me the updated schedules and the paperwork for the last round of state evals by the end of the day," he said loudly before turning and nodding at the secretary. "How are you, Lettie?" he said.

"Fine, sir," she answered.

"Beautiful day," he said, and closed the door on Elena.

4

The police showed up at her door earlier than Elena expected.

She had been waiting for it to happen. It was the only possible outcome only a moment after Mr. Higgins – *David* – left the office. But it still sent a thrill of fear up and down her spine. Something expected and something hoped for weren't always the same thing.

But she did the best to put on an innocent face as she opened the door, and thought she sounded calm as she said, "Yes?"

"Ms. Ruiz?" asked the cop closest to her, a six-foot-tall man with a mustache right out of the seventies.

"That's right. Can I help you?"

The cop was dressed in plainclothes. A detective, which she'd expected, given what had happened. He reached into his pocket, withdrew a wallet, and flipped it open to show a badge and an ID. "I'm Detective Ehlers, Ms. Ruiz. This is Detective Clay," he added, nodding to his partner, a skinny black woman with hard eyes whom Elena immediately pegged as the one she would have to tread most carefully around.

"What can I do for you?" asked Elena, trying to get the right mix of curiosity and worry into her voice.

"There's been an accident, Ms. Ruiz," said Ehlers. His mustache twitched a bit, like he had almost said something else but decided otherwise at the last moment.

Elena still controlled herself, but let a hint of trembling creep into her voice. "What... what do you mean?"

"You work at the Eighth Street Children center, right?" asked the other detective, Clay.

"That's right."

"With David Higgins?"

"That's right." She flicked her gaze from one cop to the other. "Why? What's going on?"

Ehlers looked at his partner. He looked like he was gearing up to say something – probably trying to figure out how to soften the blow as much as possible.

Detective Clay apparently didn't worry about such things. "He's dead," she said simply.

Elena gasped. "Why... how...?" Her legs wobbled a bit, then she felt strong arms on hers, Detective Ehlers guiding her to the chair nearest the door.

That was good. She'd let herself go weak-kneed, wondering if one of the detectives would help or if they would just let her stand there and either regain her balance or topple to the floor. The fact that Ehlers had moved so quickly and now helped her so gently was a good sign. A very good sign.

Unless they're playing me. Trying to lull me like I'm lulling them.

Detective Ehlers got Elena settled into the chair, waited a moment, then said, "He killed himself." A long moment later, a moment during which Elena gasped but said nothing, he added, "I'm sorry."

"'*Sorry*'?" said Detective Clay. She wasn't asking a question of Elena – another good sign. Instead, she aimed the question at her partner, her voice overflowing with an incredulous shade of anger.

Elena heard the tone, and immediately reappraised the situation. Detective Clay was going to be a cinch. "What... why are you here?" she asked them both.

"Like I said," Detective Ehlers said, "Mr. Higgins killed himself."

"But why are you *here*?" Elena wiped her eyes with the back of her hand, surprised to realize she was actually crying – though for a far different reason than the detectives would suspect. "I mean, why come by like this and –"

Ehlers looked at his partner, and again Clay did the heavy lifting. "What was your relationship with Mr. Higgins?"

Elena shrugged. "He was my boss."

"Anything else?"

"No. Just that. Why?" Elena frowned, and now injected a bit of anger into her voice. "What is going on? Why are you here?"

"Mr. Higgins was found dead in his car."

"I don't understand... was he in an accident or –"

"It looks like he killed himself. He was found in his garage with the engine running, and he was holding a number of photos."

Elena looked from Ehlers to Clay, then back to Ehlers. "What kind of photos?" she said in a small voice.

Ehlers shifted uncomfortably. She wondered how he'd gotten to this point in his career without being inured to this kind of thing, and liked the fact that he had done so. "Photos of you," he finally said. "They looked like they were... *ahem*... taken without your consent."

"I don't understand."

"The pictures looked like they were taken by a low-grade camera," said Detective Clay. She looked at the small room that was living room, kitchen, and dining area in her small apartment. "They looked like they were taken in here, in fact."

Elena shook her head. "But I never –"

"You were in your underwear in some. Naked in a few others."

Elena gasped, then her face wrinkled in disgust. That expression wasn't hard to fake – it wasn't fake at all, in fact; she just let her real feelings for David Higgins show through. "You mean he...." She looked around as though terrified she was being watched in that very moment.

"It's okay," said Detective Ehlers. He squeezed her shoulder. "We found a camera in his bedroom that we think was the one he used in here. We also found...." His voice trailed off and he looked at his partner again.

She rolled her eyes, but Elena could tell that Clay felt the same way about her partner as Elena did: he was sweet – so sweet he shouldn't have made it this far as a cop, and sweet enough that it was easy to help him during the tough moments. "We found some things we think are yours. Did you ever notice anything missing from your home? Ever have a break-in?"

She gave a tinny imitation of a laugh. "No. No break-in, but I'm not great about locking my door."

"Anything ever missing?" asked Clay again.

Elena thought, then shook her head. "Not unless you count socks. But that's just life, right? Everyone loses one of their socks and wonders why, then...." She had been speaking quickly, almost babbling as she tried to convey nervous horror. Now her voice petered away. "What?" she said. She tittered. "You saying he took my socks?"

"No. But he *was* wearing something that matched something we saw in the pictures."

"What? You mean, when he was found? What was it?" She looked around as though trying to spot what might be missing. Though of course she knew what the officers were about to say:

"He was wearing... some underwear."

"That's not unusual, is it?" She tittered again.

This time, finally, it was Detective Ehlers who delivered the hard news. "It was women's underwear." He grimaced. "Didn't fit him very well, but he crammed himself in it." He fixed her with a sudden, hard stare, and now Elena wondered if she had severely misunderstood – and underestimated – the apparently genial cop. "Looked like yours. What you were wearing in several of the pictures."

Elena gagged as though about to vomit. "Why would he... why would *anyone*...?"

Detective Clay glanced at her partner, and now Elena was certain that his kind-hearted sap vibe had been intentional. Detective Ehlers nodded at his partner, his eyes showing that Elena had passed some kind of smell test. "We think he was probably a creep who took pictures of you and stole some... *personal* effects for sick satisfaction."

"And then he offed himself when he realized what a horror he'd become," added Detective Ehlers, his voice flat and emotionless.

"Either that or it was an accident," said Detective Clay.

There was no reason to fear. Elena knew that – intellectually if not emotionally.

It had been only too easy to set it all up. Not hard at all to take several pictures of herself – using a cheap camera she bought over a month ago for cash at a Walmart fifty miles away – strutting naked or near-naked across her front room. Taking some of the underwear she'd worn in the pictures and going to his house.

David was a pig. She knew that. She knew also that pigs didn't turn into angels when confronted with a new kind of slops. So she had come onto him. A small matter to get him drunk, a smaller one to urge him into the car with the promise of sex; she told him she had "a thing" for cars. He was already on the verge of passing out, so it wasn't hard to take his keys and lock him in the car, then wait until he was good and under before unlocking it, starting the car, leaving the garage, and just waiting.

Hurrying back into the garage was the hardest part. She ran in, holding her breath, and jammed the panties halfway up his pants. She ran into the house, took a breath of clean air, then back into the garage, where she used David's dead hands to put fingerprints all over the car keys, the pictures, the panties, and the cheap camera that she then took back inside and left "hidden" in a drawer in his bedroom.

Then she wiped down everything she had touched – it hadn't been much, other than the wine and the glasses they drank from. Easy. A drunk pervert gets trashed and either offs himself intentionally or just has an "accident."

She took her wine glass – she wasn't about to get nailed for something as stupid as leaving a glass with her DNA all over it at the scene of the crime – and left.

Easy.

But Detective Ehlers was staring at her blankly, and Detective Clay now wore an expression she didn't like, either. Elena realized suddenly that she hadn't responded to Clay's last comment. She did now, hoping that she hadn't waited too long; that they would chalk her response up to stress.

"I… thought you said it wasn't an accident. But it *was*?"

Both cops relaxed somewhat. "Yeah," said Detective Clay. "We're probably looking at suicide, but it could have been an accident. He had a blood alcohol level high enough to knock out the technicians on scene."

Elena thought about following up on that. Decided quickly against it. Why feign interest? Why would a person who was supposed to be in her shoes care about anything but what had been done to *her*? So she shuddered and looked around again and said, "Can someone… can someone check the house for any more cameras?"

The responses of the two cops showed her she had guessed correctly. "Sure," said Detective Ehlers, and his voice was kind again. She didn't buy it this time – not completely – but it certainly sounded genuine. "We need you to come down to the station, if that's okay. We have to have you i.d. some of the things we found, for evidence purposes."

"Sure," she said. "Of course."

"We'll have someone come in and check your place for any more hidden devices," said Detective Clay, adding carefully, "if that's okay with you. It means they'll have to look around pretty carefully."

Elena pretended not to notice the second thing she was agreeing to: saying they could come and look for a camera would be allowing them to search her home. No claims of false seizure should they find anything. But she didn't care about that: she had nothing to hide. The only thing she'd taken with her was the wine glass, which she'd thrown against a wall three miles away from David's house, shattering it into just a few more pieces of glass in a nameless alley where they would never be *found*, let alone tied to her.

She got up. "Can I get a coat?" she asked.

"Of course," said Detective Ehlers. Then, as she turned to go, he added, in a voice too casual to be anything but rehearsed, "I just wish I knew where he printed out those pictures of you."

Elena didn't stiffen; her voice didn't stutter. She had prepared for that, too. She shook her head sadly. "I don't know, but I do know that he was always turning off his monitor when anyone came into his office." She wrinkled her nose. "I thought – we all thought – that he was looking at porn. You don't think he…?"

She looked at the detectives, her face a canvas painted in bright colors of disgust and panic. "He wasn't just printing them in there? On his computer?"

The detectives shrugged. But they would check the printer to see if it had printed out the pictures. And she knew it would.

There was a small risk they would go over his computer as well. But even if they did – and the risk was small, given how obvious a suicide/accident had caused his death – she knew they wouldn't find much. She had no idea what the new passwords were, but that meant neither did the police. And if they took the time to break into the hard drive, what would they find?

Nothing. The porn she had alluded to – not a lie at all, and something every single staffer at Eighth Street Children was aware of David doing – and probably nothing else. It would take a pretty deep dive, she figured, to uncover his offshore accounts. Again, not much chance of that, and if they did... well, there was nothing there linking her to any of it.

Nothing but the luggage with the panties. And if they were found – a pretty big *if*, because she doubted David actually had the thing – there was now a solid reason they could link to him, not her. The luggage was stolen, the underwear in them *was* hers, but also stolen.

He would be branded as what he was. And Elena would come through it just fine. Maybe she could even take over for David. That would be best for everyone, she knew. The kids especially. One or two might go missing, but that was infrequent. Unlike David, she wouldn't take much off the top, and the rest could go to keeping Eighth Street Children afloat, and keeping the rest of the kids cared-for.

She only wished she could have acted sooner. It had taken a bit of time to set this all up, and she had wanted to put a bit of distance between what she had to do and the last deal David had brokered.

She gathered her coat and went with the police. She looked sad, and that was a real emotion. There were so many more kids she could have helped.

5

Unlike Mr. David Higgins, un-dearly departed, Elena took barely anything at all off the top. Just enough to move from her one-bedroom apartment to a condo in West Hollywood. Nothing fancy.

Which meant that almost one-hundred percent of the proceeds she gained went to the home. She *was* the one tapped to take it over; largely, she suspected, because no one else wanted the job.

She lobbied for – and got – a name change as soon as possible after getting the job. Again, no one much protested. There was a board of directors, but their titles were more vanity than reality, and they deferred almost every major decision to Elena. She was, after all, the one who had come on at just the right time to save the place. She had taken over from the disgraced previous director, and had overseen a sudden uptick in anonymous donations.

The name "Eighth Street Children" had overtones of what she came to think of as *Higginism*, and she wanted none of that. "St. Jerome's" was a much better name. The board *did* balk a bit at the suggestion, worried that people might misconstrue the home as some kind of religious haven, but Elena reassured them. St. Jerome was a patron saint of orphans, but she told them that was just a helpful branding, and that none of the logos or other identifiers would give the slightest hint of religion.

Only a small fib there. Elena was a good Catholic, and she liked the idea of working for the saint who had himself cared so selflessly for so many orphans, just like Elena herself.

That was years back, and she had thought of Eighth Street Children not a single time since. She was busy with St. Jerome's, managing finances and overseeing "donations" that came in every six months or so. Sometimes it was as far as a year between the times when she got a list of needs and looked at her children – her lambs, as she came to think of them – to see if there were any who fit the bill.

There almost always was.

Still, because she was careful, the lean times *did* come. And they had come again in the last month or so. She couldn't dictate demand, only supply. Even so, she felt more and more the urge – the *need* – to reach out and see if there was anything she could do. She knew the lambs who disappeared from her flock were lost, but she continued to console herself with the knowledge that they were going to a greater reward, in service of others.

So she sat at her computer – still in the same office as before, because she was a person who had not the ego of someone like Mr. David Higgins, and so had not the need for a large office at the corner of the building – and mused. Reaching out was dangerous. It wasn't something she liked doing, not only because it was a breach of procedure, but because the anonymous broker at the other end of the chain disliked it and had told her that doing such things opened them both up to needless risk.

And yet… the ledger sheet was dripping with red. It had been over a year since the last "donation." St. Jerome's was on the verge of having to make some very hard choices, and that meant the directors were breathing down Elena's neck. Sometimes it bothered her that she relied so much on her "extra" work. She passed money to the people who volunteered for foster work, knowing that they would never have to take care of a child and could simply pocket the money sent by the state and by Elena herself in return for a few days or weeks of little or no work followed by a cursory investigation by police and social workers who saw so much in the way of runaways that they hardly blinked at the event.

So she finally opened her email and typed in the Gmail account she'd been given. A simple query, and one she didn't really expect an answer to: "Any needs?"

She clicked over to the accounting reports. She knew what they said, but couldn't help looking. The reports showed a total available funding in the amount of $666.17. She couldn't help thinking of the first part of the number as a bad omen, and even murmured, "Bad luck."

A low knock sounded at the office door and Lettie walked in. She had taken over Elena's old job when Elena rose to the throne, as it were. She was bright – bright enough that she somehow recognized, or maybe just intuited, that there was something strange about the donations that popped up every once in a while. Tens of thousands of dollars, and St. Jerome's would have bought itself another few hours of life.

She figured it out. And Elena worried she might rush to the police – perhaps even to the overly-earnest Detective Ehlers and his partner, the hard-eyed Detective Clay – but Lettie did no such thing. She didn't even ask for much of a cut, all things considered.

Now she stared at Elena, lips pursed as she finally said, "You look over the figures yet?"

"Yeah," said Elena. She pursed her own lips as she looked at the number again. "Bad luck."

"Hopefully your benefactor shows up," said Lettie. Her eyes were sad, as though the fate of St. Jerome's were all that mattered to her, even though Elena knew the younger woman had been eyeing a new car and probably needed a bit more cash to make it happen.

"It doesn't work like that," said Elena. "Besides, we sent the last one out just a few weeks ago."

"Well, *something's* got to happen," said Lettie, and left the room. "The last one just got us current, and we're already behind again."

The door clicked as it shut behind her, and Elena realized abruptly that she couldn't remember the last one's face, or age, or anything else about the child. She couldn't remember *any* of them, really.

Not my job. I don't think of the lost lambs, I think of the ones who are saved.

And that was as it should be. She was saving so many, and surely she would be allowed to turn her mind from those who had sacrificed for the greater good.

Shouldn't she?

For a moment she didn't know. For a moment a dormant part of her mind started to claw out of the box Elena usually kept it in, and scream for attention.

(What are you doing?*)*

Then the thought fell away as Elena's computer beeped to announce an incoming email.

The sender was blocked, as always. But the message was easy enough to discern: "You're in luck."

As always, there was a website link – a long series of numbers and letters that Elena knew would lead nowhere at all if typed into a web browser like Explorer or Chrome.

She opened instead the TOR web browser she had been instructed on soon after taking over – in every aspect – for David. She hadn't liked the thought of going onto the dark web at first, and the first few visits had sent her into a cold sweat until she realized that most of the things on the dark web were actually quite banal, boring. Mostly it seemed to be people who were paranoid about government or big business looking over their shoulder, so ran to the dark web as the last bastion of privacy.

She copied the address into the TOR browser, and it opened to a website she had grown to know quite well: Portobello Road. The site she had been guided to showed a list of needed items, along with the stats that would be required to fill them.

Elena opened up the roster of current lambs. She scrolled through it, marking each one internally as either a "pass" or a "possible."

The door clicked. Opened. Elena didn't look away from her work. She just said, "Good news, I –"

Then there was a sound like a wasp, and pain erupted from a central point in her chest. She had an instant to see what looked like wires trailing off her, then the pain intensified, the *buzzzz* sound grew… and then nothing at all until the white room.

6

As bad as waking up in the white room had been, nearly as bad was the feeling that she had seen several of the people she woke up with. Solomon Black and Clint Walker both looked familiar, and she wondered how she knew them. Solomon remained an enigma, right up to the point where she killed him. A sad moment, that, but necessary. She had a baby in her arms, and had to get moving or she might die... and who would take care of the baby then? Who would take care of *all* her lambs?

So he died, and she never knew why she felt a familiarity – and more than a little dread – every time she looked at him.

As for Clint – he had been at Eighth Street? And called it a *hellhole*?

Surely he couldn't have been referring to *her* Eighth Street Children. Even when Higgins had been in charge, she hadn't thought of it in such stark, ugly terms. Unless...

Of course! He must have been there before her arrival. Back in the bad ol' days, when money had been much tighter before her unique and creative way of raising funds to care for the lambs. Of course, he would have had to have been quite young. A baby, even.

There weren't many of those passing through the home. But there had been a few through the years. So he must have been one of them.

But how would he remember it as a hellhole?

She ignored that thought; told herself that he *must* be remembering a different place, or that he *must* be misremembering in the first place, or that he *must* be wrong in general.

The thoughts calmed her. She was a good shepherd, watching after lost lambs. She was a good person, taking care of people too young and innocent to take care of themselves. Nor did she feel bad that she didn't remember him; how could she be expected to remember all the faces of all the children she had helped over the years?

Not that any of that was much consolation. Not now, stumbling along with the last remains of Chong and Two-Teeth still drying on her clothes; on her hands and arms and even her face. Not now, running through dark streets, diving behind mailboxes and parked cars in order to avoid the police cruisers that hurtled down the street with sirens blaring and lights blazing.

Not now, wondering if all she had done and all she had made of herself was to come to nothing.

The latest in a long line of police cars roared past. She stood as soon as it was gone and continued running. Noelle and Clint were right at her side, all of them moving as quickly as they could, all of them knowing that they had to get as far from Heart Street as possible, knowing that to be caught by the police was against Mr. Do-Good's explicit instructions.

The communicator on her wrist beeped. "Do-Good says, *TURN RIGHT!*" She did. Another tone a moment later, more of Do-Good's instructions as he said, "Do-Good says, *TURN LEFT!*"

She followed the prompts, as did her fellow players. She couldn't think of them as anything other than that: players. Not contestants – they weren't competing against anyone that she could see, other than Mr. Do-Good's rules and instructions. They weren't survivors, either – that would imply that they, that *she*, might not make it through this. And she could not accept that as a possibility. Not at all. There was too much depending on her; too many children, too many lambs.

Another beep. Another. Another. Then a quick succession of rights and lefts that ended with the three of them standing in an alley.

She stared at the device on her wrist. "I don't understand," she murmured.

She had expected another house. Somewhere else to perform some vile act, or to watch someone else be maimed or killed. Instead, they were around the side of a crummy bank.

She waited.

"What now?" said Clint.

He wasn't talking to anyone in particular, but Noelle answered. She shoved her hands in her pockets – and Elena noticed how much cleaner Noelle had come through the explosion, and thought how very unfair that was – then said, "Maybe we –"

A voice cut her off. Elena started, jumping a full foot to one side, her head whipping back and forth as she looked around in a panic. But it was just Do-Good, still speaking from wherever he was hiding, still pushing them side to side like a toddler playing with toys he intended to break when finished with them.

"The nature of the game starts to change a tad at this point." Mr. Do-Good laughed, a warbling, nearly pained laugh. "Did you do that on purpose?"

Elena would have thought it impossible for the night to get any stranger or more terrifying. But the sound of that laugh pushed her fear to yet another new level. Mr. Do-Good had sounded cracked from the beginning, like the words he said were a constant fight with something inside him. Now, though, he sounded even worse.

"He's losing it," Clint whispered to Noelle.

Noelle obviously agreed, but she shook her head and motioned for him to shut up and listen.

Mr. Do-Good cleared his throat. "Right. Back to the script. Where was I?" Another throat clear. "Oh, yes: the game starts to change now, and this challenge is also a bit more complicated, so I'm going to walk you through it." He paused, cleared his throat once more, then muttered under his breath. Another unpleasant noise, one that reminded her of some of the kids in the home. They had classes, of course – one of the things the "donations" bought was excellent teachers for the lambs – and once in a while she sat in one to monitor the quality of instruction. A lot of the children were understandably behind in their schoolwork; often she heard even kids in their mid-teens sounding out the words in a story they were supposed to read.

Mr. Do-Good sounded like that now. Like he was reading from a script of his own writing, but that was still unfamiliar. He was fragmenting; breaking apart as they listened.

"Walk you through it," he said again, followed it with another throat clear, then said, "Elena, there's a wood pallet nearby. Grab what's beneath it."

She cast her eyes about automatically, unsure what this change in the game would mean. The pallet was right there, same as you could find in dozens if not hundreds of Los Angeles alleys. "Go ahead, I'll wait," said Mr. Do-Good. Elena didn't move, though. Terror had rooted her to the spot. "Nothing's going to bite you," he added.

Elena looked at Clint and Noelle. Both stared back at her, eyes wide and unsure, obviously trying to figure out what Mr. Do-Good was about to do and how to keep it from killing them all.

Elena raised her eyebrows, a silent plea for aid. She didn't know what she expected Clint or Noelle to do, but hoped for *something*.

Clint shook his head.

Noelle did the same, her head whipping back and forth so her tragically-nineties feathered hair was a blur around her.

Elena sighed. She went to the pallet and moved it aside. Underneath it lay three large plastic sleeves. She knew what they were, even without the words "AFTER-HOURS DEPOSIT" stenciled in large letters on one side.

Elena picked them up, holding them to show the others.

"Is the money supposed to go in there?" asked Noelle.

For a moment Elena didn't understand. What money?

Then she realized that she was still holding the backpack full of the money they had taken from Two-Teeth. She hadn't even realized it was there, but now she remembered it. Remembered hitching it up on her shoulders, the motion automatic and smooth as she ran and walked and dove for cover.

She shrugged the backpack off, even as Mr. Do-Good's voice came from her wrist: "Very good, Noelle! Money in the deposit sleeves, if you please, Elena!"

Elena started pulling the money from the pack, then cramming it into the bags. There was a lot of money, and she had to really shove to get it all in.

She actually thought about trying to swipe a few bills. Not much, but any little bit would help her kids...

And who will help them if you're gone? Who will raise the money to protect the ones who are left?

She pushed the last few bills into the last bag. Each bag had a Ziploc-style seal, and she ran her fingers along the seams, hearing the subtle snap as the bags locked closed.

"What now?" she asked.

Mr. Do-Good answered so quickly it was like he had been waiting, breathless with anticipation, for just that question. "Now for the fun, Elena. The game is changing a bit. You have a choice between two tasks."

"What are they?" she asked quietly. Afraid, but needing to know.

"Drop the money in the slot and walk away, leaving your two companions to fend for themselves, or you can keep the money and the three of you will keep playing together."

Clint stepped forward, his expression cold, obviously about to tell Elena she couldn't go; couldn't leave them to the game and to Mr. Do-Good's continued tortures.

Elena almost told him not to worry. After all, Mr. Do-Good said she could keep the money if she kept playing. That was a lot of cash, and it would help many of her lambs. It would mean more danger for her, but...

But isn't that what I expect of those children who sacrifice themselves so that their friends may live better, live longer, live well?

For a moment, she wavered. She might die. But the children would have –

Nothing. They would have nothing. *Even if Mr. Do-Good is willing to do what he says, what will you have to risk, Elena? What if you die? Who will take care of them?*

Clint took another step in Elena's direction. He reached for her. She didn't know what he would do if he grabbed her, but she could see the anger in his eyes.

And for a moment – just a moment – she felt like she could place him. She felt like she had seen him before. Like he *was* one of the lambs.

Then the moment fled as Noelle pointed to Clint's collar, which had begun to flash as he approached Elena. "You want to get in the way of Mr. Do-Good's game?" she asked.

Clint paused, looking from Elena to Noelle and back again. He looked around, obviously trying to spot how it was that Mr. Do-Good could see them; how he knew so much.

Elena felt an insane urge to yell, "Cameras, kid! You can hide a camera *anywhere*. Believe me, I know! Dave *Higgins* knows. *Everyone* knows!"

Instead, she pulled away from Clint. Held the three packets full of money close to her chest.

Clint stopped reaching for her. He said, "We get through this, I'm going to kill Do-Good," but the way he looked at her, Elena suspected he wanted to do the same to her.

"Let's focus on the 'getting through this' part first," said Noelle. Then she switched her gaze to Elena. Shoved her hands in her pockets but for once the quiet, fearful girl didn't look away.

A long moment stretched out, a moment that seemed to make the air between Elena and the others heavy and dangerous. She worried that Clint would come forward again, would grab at her... and this time, he wouldn't care about the consequences.

Her watch beeped. She looked at it. Mr. Do-Good's electronic smiley face spun on its axis as a countdown started.

0:30...

0:29...

Elena looked at Clint and Noelle, feeling the familiar pain. The ache in her heart that came every time a sacrifice was necessary. The knowledge that she was helping more – many more – than she harmed didn't mean she felt no pain. She knew that the piper had to be paid, but handing over the payment was still a trauma for her.

"I'm sorry," she said, and stepped toward the night deposit slot on the side of the bank.

"Either way," Mr. Do-Good said suddenly, "you're going to live with the consequences. Think carefully on –"

She didn't hear the rest. She just heard the heavy, solid sound of the night drop door pulling open. She heard the nearly-as-heavy thud of the first full sleeve of money falling into place. She heard the pregnant slam of the door shutting, and the muffled whisper of the sleeve cascading down the chute in the wall.

She opened the chute again. Deposited another sleeve. Like the first, it was so full it barely fit in the space provided. But fit it did, and she closed the chute door again and again heard the sound of money falling and then coming to rest.

She took longer with the third sleeve. She stared at it for a moment, aware the final seconds were counting down. What remained was still a lot of money. Not enough to take St. Jerome's out of debt completely, but enough to make a dent. Enough to make a difference.

And not *keeping it will make a helluva difference right* now. *To me.*

She dropped the sleeve into the chute. Thunk, whisper, thud.

Gone.

She stayed there, hand on the cold metal handle of the night deposit drop. She waited as the timer froze at two seconds. Waited, waited.

Finally, she turned and looked at Noelle and Clint. Both young people stared at her with expressions that were strangely wounded. Like they had expected more – expected *better* from her.

"What else can I do?" she asked. "What would *you* do?"

Clint answered quickly and decisively: "I wouldn't leave someone who needed help."

Elena looked away. As she did, she heard a *beep*. She went rigid as she realized the sound had come from her neck; from the collar there.

Do-Good lied. He lied, *the bastard, the sonofabitch, the Higginsian asshole, the* –

A click sounded. She felt something drop away and looked down to see the collar she had worn since the start of this misadventure. It lay on the ground. A moment later, the watch on her wrist fell away as well.

She took a step away from them. Her body clenched, expecting a double-cross – a final bright light and dark sound and then nothing at all. But nothing happened.

She looked at Clint and Noelle again. "I'll… I'll find help for you." Noelle nodded, and Clint didn't move at all. But Elena could tell that neither of them believed her. "I promise," she said. "I'll help."

Then she ran. She ran and ran and ran, and it wasn't until she was home and showered off the last bits of blood and flesh – and then wiped the shower clean and bleached it and cleaned it a second and third time – that she realized she was safe.

She was done.

She could do her work. She could save her lambs.

She smiled at that. There was always work to do, there were always lambs to save… and perhaps that was what had saved *her*. Perhaps Mr. Do-Good had sensed the good work she did, and was unwilling to stop it.

That made sense, cosmically.

And it didn't matter, subjectively. She was alive. Alive, and with much work to do and many lambs to save.

Interlude

1

Thaddeus Sterling had made many hard choices in his life. That was part of being a powerful man, in fact. Normal men and women could go to work – or not; could pay attention to everything around them – or not. The effect either way was largely the same.

But when a man like Tad, a *powerful* man, didn't go to work, or didn't pay attention, people's lives suffered. His decision to go into business with another company meant a seismic shift that changed the economies of cities and states. His preference to avoid a product meant that product would likely wither and die.

Hard choices. But Tad was used to them. He had come to relish them, in fact. Hard choices meant something hung in the balance; and that meant that there was something to be gained. Something to *win*. That was why he took some businesses over and ran them, and others he shattered to bits and sold what was left. It was why he persecuted some in his company when they broke rules and laws, and turned a blind eye to others.

It had even been why he shoved his wife away so hard when she got between him and his daughter. Hard enough that she hit her head when she fell, and died in the same hospital where his daughter almost did the same.

All decisions he'd made. And he regretted none of them.

Now, though, he worried that his hardest choice – and the decision he finally made – had been one of the rare situations where he lost more than he gained.

He looked at his daughter. She had turned twelve last month, and she was beautiful, even with the huge scar that ran a third of the length of her body. She had always been beautiful and, he knew, always would.

But there are different kinds of beauty, and hers had changed in the last few years. She had grown cold and aloof. She had stopped speaking to him unless it was absolutely necessary, and now days often passed without her addressing him.

She was courteous. She never snapped or raged or mocked. But even the staff had grown aware of her apparent derision of her father – of the man who had done everything for her, and had saved her in ways and at costs she could never hope to understand.

If the *staff* knew things were bad, then something had to be done.

Tad hadn't decided what would happen. It was another hard choice, and those always deserved careful attention, thought, and planning. But he knew that he could not stand for a life in which his daughter, his dearest treasure, hated him. Or at least, for a life in which she *obviously* hated him.

Tad wasn't a monster. He understood that people had feelings, and those feelings couldn't always be controlled. But he also understood that whether a person felt strongly about something or not, they could always at least *act* with courtesy. Could always *act* as if they loved him.

Tad was a powerful man. He had realized long ago that everyone seems to love a powerful man. He had realized that the act was very rarely backed up by real feeling. And he had, ultimately, realized that he didn't much care if the act was real or not. He watched people carefully for treachery, certainly, but beyond that he didn't care if people *actually* loved him or just *pretended* to love him. The outcome was the same for him either way.

He had enjoyed a perfect life, surrounded by smiles and care. And if he had to crush a dream or two, or destroy a life or two, in the course of his business, why... that was bearable, wasn't it? So long as he came home to the biggest smiles and the greatest love?

That was why this all hurt so much. Aside from the fact that he had saved her life, he simply did not deserve the silent treatment from anyone. Least of all his Hope.

She was in her room now – of course she was. It was in another wing from his – she had insisted she be allowed to move to the new room a year ago, and he had relented, more fool he. So when he decided to challenge her about her attitude problem, he had a long walk to get to her room. A long walk in which to brood, and wonder how she could act this way to him when everything he had ever done was for her.

She was at her computer. No surprise there, either. As she had withdrawn from him and the real, grounded life he represented, she had grown closer to the ephemera of electronic "realities." Online games, instant messages, shopping. She lived in a world not of beating hearts and pulsing blood, but in the short spaces between ones and zeros.

She was at her computer again – computers, he corrected; she had added three more monitors to her set-up. A driving game was splashed across them, with the other two computers showing what he assumed were ongoing chats between the racers.

"Hope," he said.

She didn't turn away from her game. She just pointed at something to her right. "I've been learning to draw," she said.

Tad looked at the picture. It was on an easel, a simple drawing done in colored pencil. Nothing special, but he knew better than to say such a thing to a child.

"Very nice," he said. "Hope, we have to –"

"Do you know who it is?"

Tad blinked. He wasn't used to people interrupting him. "I assumed...." He looked at the picture a bit closer. "I assumed it was you."

"Not me," she said. On her screen, the car she was driving spun out of control. It took out five other vehicles as it crashed – quite the epic pile-up, and Tad made a mental note to look into the game's graphics engine to see if it could be exploited for use in a military VR training package one of his companies was putting together.

The virtual explosion sputtered out. "YOU DIED" splashed itself across the screen in letters of flame.

Hope turned to him. "You really don't know who it is?"

Tad looked harder at the picture. He could see now that his daughter was right: it wasn't her. Too young, for one thing. The lips a bit thinner, the cheeks hollow with a hunger Hope had never known.

And that was when he understood: it *was* Hope. But Hope as she saw herself. As a Cinderella figure, ill-used somehow and so made to suffer unjustly.

"Look," he said softly. "I know that you think you're going through something. I'm not sure what, but obviously it's important to you." He gestured at the picture, trying to will her to understand how much he loved her, understood her, and was willing to support her – no matter how ridiculous or foolish she was being.

Hope looked at the picture she had drawn. The darker reality of herself.

"I think I'll be going to school in Europe this year," she said.

Tad was not used to hearing people tell him what they were going to do. He was used to hearing people ask him what they *should* do, and then following his orders. So the next words – whatever they might have been – died in his throat. His mouth twisted. "Will you, indeed?"

"I need to learn the ins and outs of your business if I'm going to take over someday, right?" she said, and smiled – for the first time in weeks, she *smiled*.

The sight warmed Tad. This would all be all right. His life would continue perfect. That was as it should be.

"I think I can arrange that," he said.

"Could you let me, I don't know, *intern* or something? I think that the business holdings in Switzerland are fascinating, and I'd love to see more of them."

"Computers," he chuckled. "I should have guessed that was what was going on. You want to take over that arm of the company this year?"

She blinked, suddenly demure.

(And a part of him wondered if this wasn't his reality – if the affection she was showing wasn't real as so many affections weren't real; if she was acting falsely to give him what he wanted.

And a larger part of him didn't care.)

"Well," she said, "I don't want to take over *this* year." She laughed. It was bright. It was happy. And real or not, it was perfect.

She went. And Tad was happy, because he had given his daughter what she needed – yet again – and could sleep peacefully knowing that he was a good man.

2

FBI REPORT FILE FA2017R2

Appendix C

Reproduction of comments on partial videos recovered from designate Portobello Road – see Appendix AC for list of videos recovered from Portobello Road, and report sections 21 through 22 in re actions taken to recover videos and reconstruct corrupted files where applicable.

See also Appendix AD list of possible Portobello Road users who may have commented on applicable videos

For list of known homicides possibly attributable to Portobello Road users, please see report for File FA 2018R2.

See also Appendix AD and files referred therein to list of Portobello Road videos, comments, and homicides. N.B.: Hard copies of the files must be relied upon, as *all electronic files are subject to corruption by parties unknown*. See Internal Report FA 2019R43.

<u>Comments to Portobello Road video designated PR19</u>

---

3 COMMENTS   SORT BY

Name: XXXXXXXXXX
Comment: This is the first time I've felt happy in three years.

Name: XXXXXXXXXX
Comment: Four years for me.

Name: XXXXXXXXXX
Comment: 7 years, 6 months, 2 days

FIVE

1

"She left. She just… *left*."

Clint could hear his voice, but it sounded distant, like it had followed Elena as she ran away, disappearing around the corner with her and then being swallowed by the night.

He took a step, wanting to follow her. Knowing even before his collar began to beep that it wasn't going to happen. She was leaving. Everyone good left, that was just the way things worked.

Elena's footsteps lasted longer than she did, the *clack-clack-clack* of her no-nonsense flats clattering against the pavement and then, like Clint's voice, like Elena herself, they disappeared.

Beep.

A sharp tone, and Clint felt his body clench. He wanted to vomit, and knew that anytime he heard an electronic tone like that for the rest of his life, he would have to struggle against his own gorge. If the rest of his life lasted long.

Maybe we'll make it. Maybe we'll get out.

Elena did, right?

Yeah.

Right.

He looked at Noelle. She had pulled one hand out of her pocket to better hear whatever was coming, and Clint followed suit.

"Do-Good says, ALMOST DONE! Next challenge: find the brown horsey and go for a ride. You have five minutes…."

Noelle looked at him, her brow furrowed. The nineties-style feathering of her hair had fallen out a bit during the night, and Clint was struck by the odd realization that she actually was a very pretty woman. An odd thought, but something about her in that moment was more comforting than anything else he could stand to think of.

"What does Do-Good mean?" she said.

"I don't know." He looked up and down the alley. It cut off at a dead end about fifty feet behind them. "No horsies in here, though, that's for sure."

He took her hand and ran with her to the street. They both looked up and down. The night had lasted a long time, but not long enough to end, it seemed: no sunshine broke the horizon, no dawn lit the area. There were streetlights, but they were mostly flickering or dark or broken. The area was dim.

And even if it wasn't, Clint mused, what did he expect to see? A random horse trotting down the street a few miles from Skid Row? Sure. That happened all the time.

Now it was Noelle's turn to grab his hand. She pulled, yanking him along with her as she fastwalked down the street. She was looking around, her head jerking right and left so fast Clint worried she was going to hurt herself.

"Horsey, horsey," she murmured.

Clint looked around as well. There were cars, shuttered storefronts. "Where the hell are we going to find a horse in the middle of Los Angeles?" he muttered.

Noelle began running. "Maybe... maybe a picture?" she panted. "Some kind of clue that will lead us to –" She let go of his hand, seeming to forget him in her panic.

Clint followed after her, looking for something – anything – that might help them meet Mr. Do-Good's latest deadline.

Cars. Storefronts. Fire hydrant. Mailbox. More cars. Newspaper –

"Wait!" Clint shouted.

Noelle jerked to a halt. He ran toward her, and she felt at her collar, automatically checking it as though worried she had done something to earn Mr. Do-Good's full and final displeasure.

Think of Elena. We can get out. She *did, so we can, too.*

"What is it?" asked Noelle as he ran to her. "Did you see –"

She stiffened slightly. Clint couldn't blame her: he had come right into her personal space, sliding his hand around her side as though to embrace her. And yeah, she was pretty – beautiful, even – but he had no intention of trying to cop a feel or hug her.

She was just standing in front of what he needed to see.

He tapped on it, and Noelle swung around, sidestepping at the same time so she could see what he had put his hand on.

She frowned. "What do you –"

"Brown horsey," Clint said, tapping the car's brown roof, then pointing at the symbol at the center of the car's wheel rims. "Mustang."

Noelle frowned. "We can't use cars. That's one of the rules."

"'The nature of the game starts to change now,'" he said, quoting Do-Good's last instructions to Elena. He said it absently, not at all sure he was right. He looked inside the car. Keys hung from the ignition. That just about clinched it: *no* one would leave a nice car like this, with the keys just hanging in the ignition, in a part of the city like this. No one but a madman.

No one but Do-Good.

As he looked in the car, a screen near the dashboard lit up. A smiley face spun once, winked, then disappeared, replaced by what looked like turn-by-turn directions.

"Where does that lead to?" asked Noelle.

"No idea," said Clint. "But we'll find out soon enough."

2

Noelle drove. Neither spoke a word as they got in, neither asked, "You driving, or me?" Clint was closest to the passenger door, so he got in and that was that. Noelle hurried around the front of the car, then slid into the driver's side seat and slammed the door shut.

She turned the key. The engine hummed to life. It was a late-model Mustang, and had obviously been taken care of. The engine sounded not at all like a horse, but like a pride of lions all purring contentedly.

"Lucky it wasn't stolen before we got to it," said Noelle as she pulled away from the curb.

Clint shook his head. "No luck in it." He peered out the window. "Not in this neighborhood."

"What do you mean?"

"I mean Do-Good's had eyes on us since this started. He's been watching, or having us watched. I bet the same goes with the car. Anyone who looked too interested in it before we came along was probably moved away."

"Moved... like, killed?" Noelle's fingers curled so tightly against the wheel that her knuckles glowed a ghostly white. The light from the electronic dashboard displays cast blue-white glow against her face, heightening the feeling that Clint was looking at a dead woman.

And what does she see when she looks at me?

The same. Dead man walking.

Out loud, he said, "I don't know. I doubt it. I think Do-Good's only interested in killing the people who play his game."

"Who fail it, you mean."

"Huh?"

"Elena. She won. She got out."

"Yeah." Clint bit his lip. "She did." He didn't want to think about that. Not just because it reminded him that he was still in the game, but because the idea that she had won might give him hope. Hope was the most dangerous of feelings, because it was the only one that existed in places where you had nothing *but* hope... and so it was the only thing that could still be taken away.

He looked at the GPS. It scrolled up as Noelle took the first turn, allowing another line of directions to be seen. It was plugged into the dash outlet, but the device wasn't part of the car. Just a small plastic rectangle hanging off one of the air conditioning vents. There were no buttons on the front, and when Clint pulled the device from the holder that clipped it to the vent, he saw no buttons on the back either.

"Do you have any idea where this is taking us?" he asked.

"No. Maybe Mr. Do-Good will tell us."

Clint bit back a humorless guffaw. "I don't think that he's in the habit of helping."

"No."

They drove in silence after that. Turn by turn, they left the overbuilt center of Los Angeles and started out of the city proper. Every time that Clint left any big city – and this big city in particular – he always felt a sense of relief. Like he'd lived through some battle and now was on his way home. Or if not home, at least away from the front.

Not this time. As the skyscrapers diminished in the distance, he grew only tenser. He kept glancing at the watch – or whatever it was – on his wrist. Kept sneaking glances at Noelle's watch, too, and at her collar. Like he expected any or all of them to beep for his attention, one last moment before light and sound would blast him to pieces.

But they were silent. Directions kept scrolling on the GPS screen, but other than that, Do-Good might as well just have been a dream. A nightmare. Or, worst of all, a memory.

And with that thought, he realized why he was so tense. It wasn't just what had happened in the last few hours. It was what came next. It was where they were going.

He sat up straighter, looking around with something teetering on the edge of comprehension.

"What is it?" said Noelle.

Clint shook his head. "Not sure...."

"You know where we're going?"

"No."

Noelle looked at him, staring directly at him long enough that he started to worry about them driving off the road. Then she aimed her gaze straight ahead. Her jawline firmed. "You look like you know something," she said. Her voice was flat. Clint knew that sound: the sound of someone who had just written him off. Who had decided he was a liar, or lazy, or any of a thousand red marks that went on a person's soul when they had grown up in a system instead of a home.

Clint was used to seeing that expression, to hearing that tone. And was surprised to realize that it bothered him. It usually didn't – not anymore. But he didn't want Noelle thinking that of him.

"I have no idea where we're going to end up," he said. "But I've driven this route before."

"When? To do what?"

Clint wanted to tell her. But he closed his mouth and set his own jaw. Something inside him whispered that telling her what he feared would make it happen; that saying it would make it so.

He said nothing.

He watched the turns scroll by on the GPS, watched the world pass by as Noelle drove. And that was how it felt: like the world was passing by. Like he was holding still, watching everyone and everything move past him.

Turn, turn, turn. The world spun on its axis, and spun the Mustang slowly closer to the place he worried – and then knew – they were headed.

"Clint, is this… is this where…?"

Noelle didn't finish the sentence, and Clint didn't respond to her unasked question.

The GPS stopped scrolling. The last line read: "Destination reached."

Clint stared at that line in horror. "Destination reached." Not normally the kind of thing that would strike fear into a person, but here… here it meant something much more final.

Noelle stopped the car, then turned off the engine. She looked around, and said, "What now?"

Clint couldn't tell if she was speaking to herself, or to Clint, or to the undoubtedly-listening Mr. Do-Good.

"You know where to go," said Mr. Do-Good, speaking again out of the microphones on their wrists.

"*I* don't," said Noelle. "What do you –"

"You know where to go," Mr. Do-Good said again. "Don't you, Clint?"

Clint didn't answer. He just got out of the car and began walking, trusting that Noelle would follow as he pushed up the hill, swerving to avoid the blocks of metal and stone that jutted up from the ground like witch's teeth.

Halfway up the hill, he began to run. His collar didn't beep, which meant that Noelle must have kept up with him. But even if it *had* started making noise, he doubted he would have stopped running. He had to see. He had to know.

Then he did see. He did know.

He fell to his knees. "No... no... no...." The word came out as a whisper, a plea, a prayer. All of which went unanswered or ignored in the final moments of this long night.

3

Clint heard Noelle running after him, and heard her gasp as she saw what he saw. "Is this…?"

Clint shook his head. Not answering her in the negative, just denying that what he saw was real.

But it *was* real. He stared at a simple metal rectangle, set flush with the ground.

CLAIRE – 1999-2007

The words and numbers were short and to-the-point. Partly that was because the charge for the inscription had been per-character, but even if Clint had had millions of dollars to spend, he suspected he would have put nothing more than that. She deserved more, sure, but there were no words he could think of that would meet the level of praise he wanted to give her. So it would just be her name, and the dates of her birth and her –

(Death.)

– disappearance.

He had been there the day before Mr. Do-Good's game. He had stood in this exact spot, and looked down at this exact plaque. Only the day before, it had been a plaque marking a long green rectangle, a gravesite covered by grass and a few wildflowers that waited to be found and trimmed.

Now, the plaque marked a different rectangle. Not grass and flowers, but dirt. The place Claire's memory had rested was gone. *She* was gone.

"No," he said again.

Saying it didn't change anything. Didn't change the fact that where a memory's grave had been, now there was only an *absence*. A desecration.

Beside the hole, a tall mound of dirt further evidenced what had been done: someone had dug up the grave and piled the dirt to one side. Two shovels – presumably belonging to whoever had so desecrated Claire's gravesite – stood upright in the mound, blades shoved deep so only the handles stood visible.

Noelle stared at the pile of dirt, her face a study in horror. "Your sister?" she murmured. Clint nodded.

Swallowing hard, he said, "Why would Do-Good do this? She wasn't even buried here." He looked at the empty hole. "The only thing here was a marker."

He knelt and touched the plaque. It was cheap. It was all he could afford. It was precious to him. "I never found her," he said. "She was there, and then she was gone." Some of the lead in his gut seemed to move to his eyes as he felt the tears come. "I couldn't even look for her. Not until it was too late, and the only thing I could do was give her memory a place...." His fists curled. "I wanted to kill whoever took her. Wanted –"

A muffled moan sounded. Clint stiffened, looking automatically at his watch as Noelle grabbed in semi-panic at her throat. The sound they'd heard wasn't an electronic tone, but it didn't belong in this place – so it had to be Do-Good.

The sound repeated. "It's coming from over there," said Noelle. She pointed.

The cemetery was nicer in the direction she pointed. The rich lay beside the poor in this place, as though whoever had designed it wanted it known that death was no respecter of persons, and the rich and poor would lay together in the eternities.

Of course that was a foolish dream. Because the cheap plaques in the area where Clint had buried his sister somehow became even cheaper when compared to the ornate tombstones and crypt-like structures only a few feet away.

The rich stay rich, even when they're dead, he thought.

The moan repeated. Noelle took Clint's hand and led him toward the noise. One of the larger tombstones – six feet long, nearly as tall. A name on it, which blurred in and out as the tears continued to flow even as he left his sister's grave.

They went around the tombstone.

Mr. Do-Good was waiting for them.

4

Clint saw the man, and there was no doubt it *was* him. Same suit, same blood-smudged cutout face. But he wasn't holding a phone or whatever he'd been talking into, ready to provide another impossible task. He wasn't at a computer, programming the watches to spit out more bad news.

Instead, he was tied hand and foot, his wrists bound behind his back, his ankles crossed with the same heavy line. Another length of rope tied ankles and wrists to each other, then to his neck so that if he straightened out of a kneeling position he would choke himself.

One of his knees was... *gone.* A bloody mess through which Clint could see mangled flesh and the sharp yellow angles of shattered bone.

Do-Good was laying on his side, his head obscured behind the mask, which began to shake as they approached, the moans redoubling as he did so.

For a moment, Clint felt a surge of hope that wiped away the still-falling tears. The game was over! He didn't know how, but that didn't matter. All that mattered –

"I told you the nature of the game had changed." Clint stiffened as Mr. Do-Good spoke. But not from the ground. His voice was coming, as it had before, from Clint's watch. "But it *is* still going on." Do-Good laughed from the watch, even as he writhed and moaned on the ground. "Final round! Last challenge: bury me! You have ten minutes!"

The countdown began.

On the ground, Do-Good kept shaking his head. He was moaning, but the moans had changed from the sounds of a man swimming out of unconsciousness to something more urgent. More terrified, but still muffled. They sounded like he was gagged behind the mask.

"This doesn't make sense," Clint whispered.

"Nothing about tonight has made sense," said Noelle. "How do we even know it's him?"

Mr. Do-Good's voice again came from the watches, as Mr. Do-Good simultaneously continued moaning. "It's really me. And I'll add a bonus to this round: complete the challenge in *five* minutes or less, and I'll tell you what happened to your sister."

Clint had been shaking his head. But Do-Good's last words transfixed him. A dark veil seemed to drop over his vision, and when it half-cleared he found himself dragging Do-Good by the ankles toward the empty hole. The man was no longer moaning, gagging noises now the only thing coming from behind his mask as Clint's movements dragged the rope ever tighter around his throat.

Another darkness, in which he thought, I never buried her. I never found her. Now someone promises to tell me....

It made little sense. But Noelle was right: nothing about the night had made sense.

The darkness cleared again, and now Do-Good was laying in the place where Claire had never lain herself. Clint had a shovel in his hands, and started shoveling dirt over the man who had led them on this chase, who now craved death – a craving that Clint was happy to satisfy.

Noelle was watching, her hands jammed in her pockets, terrified. "What are you doing?" she asked in a small voice.

It was obvious what Clint was doing, but he knew she wasn't asking about the fact – she was questioning something deeper. People, confronted with a truth so ugly and so inevitable that it shakes their worldview, are more likely to pretend that what they know is less important than what they feel. So they feel a need to deny what they see, and that denial *becomes* their reality.

That was what she was doing now. Noelle wasn't asking what was happening, she was asking herself if it was real.

Is this real?

Can I do this?

"What are you going to do?" Noelle asked, her voice even quieter. Even lower.

Clint slowed. He looked at his watch.

6:14...

6:13...

What am I doing?

What am I going to do?

He slowed, but did not stop shoveling dirt over Do-Good's rapidly disappearing form. He shoveled two more piles. Do-Good writhed.

What would Claire want me to do?

That was the real question, wasn't it? She had come into his life as an orphan – another girl in one of the orphanages that came and went. A child so bright and so lovely that he adopted her as a sister. It wasn't real, of course. Nothing was really real at all in a place defined by severed connections. But in her he found someone to love, and someone who loved him, and it didn't matter that he was black as night and she as white as snow. It didn't matter that she had blue eyes, he had brown, or that his hair was tight and close to his head and hers was blonde and straight and hung to the middle of her little back.

She was his sister. He was her brother. They promised to stay together, and on the rare times where they were separated, they had both acted so horribly that the foster parents were forced to return them to their group homes and they continued together until…

Until we went to sleep one night.

Until I woke up and she was gone.

(I can find out what happened to her! I just have to do this one little thing!)

He couldn't do it. Claire was gone, and he had no doubt she was dead. But he knew she wouldn't want him to know where she was if the price was another life – even one as worthy of extinction as Do-Good.

He slowed.

5:49…

Slowed.

5:48…

Stopped.

He looked at Noelle, who was looking at her watch, then shifting her gaze to Do-Good. "He's the one who did this," she said.

Clint knew what Claire would think; what his *sister* would say. "And he deserves to pay. But not like –"

Noelle rushed forward. She grabbed the second shovel and now she restarted what Clint had decided to end. She tossed shovelfuls of dirt onto Do-Good.

"No!" shouted Clint. "We can't just kill –"

Noelle seemed to have become another person. "It's all him!" she shrieked. "It's all his fault! All this! He –"

Clint dropped his shovel and grabbed hers as she was about to drop another pile of dirt over Do-Good. She resisted, so he wrestled the shovel away from her. Twisted and turned and then the shovel was in his hands and she was ten feet away, fallen against another tombstone.

He turned and jumped into the hole beside Do-Good. The man had disappeared from the waist down. But he still groaned and writhed.

Clint reached out and flipped the bloody mask away from the man's face, revealing a man who looked to be in his fifties, with a tan and a lack of wrinkles that somehow screamed wealth. His mouth was covered in duct tape, which Clint ripped off. It wasn't like the movies: the duct tape didn't just come loose easily. It came off in uneven strips, each one peeling a layer of Do-Good's skin away with it.

"I won't bury you, but I'm not going to leave your side. So you have maybe six minutes to turn off the explosives before we both go *boom*. Then you got about twenty more seconds to explain what's going on. After that...." He worked the last bit of tape free. "... the story better be a damn good one."

The tape gone, Clint would have expected Do-Good to start screaming in rage or madness, or to keep that strangely giddy tone he had spoken with throughout the nightmare as he laid out a *new* challenge, a *new* bit of the scavenger hunt.

He did neither. Instead, he looked past Clint. "What the hell are you doing here?" he demanded, in a voice that Clint knew well – the voice of the man at the root of all the night's death and pain. "What's going on?"

Clint squinted, confused. He followed Do-Good's gaze, looking behind him to see that Noelle had grabbed the shovel Clint dropped before. Dirt began raining down again – on both Do-Good *and* him.

"Noelle! Don't do this!" shouted Clint.

He looked from Do-Good to Noelle. He didn't understand, and something in his brain was finally shutting down, going dark. Too much confusion, too many horrible choices.

Do-Good started gagging as dirt – at least partially blocked by his mask before this – started raining directly into his mouth, nose, eyes.

Do-Good sputtered, then gasped as Clint clambered out of the hole. He shoved Noelle, trying to stop her from whatever mad course she had decided on. She went down on her ass. Clint tried to keep an eye on her and Do-Good at the same time.

"I'm not going tolet you do this, Noelle. I won't let you –"

Noelle spoke, and the sound of her voice stunned Clint almost as much as had the sight of Claire's desecrated grave. Her voice changed, the coarse tones of lower-class Boston slipping away and being replaced by something much more elevated and elegant. "I'm glad you didn't want to bury him, Clint. I knew you were a good person."

Then she reached behind a nearby tombstone, and withdrew something that Clint's over-stressed mind literally couldn't process.

She held the implement in both hands, arms straight ahead of her. She moved slightly.

The Taser lurched in her grip, and Clint heard a sound familiar and dreadful. The noise that had marked his entry into the night's game.

Buzzzzz.

Clint jerked in place. Then he fell. A new and much thicker veil dropped over his sight. He saw nothing, then he heard nothing, then he *knew* and was swept away into darkest dark.

5

The darkness rent in bits and pieces, like a threadbare blanket that wore through in some spots before others.

Clint hid under just one of those blankets. Stared at the girl under the blanket with him. They had stolen – no, just borrowed, really – a flashlight from the emergency kit in Mr. Higgins' office. And now Clint was reading to her.

"… were disposed as follows. The lost boys were out looking for Peter, the pirates were out looking for the lost boys, the redskins were out looking for the pirates, and the beasts were out looking for the redskins. They were going round and round the island, but they did not meet…."

The threadbare strands of memory shifted, and the darkness fell and then rose again and now he was not huddled with Claire under the blankets, not reading in a rare moment of bliss. Now he was staring at the director of the orphanage. The man looked at him with a blank, bland face as Clint tearfully said that something had happened to his Claire. The man shrugged. She had gone to another home, he said. She was lucky to have people who would love her, he said.

But his eyes were lying.

Darkness fell, and light came, and now Clint was in the back of a police cruiser. He had stolen out of the home, and had gone to the nearest police station he could find. He had told them of Claire. "She wouldn't leave without saying goodbye," he said. "She wouldn't leave in the middle of the night." And the desk sergeant nodded kindly and called another man who looked scary and frowned at Clint a lot as he put him in a car and took him back to Eighth Street Children.

Dark. Light. Dark. Light.

Getting out of the final home. Not to a new family; he was just eighteen and it was time to leave. Adult, but he still felt like that little child. He still missed his Claire.

Dark.

Then, finally, light again. He had caught up to *now*, it seemed. He saw flashes, just like he had at the beginning, when he woke in bits and pieces in the white room.

He saw Noelle, grabbing duct tape from behind the same tombstone where she had secreted the Taser she used on Clint. She wrapped his hands and ankles. No rope binding feet to wrists to neck, but she tied the tape so tightly he knew there was no use struggling.

Darkness.

Light.

Flash, flash, flash.

He thought he saw Claire's eyes in one of the flashes.

Then he woke to Do-Good's screaming. Noelle shoveling dirt into the grave where he still lay helpless. The shrieks turned to whimpers as the dirt covered more and more of the man being buried alive. The whimpers became gagging. The gagging became nothing at all.

Clint screamed, "Help! Someone help!"

Noelle put the shovel down. There was still a huge mound of dirt beside her: she hadn't filled in the hole. Just covered Do-Good. "No one's coming," she said to Clint.

She looked down into the hole. "I can see one eye," she said, not to Clint, but to Do-Good. "I wonder if you're finally seeing the mistakes," she said. "You probably think even now that you're going to get out." She shrugged. "That's what being rich means: you can make anything happen, can't you?" Her eyes went to someplace far away. "I remember hearing someone say that," said Noelle quietly, her tones still rounded and rich. She pushed her shovel into the mound. Lifted away a tall pile of dirt, then dropped that final bit of earth onto Do-Good.

She turned to Clint. Grabbed his ankles and with surprising strength began dragging him down the hill. He struggled, and actually managed to kick free and roll a few helpless feet down the hill. She stared at him with sorrow. "Why do that, Clint? I'm trying to help you."

Then she brought out the Taser again – maybe the same one, maybe a different one. Clint didn't know and it didn't matter. All that mattered was that she pointed it and pulled the trigger and the blanket fell over him again.

6

Higgins stares at him.

"She's dead, isn't she? My little sister is dead."

"She's not dead. She was placed with a family." Higgins opens a file. "You'll have to be punished for sneaking out."

"I snuck out to go to the *cops,* since no one here cares –"

"She was *placed with a family.*" Higgins stares at him over the top of the open file. It is a thick file. It has Clint's name on it. "Hardly a matter for the police."

"She wouldn't have gone without saying goodbye. It ain't right. My sister –"

"She *wasn't your sister.* And she's better off wherever she is."

Higgins puts the file down and smiles. The smile does not touch his eyes.

"Besides, good news comes in pairs, it seems. You have a new placement, too – easier with the two of you apart, as I continue to tell you. And if you go without a fuss, that punishment I mentioned could be... forgotten." The false smile disappears, replaced by the only sincere look Clint has ever seen grace the man's face: disdain, like the look a venemous snake would give a mouse caught in its cage. "I'd pack quickly if I were you."

In the reality of what happened so long ago, Clint does not say anything. In that *reality,* Higgins nods and a woman who started working here about a year ago and is usually nice to the kids she calls "her lambs" comes in and glares at Higgins and says, "We have to talk. Soon," and then takes Clint away.

That is what happens in the reality of the memory.

But this is not the reality. And in this version of memory, before the woman can take him away Clint opens his mouth and screams louder and louder and every moment his mouth opens wider to let the scream out and the scream gets louder and louder and his mouth gets wider and splits his head in two and opens up his brain and Higgins reaches in and pulls Claire out of his mind and Clint cannot remember why he is screaming but he still screams and he –

7

– didn't realize for a good five seconds that he wasn't screaming anymore. He wasn't in Higgins' office, either. No office, no woman coming to take him away and help him pack his meager belongings.

He was, instead, back where this night had started.

He was in the white room.

8

There was the iPad on the wall, dark now, hanging behind its mesh like a closed eye. Clint wondered if Do-Good's eye had looked like that as it closed. As Noelle dropped that final shovelful of dirt over his last inch of flesh.

The same water cooler sat on the floor, though the Dixie cups were gone.

Noelle was in here, and that was as it had been at the beginning, too. Only she wasn't talking to Clint, coaxing him back to wakefulness. She had her back to him, speaking to a camera that sat on a tripod a few feet away from her. A red light blinked above the long lens of the obviously-expensive equipment. Recording as Noelle stared at it and said, "I've shown you how it can be done. Whether you do it is up to you."

Clint tried to sit up. He couldn't. He looked to the side and saw he was still bound. Not with duct tape this time, but padded straps. They didn't hurt at all, but they left him nearly no room to move.

As he shifted, Noelle reached forward and turned off the camera. She turned to him and smiled wanly. "No fun to wake up in a place like this, is it?"

She picked something up from the floor. A Do-Good mask, covered in dirt and blood. She stared at it for a moment, her expression unreadable. Then, as Clint watched, she dropped the mask. She lifted her hands to her ears, and removed the bangly earrings from her lobes, then ran a hand through her hair. The feathering fell away, revealing something that was still far from high-fashion... but with the tacky earrings gone, the feathers combed away, she looked like a different person. Less trashy. More in line with her voice.

"I take it you were never a waitress?" said Clint.

"No. I do own several restaurant chains, though." She shrugged. "Close enough."

She dropped the earrings. They tinkled as they hit the metal floor. Then she reached down again and picked up a knife. Even confined ten feet away, Clint could tell that the six-inch blade was honed to a razor edge.

"Noelle," he said, as calmly as he could – which wasn't calm at all. "Please tell me what's going on."

She smiled, half at him, half at the knife. "How much do you want to know?" she said. Her eyes flicked over, totally focused now on him. "How much do you *really* want to know."

Clint didn't speak. But he stared at her, his gaze never wavering from hers. *All of it* was what he knew his eyes were saying.

She nodded, then looked around. "I woke up in the white room."

"We all did."

"No, this was a different one. A long time ago. I hurt all over. My chest…." She put a hand on her chest, her eyes gazing upon something that Clint could not hope to see. Then they hardened and she looked around again. "These aren't exactly the same beds I woke up in. But they're close."

Clint's brow furrowed. "I don't underst –"

"Neither did I. I knew I'd been sick. But I didn't know more than that. Of course, there were obvious signs of something major. But Dad never talked about it. I knew something was wrong. So I looked. He tried to stop me, but... I've always been very good with computers. I can hack into just about anything, from dark web sites to off-the-book ledgers."

Clint shook his head. "You're not making sense."

Noelle turned a bright grin on him. "It's pretty simple. Most things are, when you have enough money. Even things that would kill most people...." Her hand went to her chest again. "Your heart gets sick, deathly ill, and most people would just die. Most people would just end there. But I've never been most people. Not my fault; I was just born to it."

She approached Clint. As she did, she absently ran the ball of her thumb down the knife. Blood welled instantly, dropping down the side of her hand and in a thin trickle over her wrist and forearm.

"My dad didn't want his little girl to die. So he made it happen. He called the right people. The broker was careful, and Dad was always careful, too." She frowned. "Not careful enough to keep them from me, though." She brightened again, though Clint now saw deep sorrow below the brightness. A dark patch on her soul. "After he decided to save me, it was a done deal. That's what being rich does. Things just *happen*. Dad contacts people, who put him in touch with a man who runs an illicit website that specializes in putting together buyers and sellers."

"What does any of that have –"

"It was Chong, of course." Noelle laughed. "Daddy paid Chong, Chong paid the man with the goods."

"What man with the goods?" Clint asked quietly. "What did Chong buy?"

"Chong had friends everywhere. Most of them he didn't know at all. But some of them he did. He knew, for instance, a guy named Two-Teeth. And Two-Teeth knew a guy named David Higgins. And David Higgins would answer Two-Teeth's calls and send out a child – usually to a woman named Dee-Dee, who was on paper quite the saint."

"Dee-Dee?" Clint shook his head. "She was a *foster parent*?"

"Sort of. More a waystation. She'd keep the child – or the baby, like you saw tonight – for a day or a week or a month, then the child would be brought by Two-Teeth or one of his men to a point Chong designated."

"One of his men," Clint said, and swallowed. "Like Solomon Black?"

Noelle nodded. "Him and a few others. And no one the wiser. Except one little boy, and no one was going to listen to *him*. Not even when he went to the police. Because powerful men can buy anything. Even corrupt cops who –"

"The cop, the one who got killed tonight," said Clint. His eyes widened. "I remember. He was the one who took me back to the home."

Noelle nodded. "Detective Pattinson's lies took so many people away. So I thought it appropriate that he end with Solomon Black, and that he end by having his lying mouth blown to pieces." She paused, then leaned in close and whispered, "Do you want to guess what a human life – a rush order – costs?"

Clint began weeping. "Two-hundred and fifty thousand," he said, remembering the piles of bills on the bed, the baby in Dee-Dee's house. Trying not to think of

Claire, and whether she had been taken to that place all those years ago, or if she had just been spirited away for the "rush job" Noelle was talking about.

"Actually, it's how much *part* of a life cost. Not all of it." She pulled at the neck of her t-shirt. The cotton stretched easily, pulling halfway down her chest, the "v" of the edges not exposing breasts, but more than enough to show the long scar that bisected her chest. "Just a piece," she said. "Just a little girl's heart."

Clint wanted to scream. For a moment he thought about the dream scream, the one that opened his mind and allowed Higgins to pluck away the very memory of Claire. Instead he said, "Why would you do all this?"

Noelle smiled, and unlike Higgins' lying grins, her smile was sincere. "Don't cry over any of them. Everyone who died was part of what happened to your sister."

"So why not just kill them? Why do this to us? To *me*? What did *I* do to you?"

Noelle touched her watch. The iPad on the wall blinked to life, and Clint blanched, part of him expecting to see Do-Good staring out at him. Instead, a series of vignettes appeared. The group of contestants running from the white room. The run across street after street. The cop's face disintegrating along with Solomon's hand and wrist as the explosive there went off. Two-Teeth and Chong, disappearing in a flash of light and smoke and spattered flesh.

All of it.

"Cameras along our routes, and secreted in some of the houses, caught everything we did. Recorded it all."

Clint still didn't understand. *"Why?"*

"Because you weren't the only one they did it to. Claire wasn't the only one taken. Even after the Eighth Street Children closed, it just reopened. Different name, different management."

Clint understood instantly. "Elena."

"She just moved into the space that Higgins had occupied. He *is* dead, by the way."

Clint jerked in place. "How?" he asked, morbid curiosity momentarily overtaking his fear.

"Elena did it, years ago. I wish she hadn't. I wish he'd gotten something better. Something more befitting." She shrugged, a *"what's a girl gonna do?"* gesture.

"And Do-Good?"

"Thaddeus 'Tad' Sterling. Billionaire, mover of mountains. I just called him Dad." She chuckled. "He was the easiest to grab, and the easiest to manipulate."

"Your *father*? And what, he just went along with a plan that ended in his death."

"No. But shoot a man in the knee, then work him over with brass knuckles for a few minutes before aiming the gun at his other knee; then ask him to read a script, and believe me, he reads."

Clint remembered the jittery, halting way Do-Good had spoken. He remembered, too, the way Do-Good had laughed. An insane laugh? Or pain as he was made to deliver lines that would be given at points in a timeline crafted by his daughter?

He remembered, too, Chong attacking the iPad in the white room. The iPad glitching – only was it a glitch, or a change to a different video file?

He remembered the strange way Do-Good flinched. And now Clint thought: *Not flinching from Chong. From his daughter. From* Noelle.

And then Do-Good whispering, "Stop. Please just *stop!* Stop, stop, *STOP!*"

Then another glitch on the screen, and Do-Good saying, "When I give an order, I expect it to be obeyed." And finally, toward the end: "The nature of the game starts to change a *tad* at this point." And Do-Good laughed his pained laugh and said, "Did you do that on purpose?" before clearing his throat and saying, "Right. Back to the script. Where was I?"

Clint shook his head, stunned. "All him talking to you? Recorded?"

Noelle nodded and put her hand in her pocket, withdrawing a slim keypad. "And it wasn't hard to key in instructions, to activate audio and video. Even to trigger explosions when it was time for the game to end for certain people." As she spoke, Clint remembered all the times her hands had been in her pockets. Had it been every time Do-Good spoke? Every time someone died?

He thought it had.

Then he shook his head. "No," he said, talking mostly to himself. "He spoke to us. He didn't just say things in a vacuum, he answered the things we said."

"The things *we* said, or the things *I* said?" asked Noelle. She laughed at the expression on his face. "I thought

328

it would be a bit less... *organic* to just have him talking *at* us, so of course I prerecorded parts that required a bit of back and forth. Which was easy since I had written the dialogue, so I knew when the pauses came and how to answer them."

Clint gaped at her. "And you did this to your own father."

Noelle nodded, then laughed long and hard. "But want to hear the fun part? I know it's not a big thing, just a detail, but I was rather proud of it." She leaned in toward him again and said, "Who do you think dug the hole he was buried in?"

Clint started to say, "You," then stopped himself. He remembered a half-noticed detail. The blood on Two-Teeth's clothing when he had come for Dee-Dee – and more after he finished with her – had taken up most of Clint's memory of the man. But there was also... "Two-Teeth was covered in dirt the first time I saw him."

Noelle smiled. "Bright." She cocked an eyebrow at Clint's expression, and the smile turned to a mocking pout. "Don't approve? I thought it was rather poetic – everyone who did this to you and your sister helping set up tonight's game. Don't be sad for them. Everyone who died... they *wanted* to play this game. Do-Good presided over the closing rounds, but all the players began the scavenger hunt a long time ago. Searching for bodies, for parts to supply the rich who didn't want to wait their turn, take their chances." She grew quiet, then whispered. "Everyone here wanted in the game. They just didn't realize the way it would end up being played."

Clint thought of something: "Solomon didn't recognize Dee-Dee. What if she wasn't even a part –"

"She was. He didn't know her because Two-Teeth kept the different parts of the job separate. Same with the others Two-Teeth killed –"

(And Clint remembered the blood all over Two-Teeth, remembered him saying to Dee-Dee, "SFD didn't do it. And he won't paw you no more – or anyone else. Neither will Zonker or Mako.")

"– which was another careful move that didn't matter in the end. Not to someone like me."

She looked behind her, intent for a moment on the mask that lay on the floor. "I drew her once, you know. Drew her face, and showed it to him, and he didn't even recognize it."

Clint blinked back the tears that wanted to come, thinking of his sister, unknown by any save him and this madwoman. "And me? Why was I in the game?"

Noelle smiled. Then raised the knife she still held and in a motion too fast to be seen, she stabbed down and buried the knife up to the hilt in his chest.

9

Clint gasped, expecting the pain to come hard and fast and sharp. There was nothing. A strange numbness, a tingling that spread out from his hand of all places.

He looked down. Saw the knife sawing away, but not at him after all. Noelle slashed through the bonds on his right wrist. Then she lifted it and Clint flinched again as she brought it toward his face. But she reversed it, holding the blade as she extended the knife toward him.

He took it. Made sense to do so: always better to be armed when facing a crazy person. But he suspected she could have handed him a handful of used toilet paper and he would have taken that, too. He was acting automatically, his mind barely keeping up with what was happening.

Noelle – was that even her name? he wondered – pulled her shirt down, again exposing the scar that held –

(don't think about it don't think about what's in there or you really will go crazy)

– the evidence of what she had been a part of. "You were the only one who didn't choose to play," she said. "You and Claire, and the baby we saved earlier tonight."

Clint looked at the knife. "The baby could have died."

Noelle shook her head. "I knew one of the players would take the baby. Would take her and save her, even if they didn't know what they were saving her *from*. I would have suggested we take her to the fire station if you hadn't thought of it, but I knew you *would* think of it, because it was what had been done to you." She nodded at the knife in Clint's hand, then looked at her scar. "You can have it back," she whispered. "You can cut it out. I lived stolen years, and I don't want them anymore."

Clint cut his other wrist free. Then he exploded from the bed, knocking Noelle down. He rode her as she fell, ending up astride her, the knife at her throat.

"Just for my own curiosity: why did you let Elena go?"

Noelle smiled beatifically at him. "Who said I did?"

"You *did*. I saw her –"

"You saw her walk away. But neither of you noticed the evidence I left. DNA and fingerprints at a murder scene."

"What the hell are you –" began Clint. Then he stopped. He looked at the water cooler. At the space on the floor where the Dixie cups had been. He remembered Noelle handing Elena a cup, then Elena putting it down.

Then later, Two-Teeth striding across the trash in Dee-Dee's apartment. Including a cup.

A paper cup.

He remembered Elena as the only one to touch the money on the bed, the only one who dropped the deposit bags into the bank.

"I left a baby whose footprints would tie to her."

"How would –" Clint began. Then realized. "Babies who are orphaned or abandoned have their vital stats taken, including their footprints." He exhaled, sudden rage taking him. "She came from St. Jerome's." Then he frowned. "But she didn't even recognize the little girl. Or me, either. I'd swear she didn't."

"Do you think someone like her would remember the ones who made her life easier?" Noelle shook her head. "I left evidence that she was at every place where a murder happened, along with a huge amount of cash that she didn't notice was going to her personal account...."

(*Clint heard the sounds of the envelopes sliding into the deposit chute. Thud...thud...*)

"... and which had a newly-deceased man's prints all over it."

(*Thud... and the money was gone.*)

"They picked her up a few hours ago," said Noelle. "They're going to find files showing transfers of money like the one in the safe. She's going to say she did it for the orphans – evil people always say they're acting for the greater good, and the worst of them actually believe it – but they won't believe her. She's going to jail, and the right people have already been alerted. Some very bad things are going to happen to her once she's behind bars, so she'll know what it's like to be powerless, forgotten... and used until there's nothing left of her."

"What about the others? At St. Jerome's?"

"The kids?" Noelle grew sad, even as she said, "They're going to be taken care of. For real this time." She laughed, but tears bejeweled her eyes. "Being rich means I can make things happen."

"What now? Why all the cameras?"

"Because I wanted it to be big. I wanted people to see, and remember, and then make a choice."

"What choice?"

She told him. Clint didn't move. The knife didn't waver. If anything, it pressed harder to her neck as Noelle spoke. Then she finished, her voice not trembling, her eyes resigned, and said, "What happens next is up to you."

Postlude

1

FBI REPORT FILE FA2017R2

Appendix A

First interview with subject, night of incident, by Detectives Hernandez and Dehghani (continued).

HERNANDEZ: Look, we know you didn't do it. Not all of it. We think there was someone behind this, but can't pin down who it was. If you know, tell us his name, please.

DEHGHANI: He could barely stand when we found him. He mighta fried a circuit or –

WITNESS: (laughter)

DEHGHANI: (addressing Hernandez) You ever see something like this?

HERNANDEZ: (unintelligible)
        (addressing witness) What about Thaddeus Sterling? He was seen near where we found you -

DEHGHANI: Not his usual stomping grounds –

HERNANDEZ: And we know he's missing

DEHGHANI: He one of the bodies?

WITNESS: (laughter)

DEHGHANI: We know that Elena Ruiz is in this up to her eyeballs.

WITNESS: Well of course she is!

DEHGHANI: I knew it! I knew you were in this. How do you know her, Walker? I swear to God if you don't –

HERNANDEZ: D., chill!
    (addressing witness) Mr. Walker. Clint. How do you know Elena Ruiz?

WITNESS: She worked at an orphanage I lived at for a while. With another girl. She disappeared.

HERNANDEZ: Who did? Elena Ruiz?

WITNESS: My sister.

HERNANDEZ: Oh shit.
    (addressing Dehghani) You don't think…

DEHGHANI: The amounts line up. And if it's true, I wouldn't want to be her, I wouldn't want to be that woman once she hits gen-pop in the prison. A person who does that... to kids.

I better make a call

HERNANDEZ: You better make a lot of them, or she might not even make it to trial.

WITNESS: I wouldn't worry too much about that. She'll make it to trial.

HERNANDEZ: What does that mean, Clint? What do you know?

Okay, let the record show we're taking a short break

(...)

HERNANDEZ: Okay we're back. Witness is still Mr. Clint Walker, Detectives Hernandez and Dehghani administering the interview of Mr. Walker.

Clint, I'm sincerely sorry for what happened to you. To... your sister?

WITNESS: My sister. Claire.

HERNANDEZ: I'm sorry. We'll follow up on that. But now I need to know: who else was involved in what happened tonight?

WITNESS: I can tell you what happened to me. But as for what else was going on, and who was behind it?

(witness shrugs)

2

FBI REPORT FILE FA2018R2

Abstract

Previous videos downloaded from Portobello Road open site, YouTube, and various other P2P and bit torrent sites continue to emerge (list of known videos and sites can be found in Appendix D; please note that though attempts have been made to remove the videos from as many sites as possible, every single one continues to emerge at different sites in various geographical locations).

To date, the exact number of homicides proceeding as a result of these videos is unknown.

The above is complicated by the fact that electronic files dealing with the case are consistently penetrated by an outside hacker, then corrupted or destroyed. As a result ONLY PAPER COPIES OF REPORTS MAY BE RELIED UPON.

3

Her name was Hope. She did not like it; she hated the name, in fact, because she knew her life represented hope stolen from an innocent.

She had enjoyed being Noelle, if only for a short time. But she would be Hope again. That was part of her penance.

She looked around, and had to resist the urge to gag for the tenth time. She hated this room. She'd been in here only once before, to hit Chong with the Taser, but even that short time in the room where so many deals were made, where so many came to purchase life for one at the cost of death for another, had made her feel like vomiting, even though she *had* spent hours in here virtually, hacking her way into Chong's systems and servers.

He was pretty good. But she was better. She'd always been good with computers, and once she realized what her father had done, and what she would *have* to do to start righting some wrongs, she had been driven to a place beyond expertise, beyond even genius. UCry2 was born then: a hacker of highest skill, and who could go anywhere and be anyone from the hidden corners of the internet.

So yes, she had been in here dozens of times, pulling information from Chong's files, subverting his Portobello Road abomination in preparation for this moment.

She looked at one of the screens. A series of thumbnails showed on it, each of a child. Beside each child were five fields:

Date of Sale – BUYER – SELLER – Price

– KNOWN FAMILY –

Another screen showed the edited version of the final rounds of the scavenger hunt, the program she was using to lighten and brighten all the scenes compiling as her voice played over the scene.

"I've shown you how it can be done. Whether you do it is up to you."

The video ended. A beep sounded and she turned to the screen. A pop-up message said, "Video compressed. Send?"

Her finger hovered over the keyboard.

She looked at another of Chong's screens. This one held no images, no video. Just text. A transcript.

WITNESS: I can tell you what happened to me. But as for what else was going on, and who was behind it?

(witness shrugs)

WITNESS: I dunno. I just hope that anyone else who made other kids disappear... I hope someone finds them. I hope someone tells their friends and families what happened, and who did it, and I hope...

Noelle didn't have to read the last line. She had it memorized. *"I hope the people who do shit like this find themselves in hell."*

Her finger stabbed down.

The videos began posting. Some on Portobello Road – which had under her hand gone from dark web repository of the worst in humanity to a website that was appearing at the top of every Google search, with pages archived that showed as many identities as she'd been able to discover.

She wasn't done, though.

She'd find them *all*. She'd post their names, too, and send the information to the relatives and friends and loved ones of the people who had disappeared like a little girl packed into a suitcase in the middle of the night.

She'd send the videos she'd made. She'd post them on hundreds of places, impossible to take down all of them. She'd give everyone who'd been wronged a visual example of what could be done.

The dead could not be brought back.

But the guilty would not enjoy what they had stolen.

Not for long.

Not if Hope had any power in the world.

A REQUEST FROM THE AUTHOR:

If you loved this book, **I would really appreciate a short review on the page where you bought the book**. Ebook retailers factor reviews into account when deciding which books to push, so a review by you will ABSOLUTELY make a difference to this book, and help other people find it.

And that matters, since that's how I keep writing and (more important) take care of my family. So please drop a quick review – even "Book good. Me like words in book. More words!" is fine and dandy, if that's what's in your heart.

And thanks again!

Author's Note

The black market organ trade earns $1.7 billion annually

10% of the total organ transplants in the world come from this market.

HOW TO GET YOUR FREE BOOK:

As promised, here's a goodie for you: sign up for Michaelbrent's newsletter and you'll get a free book (or maybe more!) with nothing ever to do or buy. Just go to http://eepurl.com/VHuvX to sign up for your freebie, and you're good to go!

*

FOR WRITERS:

Michaelbrent has helped hundreds of people write, publish, and market their books through articles, audio, video, and online courses. For his online courses, check out http://michaelbrentcollings.thinkific.com

*

ABOUT THE AUTHOR

Michaelbrent is an internationally-bestselling author, produced screenwriter, and member of the Writers Guild of America, but his greatest jobs are being a husband and father. See a complete list of Michaelbrent's books at writteninsomnia.com.

*

FOLLOW MICHAELBRENT

Twitter: twitter.com/mbcollings

Facebook: facebook.com/MichaelbrentCollings

ACKNOWLEDGMENTS

As always, first prize for thanks-deserved goes to my wife, with the second place a four-way tie between my kids. I don't know how they put up with me, but am beyond grateful that they do.

A big thank you to my Street Team (lovingly known as the Collings Cult). You all help me spread the word, and catch errors that would make me look dumb(er).

Special thanks to my friends Bobbie Bretana, Nicole Toscano, Julie Castle-Smith, Maria Cook, Heather Escobedo, Rudy McDaniel, Dan Hilton, Malina Roos, Kim Napolitano, Priscilla Bettis, Charlotte Acha, Shelley Butchart, Eric Taylor, Mary Jude Schmitz, Christine Christensen, Kimberly Busse, Christine Huff, Trevor Holyoak, and others who caught errors and continuity issues.

Thanks also to my fans and friends on Facebook, with whom I shared bits and pieces of the story before it came out, and who got me excited again when the grind of a novel got me down.

NOVELS BY MICHAELBRENT COLLINGS

DARKLING SMILES
PREDATORS
THE DARKLIGHTS
THE LONGEST CON
THE HOUSE THAT DEATH BUILT
THE DEEP
TWISTED
THIS DARKNESS LIGHT
CRIME SEEN
STRANGERS
DARKBOUND
BLOOD RELATIONS:
    A GOOD MORMON GIRL MYSTERY
THE HAUNTED
APPARITION
THE LOON
MR. GRAY (aka THE MERIDIANS)
RUN
RISING FEARS
DARKLING SMILES (collection)

THE COLONY SAGA:
THE COLONY: GENESIS (THE COLONY, Vol. 1)
THE COLONY: RENEGADES (THE COLONY, Vol. 2)
THE COLONY: DESCENT (THE COLONY, VOL. 3)
THE COLONY: VELOCITY (THE COLONY, VOL. 4)
THE COLONY: SHIFT (THE COLONY, VOL. 5)
THE COLONY: BURIED (THE COLONY, VOL. 6)
THE COLONY: RECKONING (THE COLONY, VOL. 7)
THE COLONY OMNIBUS
THE COLONY OMNIBUS II

THE COMPLETE COLONY SAGA BOX SET

**YOUNG ADULT AND
MIDDLE GRADE FICTION:**

THE SWORD CHRONICLES
THE SWORD CHRONICLES: CHILD OF THE EMPIRE
THE SWORD CHRONICLES: CHILD OF SORROWS
THE SWORD CHRONICLES: CHILD OF ASH

THE RIDEALONG
PETER & WENDY: A TALE OF THE LOST
    (aka HOOKED: A TRUE FAERIE TALE)
KILLING TIME

THE BILLY SAGA:
BILLY: MESSENGER OF POWERS (BOOK 1)
BILLY: SEEKER OF POWERS (BOOK 2)
BILLY: DESTROYER OF POWERS (BOOK 3)
THE COMPLETE BILLY SAGA (BOOKS 1-3)

website: http://www.michaelbrentcollings.com
email: info@michaelbrentcollings.com

For more information on Michaelbrent's books, including specials and sales; and for info about

signings, appearances, and media,
<u>check out his webpage,</u>
<u>Like his Facebook fanpage</u>
or
<u>Follow him on Twitter.</u>

Made in the USA
Middletown, DE
25 April 2020